THE ... BROTHERHOOD OF EVIL

THE FAMILY JENSEN
BROTHERHOOD
OF EVIL

William W. Johnstone
with J. A. Johnstone

PINNACLE BOOKS
Kensington Publishing Corp.
www.kensingtonbooks.com

PINNACLE BOOKS are published by

Kensington Publishing Corp.
119 West 40th Street
New York, NY 10018

Copyright © 2015 J. A. Johnstone

PUBLISHER'S NOTE
Following the death of William W. Johnstone, the Johnstone family is working with a carefully selected writer to organize and complete Mr. Johnstone's outlines and many unfinished manuscripts to create additional novels in all of his series like The Last Gunfighter, Mountain Man, and Eagles, among others. This novel was inspired by Mr. Johnstone's superb storytelling.

All Kensington titles, imprints, and distributed lines are available at special quantity discounts for bulk purchases for sales promotions, premiums, fundraising, educational, or institutional use. Special book excerpts or customized printings can also be created to fit specific needs. For details, write or phone the office of the Kensington sales manager: Kensington Publishing Corp., 119 West 40th Street, New York, NY 10018, attn: Sales Department; phone 1-800-221-2647.

PINNACLE BOOKS, the Pinnacle logo, and the WWJ steer head logo are Reg. U.S. Pat. & TM Off.

ISBN-13: 978-0-7860-3599-1
ISBN-10: 0-7860-3599-4

First printing: October 2015

10 9 8 7 6 5 4 3 2 1

Printed in the United States of America

First electronic edition: October 2015

ISBN-13: 978-0-7860-3600-4
ISBN-10: 0-7860-3600-1

BOOK ONE

Chapter I

Bitter cold rain sluiced down from gray, leaden skies, turning the single street of Espantosa, New Mexico Territory, into a muddy bog. It was the middle of the afternoon, but the thick overcast made it seem more like twilight.

No one was out and about except one man, who muttered curses under his breath as he attempted to run up the street. The mud kept trying to suck the boots off his feet, so his run was more of a stumble.

Petey Tomlin was plumb miserable. He wore an old slicker, but it leaked in several places. Even if it hadn't, pounding rain always found a way to work itself inside a man's duds and make him wet and uncomfortable. In less than a block, Tomlin felt like he was soaked to the skin. Water ran in a steady stream from the brim of his battered old hat and made it difficult for him to see where he was going.

He kept his eyes on the yellow glow up ahead that marked the front windows of the Gilt-Edge Saloon. That was his destination. He carried important news for the men who waited there.

Espantosa didn't have boardwalks along the two blocks of its business district. Most of the establishments opened directly onto the street. A few, like the Gilt-Edge, had covered porches, but that didn't help Tomlin stay out of the rain.

He could dry off and warm up later, he told himself, once he'd let Jack Shawcross know what he had seen at the livery stable down the street.

Shawcross had sent him to the stable to check on the horses, or so he'd claimed. Tomlin thought Shawcross had done it mostly to make him miserable. He got mean like that sometimes, especially when he'd been putting away the booze. He and the rest of the bunch had been in the Gilt-Edge all afternoon, drinking and playing cards and taking turns going upstairs with the saloon's lone bar girl.

Tomlin hadn't been up there with her yet. He was usually one of the last for anything good and the first for any unpleasant job like going out in the rain.

He would have to wait even longer for female companionship. He knew his boss would want to deal right away with what he'd discovered at the livery stable.

Maybe Shawcross would be feeling generous after that. He might even toss Tomlin an extra double eagle in appreciation for what he'd done.

He reached the steps leading up to the saloon's porch and climbed them, stomping to knock some of the mud off his boots, but the blasted stuff was just too thick and sticky.

At that time of year, the batwings were fastened back on either side of closed double doors. He grasped the right-hand doorknob, opened it, and stepped into the welcome warmth coming from a potbellied stove in the corner.

"Stop right there!" bellowed Ben Gormley, the craggy-faced bartender and the saloon's owner. "Don't come trackin' all that mud in here. Go outside and take them boots off."

The little outlaw ignored the man who stood behind the bar and scuttled across the room toward the round, baize-covered table where Jack Shawcross was playing poker with four members of the gang. Three more men were at the bar, nursing mugs of beer. The nine owlhoots were the only people in the Gilt-Edge's main room, other than the owner.

"Damn it!" Gormley said as he started out from behind the bar. "I told you—" He stopped instantly and shut up as Shawcross lifted a hand.

"Petey wouldn't be hurrying like that if he didn't have something important to tell us," the outlaw boss said.

"Sorry, Jack," Gormley muttered as he retreated behind the hardwood again.

The outlaws spent freely and generally behaved themselves in Espantosa, which they had adopted as their unofficial headquarters. Nobody wanted to get on their bad side—which, according to their reputation, was very bad indeed.

Tomlin took off his hat and tilted it so that water ran off and formed a puddle in the sawdust on the floor. The sawdust would soak it up, given time.

Shawcross turned his attention back to the cards in his hand but asked Tomlin, "How are the horses, Petey?" He snickered. "Staying dry?"

"I didn't check on 'em," Tomlin answered.

Shawcross frowned and looked at Tomlin coldly. "That's what I told you to do, wasn't it?"

"Yeah, but some fellas rode into the livery stable just before I got there. I saw 'em goin' in, and somethin' about one of 'em struck me as familiar. So I snuck up to the door and watched while they talked to ol' Ramon. I got a good look at 'em then, and I recognized one of them, just like I thought."

Shawcross slapped his cards on the table, facedown, and snapped, "Damn it. Spit it out already."

"It was Luke Jensen, Jack. I'm as sure of it as the day I was born."

Chapter 2

The name was loud in the saloon. Shawcross sat up straighter, as did the other men at the table. The three men drinking at the bar stiffened, set their drinks down, and turned around.

"You'd better not be trying to have a little sport with me, Petey." Shawcross's voice was soft, but it held a steel-edged quality that made a shiver go through Tomlin.

"I'd never do that, Jack." *Even though you might deserve it for all the times you've tormented me.* "It was Jensen, right enough. He didn't look exactly like he did in El Paso last year. He was a little skinny, like he'd been sick or something. But it was him, no doubt about it."

Shawcross turned his head and said to the men at the bar, "One of you go get Clancy." Then he got to his feet. The cards, the game, and the pile of greenbacks and coins in the middle of the table obviously were forgotten. He drew the heavy revolver from the holster at his hip, opened the cylinder, and took a cartridge from one of the loops on his shell belt. He thumbed it into the empty chamber and snapped the cylinder closed.

Around the table, the other men began doing likewise.

Shawcross pouched the iron and looked out the window at the falling rain. He was a lean, lantern-jawed man. His cheeks still bore the faint pockmarks of a childhood illness. His deep-set eyes burned with a fire that might be hate or insanity or both. "You said there were some other men with Jensen?"

Tomlin nodded. "Yeah, three more. A couple who looked younger than him, and one old-timer. I didn't recognize any of 'em."

"Doesn't matter. It's their bad luck to be here today. And to be friends with that bounty-hunter."

The man who had hurried upstairs in response to Shawcross's order reappeared with another outlaw following him. The second man was stocky and had a shaggy head of sandy hair, along with a ragged mustache of the same color. His hat was pushed to the back of his head, his gun belt was draped over his shoulder, and he was clumsily fastening his shirt buttons. His long red underwear was still visible through the gap.

"I don't understand what the dadblasted hurry is," he complained.

Shawcross called up the stairs. "Luke Jensen is in town, Clancy."

The shaggy-haired man stopped. His eyes widened for a second. "Why the all-fired hell didn't somebody say so? Let's go get him!"

"That's what we're doing." Shawcross turned back to Tomlin. "Did you happen to hear Jensen and his friends say where they were headed?"

"No, I hustled back here quick as I could in all that mud. Not many places in Espantosa they could go, though. The saloon here and the hotel are just about it. Shoot, they might still be at the livery stable. You know how that old Mex likes to talk."

Shawcross nodded slowly. "We'll find them. Grab your slickers, boys, and let's go."

The outlaws pulled on slickers, tugged down their hats, and stepped out onto the porch. From behind the bar, Gormley shook his head as he watched them go, as if he felt sorry for the man who was the object of their wrath and his unfortunate companions.

The mud made sucking sounds as the men walked along the street toward the livery stable in the next block. Both of the stable's big front doors were open, allowing lantern light to spill out into the street, but Shawcross and his men couldn't see into the building from where they were.

As they drew near the hotel, Shawcross said, "Neal, Wilson, check in there."

The two men hurried ahead, tracked mud into the hotel lobby, and returned to tell Shawcross that no strangers had arrived recently.

"And that slick-haired clerk was too scared not to be tellin' the truth, boss," one of them added.

Shawcross nodded. "They have to still be at the stable, then." He pointed to four of the men and went on. "You boys head around back and come in that way. The rest of us will take the front."

The four outlaws drifted off into the rain, quickly vanishing into the gloom. That left six men to tramp the rest of the way down the street to the stable.

Tomlin scrambled up next to Shawcross. "You reckon Jensen will start shootin' as soon as he lays eyes on you, Jack?"

"He might. He probably heard that I swore to get him after he killed Trace last year."

Shawcross and Trace Bennett had been closer than brothers. Best friends and partners in leading the gang, they had been responsible for spreading outlawry across a wide swath of West Texas and New Mexico Territory.

The notorious bounty hunter Luke Jensen had trapped Bennett in a café in El Paso, gunning him down so that Trace had died in a welter of broken crockery, tangled in a checked tablecloth. Dying was bad enough; to do it in such undignified circumstances was an unforgivable insult.

Shawcross would have gone after Jensen then and there, as soon as he'd heard about what had happened, but a bunch of Rangers had ridden into town just then and the gang had to light a shuck to avoid being captured. By the time they'd made it back a couple weeks later, Jensen had already collected his blood money and was long gone.

Shawcross had insisted that he would cross trails with Luke Jensen again someday, and when he did, Jensen would die.

In the squalid little New Mexico settlement, it looked like that day had come.

"Clancy, Wilson, with me," Shawcross said softly. "You other three spread out a little as we go in. Wait for Jensen to start the ball. I want him to know who's gonna kill him and why he's fixing to die."

The others nodded in understanding. Usually, it was best not to give an enemy any more chance than you had to, but the outlaws outnumbered Jensen and his pards more than two to one, and they would be caught in a crossfire, to boot. They wouldn't stand a chance.

As the outlaws moved into the broad, open doorway, they unfastened their slickers and swept them back so they could get to their guns in a hurry. The hard rain drummed on the roof, and the four men standing inside the stable, talking to old Ramon while the hostler tended to their horses, didn't seem to hear the newcomers enter.

Shawcross's nostrils flared as he took a deep breath at the sight of one of them. Tomlin was right. The tall man with the craggy, unhandsome but compelling face and curly dark hair was Luke Jensen, no doubt about that. He looked like he had lost some weight and his face was a little pale in the lantern light, but it was him.

A man a few years younger and a couple inches shorter than Jensen stood with him. He had sandy hair under a thumbed-back hat, and his shoulders seemed incredibly broad in the slicker he wore. The third man was a little taller than Luke, fair-haired, powerfully built, and younger still.

That left the grizzled, whip-thin old-timer who wore a buckskin shirt and an old, steeple-crowned hat that had seen much better days. Sitting next to him was a big, shaggy dog of some sort, looking miserable with its wet fur matted to its body. Somebody as ancient as the old man probably didn't represent any threat, but they would gun him down anyway.

There was no law in Espantosa to say they couldn't.

It was the dog who noticed them first. His big head swung toward them, and he bared his teeth in a snarl that suddenly made him look more wolf than dog.

That got the old man's attention. He turned to look and said in a voice cracked with years, "Looks like we got comp'ny, boys."

"Yeah," Jensen said, turning slowly to face Shawcross and the other outlaws. Recognition showed on his face. "Jack Shawcross. I didn't expect to run into you here."

"I'll just bet you didn't," Shawcross grated.

"You got some idea of settling the score for Trace Bennett?"

"You killed him!"

Jensen shrugged. "The reward posters said dead or alive. I took them at their word, especially when he drew on me first."

Quietly, the broad-shouldered man told old Ramon, "Drift on into the tack room, *tio*, and keep your head down."

Ramon swallowed hard, his Adam's apple bobbing. "*Sí, Señor Jensen.*"

Shawcross caught that and said quickly to Luke, "Jensen, eh? Your brother?"

A faint smile touched Luke's lips under his thin mustache. "That's right. This is my brother Smoke, and this is my other brother Matt. They call the old-timer Preacher."

As Petey Tomlin stood a couple yards to the right of Shawcross, Clancy, and Wilson, he felt his guts turn to water. Everybody had heard of Smoke Jensen, who was quite possibly the fastest, deadliest gunfighter in the entire West, and Matt Jensen's fame as a pistoleer was growing rapidly, too. And as for Preacher . . . well, that old man was a living legend, no two ways about it.

Tomlin wondered if he could turn around and run back out into the downpour before they killed him.

Too late. Jack Shawcross yelled a curse, and his hand stabbed toward the gun on his hip.

Chapter 3

Luke, Smoke, Matt, and Preacher hadn't been getting in any hurry to get back to Sugarloaf, Smoke's sprawling ranch in Colorado. They had been taking it easy as they rode through Arizona and New Mexico.

Luke knew that deliberate pace was mostly because of him. The other three had pulled him out of a bad spot. He'd been held captive for a good while under harsh conditions in an outlaw stronghold,[1] and as a result he wasn't in the best of shape. None of the others wanted to push him too hard.

He appreciated their concern, but at the same time it annoyed him a little. He didn't want anybody feeling sorry for him.

He had already given some thought to going his own way and letting his three companions head back to Sugarloaf without him. He was grateful for what they'd done—they had saved his life, no doubt about that—but he had spent many years as a loner and even though he had been reunited with his family, that wasn't going to change.

1. See *The Family Jensen: Massacre Canyon.*

As he stood in the livery stable that was pleasantly warm and smelled of horseflesh, straw, and manure and saw the outlaw named Jack Shawcross reach for his gun, Luke knew that if he and the others survived the next few seconds, it would be time for them to split up.

But first there was some killing to do.

He had already opened his slicker for a couple reasons. Doing so let his damp clothes air out and start drying. More important, he was in the habit of making it easy to reach for his guns.

His hands flashed across his body to twin ivory-handled Remingtons riding butt forward in cross-draw holsters. The long-barreled revolvers came out smoothly and spouted fire from their muzzles as he brought them level.

Both slugs plowed into the chest of Jack Shawcross, who had cleared leather but hadn't had time to raise his gun. He jerked the trigger as his muscles spasmed under the shock of Luke's bullets, but the slug smacked into the ground at his feet.

To Luke's right, Smoke's .45s roared. His lead hammered two more outlaws off their feet.

To the left, Matt and Preacher were about to deal with the remaining three gunmen. Matt had his Colt out, and Preacher had drawn the pair of revolvers he wore, his movements amazingly swift and supple for a man his age.

At that instant, however, shots blasted behind them and Preacher's hat flew off his head, plucked from its perch by a bullet that narrowly missed his skull.

Some of the gang had slipped around the stable and come in the back, Luke realized. They were still outnumbered and were caught in a crossfire. "Spread out!" he shouted as he triggered his Remingtons again and saw another man stagger from the bullet that ripped across his side.

Luke and Smoke went to the right, Matt, Preacher, and the big cur called Dog to the left. Smoke pressed his back against one of the thick beams that supported the hayloft. He fired in opposite directions, front and back, at the same time.

Luke ducked behind a grain bin and grimaced as a flying slug struck the bin's lid and sent splinters spraying against his cheek. He fired both Remingtons again at the outlaws who had come in the front doors and were scattering under the onslaught of Jensen bullets.

Matt dived off his feet and rolled against the gate of a stall. As he came to a stop on his belly, he fired up at an angle at one of the outlaws who had snuck in through the stable's back door. The slug caught the man under the chin, ranged up through his brain, and flipped him off his feet. He was dead when he hit the ground.

Preacher drifted into an empty stall and fired over its side wall. A gunman in the rear of the stable flew backward as if he'd been punched by a giant fist. Both of Preacher's bullets had found their mark. The man hit the back wall, bounced off it, and reeled out through the open door. He collapsed in the rain, which made dark pink streaks run around him as it washed away the blood welling from his wounds.

At the same time, Dog leaped at one of the other men, who triggered a shot at the cur but hurried it and missed. He paid for that in a heartbeat as fangs tore into his neck and Dog's weight knocked him off his feet.

Matt gunned down another man with a well-placed shot, and another volley from Luke's Remingtons blew away a sizable chunk of an outlaw's head. The gun-thunder inside the stable had been deafeningly loud, but the echoes began to fade away as all the weapons fell silent.

All that was left were Dog's snarls as he finished mauling the man he had taken care of.

"Looks like they're all done for," Luke said into the eerie hush that followed the violence.

"Any of you fellas hurt?" Smoke asked.

"I'm fine," Matt said as he got to his feet and brushed straw and dirt off the front of his shirt.

"I ain't hurt," Preacher said angrily, "but one o' them scoundrels put a hole in my hat!"

"That hat's been to hell and back," Smoke said with a grin as he reloaded one of his Colts. "I don't reckon one more bullet hole is going to do that much more damage to it."

Preacher just snorted disgustedly as he picked up the headgear in question and clapped it down over his thinning gray hair.

"Hold on a minute," Matt said. "I count . . . nine of them. Six came in the front, and I would have sworn when they bushwhacked us from the back there were four more of them. That makes ten."

Luke nodded grimly. "So one of them got away."

"You want to take a look for him?" Smoke asked.

Luke thought about it for a second. It was doubtful the lone surviving gang member posed much of a threat to them, but he didn't like leaving loose ends. "Maybe we'd better. No telling if the hombre might go in for some back shooting."

Smoke opened the tack room door and asked the old hostler, "Are you all right in there, *tio*?"

"*Sí, señor*," the man replied.

"You know who those fellas were, don't you?"

The old man emerged tentatively and nodded. "Señor Shawcross and his men. They come here to Espantosa from time to time. They do as they please because everyone is too afraid to stand up to them."

"Well, you won't have to worry about that anymore," Smoke said. "Do they stable their horses here?"

"*Sí*. This is the only place in town for the *caballos*."

Smoke nodded. "Preacher, you and Dog stay here in case the fella tries to double back and grab a mount."

Preacher didn't argue with the decision. Even though he had mentored Smoke for many years and taught the younger man practically all he knew about surviving on the frontier, there was no denying that Smoke was a natural leader and usually knew the best thing to do.

"The rest of us will see if we can find him," Smoke went on.

"Should be able to," Matt said. "This settlement isn't much more than a wide spot in the trail. There aren't that many places he could have gone."

The three of them holstered their guns, buttoned up their slickers, and slid Winchesters from saddle sheaths. They worked the levers on the repeaters, then stepped out into the rain, moving quickly so they wouldn't be silhouetted in the doorway for more than an instant.

Chapter 4

Since they were tracking just one man, they split up, Luke and Matt taking one side of the street, Smoke the other. They checked the alleys between the buildings, looked around parked wagons and behind rain barrels that were already overflowing, and poked into the alcoves of businesses that were already closed for the day. The proprietors figured they wouldn't have any customers in the bad weather.

As Smoke approached the entrance of a store that appeared to be closed permanently, judging by the empty, dust-filled window, a dark figure suddenly stepped out of the alcove and pointed a gun at him. The Winchester flashed to Smoke's shoulder, but he didn't fire. The same hair-trigger reflexes that had saved his life many times kept him from squeezing the trigger as he realized the man's gun was wobbling back and forth so violently he didn't stand much chance of hitting anything.

Still, a lucky shot could be just as deadly as a well-aimed one.

Smoke yelled, "Drop it! Now!"

The man whimpered. His hand opened and the gun

thudded to the muddy ground at his feet. It would need a good cleaning before it could be used again. "Don't shoot me," he pleaded. "Oh, Lord, don't kill me, Mr. Jensen."

The man was short and so scrawny that the ragged old slicker flapped around him like the clothes on a scarecrow. Smoke recognized him as one of the outlaws who had come through the front doors of the stable with Jack Shawcross.

Luke and Matt heard Smoke's shouted warning and hurried across the street, moving as fast as they could in the thick mud. They held their rifles at a slant across their chests, ready to use the weapons instantly if need be.

"Looks like you got him, Smoke," Luke called to his brother.

"Yeah. Question is, what are we going to do with him?"

"Please don't kill me!" the little outlaw wailed again.

"Settle down, mister," Smoke snapped, keeping the man covered. Even an hombre who didn't appear to be a threat at all could have a trick or two up his sleeve. "What's your name?"

"P-Petey. Petey Tomlin."

"I've heard of him," Luke said with a scornful note in his voice. "Even seen a wanted poster on him. He's been riding with the Shawcross bunch for a while."

Matt asked, "How much is he worth?"

"I believe the bounty was fifty dollars."

"Fifty?" Matt chuckled. "Is that all?"

"He's not exactly Jesse James, are you, Petey?"

"N-No, sir. I ain't even close to bein' Jesse James." Tomlin gulped. "Mostly I hold the horses."

Smoke asked, "Did you ever kill anybody?"

"No, sir! Leastways I don't see how I could have. The

times when we swapped lead with posses, I always tried to shoot high, so I wouldn't hurt nobody."

"But you were ready to help Shawcross gun us down just now," Luke said harshly.

"What else could I do? If I'd told Jack I didn't want to come along, he would've been liable to shoot me himself. There was no tellin' when he'd fly off the handle and do somethin' like that."

Smoke glanced over at Luke. "What do you think?"

Luke shrugged. "For what it's worth, he's probably telling the truth. If there was a marshal and a jail here, I'd lock him up and put in for the reward anyway. Fifty dollars is fifty dollars." He paused. "But there's no law, at least not that I know of—"

"There ain't," Tomlin interrupted eagerly. "The county sheriff don't even send a deputy around here."

"So we'd probably have to take him all the way to Taos to turn him in," Luke continued. "I'm not sure it's worth it."

"What about the others?" Matt asked.

"Oh, them I'll load on their horses and take with me," Luke said. "They won't give any trouble, the shape they're in now, and the price on their heads will add up to a tidy sum. By all rights, I should split it with you fellas and Preacher."

"Forget it," Smoke said. "We don't need the money, do we, Matt?"

Matt shrugged. "I reckon not."

Luke's jaw tightened. Even though he knew Smoke didn't mean to sound judgmental, Luke took it that way. What Smoke meant was that they didn't need blood money, he thought.

That was one more reason for him to go his own way.

His brother had been a notorious gunfighter and wanted by the law for a while himself. Now he was a fine, upstanding citizen, and rich from that ranch, to boot. Hell, Smoke Jensen could probably get himself elected governor of Colorado if he wanted to, thought Luke.

Teaming up with his brothers now and then was all right, he supposed, but for the most part they all had their own trails to ride.

"So what do we do with Petey?" Smoke asked. "Let him go?"

"If you do, I'll never trouble you again, Mr. Jensen," the little outlaw said. "Not any of you. I swear it."

Luke nodded as he came to a decision. "Yeah, let him go. Petey, you're coming back to the stable with us. You'll get your horse, ride out of Espantosa, and never come back here again. You understand?"

Tomlin's head bobbed up and down on his neck so hard it looked like it was about to fall off. "You betcha, Mr. Jensen. That's just what I'll do. Thank you. Thank you so much—"

"Shut up before I get tired of listening to your jabber," Luke said. "Now move."

Tomlin practically ran up the street to the livery stable with Luke, Smoke, and Matt trailing along behind him.

"Hope Preacher doesn't shoot him when he comes busting in," Matt said. "That cantankerous old-timer can be pretty quick on the trigger."

"Maybe I'd better catch up to him and make sure that doesn't happen," Smoke said. "Hey, Petey, slow down and wait up a minute."

A short time later, Smoke, Luke, Matt, Preacher, and Dog stood in the livery barn's open doorway, watching as Petey Tomlin rode away in the rain. They had dragged aside the bodies that were blocking the entrance.

The old hostler joined them and sighed.

Matt looked over at him and frowned. "What's the matter, old-timer? Seems to me you'd be glad to get rid of these outlaws."

Ramon nodded. "*Sí, señor*, they were very bad men. *Mucho malo.* They caused fights, they were rude to the women of the town, and sometimes they did not bother to pay for the things they took. But when they wanted to, they could be generous. There is not much business in Espantosa."

"And they provided a sizable chunk of it, didn't they?" Smoke said.

"*Sí.* They stabled their horses here, they drank at the saloon, they slept in rooms at the hotel, they got their supplies at the store. No longer."

Luke rasped a thumbnail along his jawline as he frowned in thought. After a moment he said, "Tell you what . . . I need their horses to carry their sorry carcasses to Taos, but when we get there I'll sell the horses and send the money back here to you. You can split it with the other merchants if you want. That's up to you. I'm afraid that's all we can do for you, though."

"It is most generous of you, señor. We will be very grateful."

"Maybe with the gang gone, more good people will come here and do business," Smoke suggested.

"It is something devoutly to be wished, señor."

"In the meantime, I guess we need to rent another stall from you for the night."

"Another stall?" Matt asked.

"Got to pile those bodies somewhere," Luke said.

Chapter 5

The hotel had a dining room, but Ramon suggested that they eat supper at the Espantosa Café instead, claiming that the food was much better there. It was run by his cousin Tomas and Tomas's wife Maria. He offered to look after Dog if they wanted to leave the big cur there at the stable with the horses.

Smoke, Luke, Matt, and Preacher followed the old liveryman's advice and found that the food was indeed quite good, with a distinctive blend of chillies. The meal was pleasant enough that it almost made them forget about the bodies waiting for them at the livery stable.

Those bodies were wrapped tightly in canvas Smoke had gotten from the general store. The store had been closed for the night, but Ramon had volunteered to roust out the owner and get him to open up.

They were all glad it was going to be a cold night. That would help with the smell when they had to lash the corpses to the horses and take them half a day's ride to Taos.

* * *

The journey turned out to be uneventful. As they rode into the old town nestled at the foot of the Sangre de Cristos, the procession of horses with their grisly burdens drew a lot of attention. People followed them along the street.

When Luke asked, "Which way to the undertaker's?" half a dozen pointing fingers indicated the direction.

The local law intercepted them before they could get there. A stocky man with a squarish head strode out into the street and lifted a hand to stop them. A tin badge was pinned to his vest. He must have heard the commotion caused by the arrival of the strangers, living and dead.

"I'm Marshal Lopez," he announced. "What the hell is all this?"

"We have some business for your local undertaker," Luke explained.

"I can see that," Lopez said with a frown as he looked along the line of dead men's mounts. "Who are they? For that matter, who are *you*, señor?"

Luke inclined his head toward the bodies. "That's Jack Shawcross and his gang. My name's Jensen and these are my brothers and an old friend of ours. Shawcross and his bunch jumped us in a little settlement west of here called Espantosa."

The lawman's frown deepened. "I count nine of them and only four of you."

Preacher drawled, "Yeah, the odds weren't hardly fair . . . for them."

"Jensen, Jensen . . ." Lopez mused. "There's a gunfighter up Colorado way named Smoke Jensen. . . ."

"That would be me," Smoke said. "I'm just a rancher now. My gunfighting days are behind me."

Preacher let out a scornful grunt that showed how little credence he put in what Smoke had just said.

Luke went on. "Marshal, I'm sure you have wanted posters on all of these men in your office. If you'd like to come along with us to the undertaker's, you can take a look at them and identify them. That way you can confirm my claim when I put in for the rewards on all of them."

"You're a bounty hunter," Lopez said disdainfully. Evidently, like most star packers he considered bounty hunters little better than outlaws themselves.

"I've never denied it," Luke said. "Now, would you like to come with us or not? These bodies need tending to."

They were fortunate that even though the rain had stopped, the day was overcast and still on the chilly side, but there was only so much cool weather would help with the inevitable processes of nature.

"Yeah, go ahead," Lopez said. "I'll be down at Claude's place in a few minutes."

Luke nodded and heeled his horse into motion again. He was leading three horses, and his companions had two each. They rode slowly along the street until they reached the undertaking parlor, where they found a pudgy, round-faced man in a dark suit waiting for them.

"I heard that customers were on the way," the man explained with a smile. "Take them on around to the back, gentlemen. My helpers are waiting to unload them."

By the time Lopez arrived a few minutes later, the canvas-shrouded corpses were all laid out on boards in the yard behind the undertaking parlor. The marshal had a sheaf of badly printed reward dodgers in his hand. Clearly, he had gone back to his office and found all the paper he had on the Shawcross gang.

Luke, Smoke, Matt, and Preacher waited off to one

side while the marshal checked each body, comparing them to the wanted posters.

When he straightened from that grim task, he turned to Luke and nodded. "All right, Jensen, I'll confirm that these men are who you say they are. You want me to wire the capital and see about getting your money?"

"That would be very helpful, Marshal," Luke said. "I'm much obliged to you."

Lopez looked at the other three. "Are you bounty hunters, too?"

"Nope, just giving Luke a hand," Smoke replied.

"I still don't see how the four of you managed to gun down nine hardcases like this."

"We're good at what we do," Preacher said.

Chapter 6

In a cantina on the edge of town, Petey Tomlin had been sitting and staring gloomily into a glass of tequila when he heard a commotion outside. He was in such a blue mood that it took several moments for the sounds to penetrate his sullen reverie.

He had ridden in the rain from Espantosa to Taos the previous evening, arriving even more soaked than he had been. Two emotions had warred within him the entire way—fear that the Jensens would change their minds and come after him and self-loathing because he had turned yellow and run away when the shooting started, then descended even further into craven cowardice by surrendering when he could have gone down fighting like his partners in the gang.

The booze he'd consumed since stumbling into the cantina the night before hadn't helped his mental state. Eventually, he had passed out and slumped over the table. The proprietor had allowed him to stay right where he was until he woke up and started drinking again.

Whatever was going on outside had drawn several men to the entrance, where they opened the door and stood looking out. Tomlin heard one of them say something about corpses, and that perked up his interest enough to make him climb unsteadily to his feet. He stumbled over to the entrance and rasped, "What's goin' on out there?"

One of the cantina's curious customers looked over his shoulder and said, "Some hombres are leadin' in a bunch of horses with bodies draped over the saddles."

"What?" Tomlin pushed into the doorway, then felt sobriety hit him like a bucket of cold water in the face. The sight of Luke, Smoke, and Matt Jensen, along with the old-timer called Preacher and that damned dog, drove the drunkenness right out of Tomlin. He took a quick step back, putting himself in the shadows inside the cantina again.

The Jensens hadn't warned him that they would kill him if they ever laid eyes on him again, but Tomlin didn't want to take a chance on that. They had reputations as tough, deadly, unforgiving enemies. He retreated to the table and his bottle and glass, shame burning in him at the knowledge those canvas-wrapped corpses were those of his former friends.

Maybe Shawcross should've left well enough alone and not gone after Luke Jensen, thought Tomlin, but what had happened still wasn't fair.

He knew that if he hadn't scurried back to the saloon from the livery stable to tell Shawcross what he'd seen, the rest of the gang might still be alive. That didn't actually make their deaths his fault, but he'd had a hand in the whole mess and he couldn't stop thinking about that.

What could he do, though, he asked himself as he tipped more tequila into the glass. How could he fix this? He was only one man.

A shadow fell over the table, and a man's voice said, "You look a mite upset, amigo. What's wrong?"

Tomlin looked up, saw two men standing there. Their stances were casually arrogant, thumbs hooked in their gun belts and hats pushed back. They had a strong enough resemblance between them for him to guess they were brothers. Just looking at them was enough to make him uneasy, because he sensed that they carried trouble with them.

"It's nothin'," he replied with a shake of his head.

"Didn't look like nothing," one of the men said. He drew out an empty chair at the table, reversed it, and straddled it. The other man did likewise as the first one went on. "You saw somebody you know out there, and you're not happy about it. Nate and me, we saw those fellas ride by with those dead bodies. Friends of yours?"

"Hell, no," Tomlin said. "They're no friends of mine."

"What about the dead men?" the one called Nate asked. "Maybe *they* were your pards."

The first man nudged the bottle, which had only about an inch of liquor left in it. "Let me get you another bottle of tequila, and you can tell us all about it."

Tomlin thought about it then licked his lips. "Yeah, sure. Why the hell not?"

It had been a mistake telling the Riordan brothers what had happened in Espantosa, Petey Tomlin thought later that day as an early dusk was settling over Espantosa. At first, he hadn't seen what it would hurt. Nate and Chuck had been so friendly, grinning and plying him with tequila and assuring him that none of the bloody violence had been his fault.

He hadn't realized at the time that all they were really interested in was making names for themselves as gunmen.

Standing in the gathering shadows just inside the mouth of an alley, nervously clutching a shotgun while he waited for his quarry to come along, he gave thought to what had happened.

They fancied themselves as being fast on the draw and dangerous, and there could be no better way of proving that than becoming known as the ones who killed the Jensen brothers and Preacher.

"Once we've done that," Chuck said, "it won't be any time at all before a bunch of hombres are wanting to ride with us."

"We'll put together a gang that'll make everybody in the territory forget about the old Shawcross outfit," Nate added.

Chuck nodded. "And you'll be our second in command, Pete, since you're the one who's going to help us get the whole thing started."

Tomlin liked the way they called him Pete. Jack Shawcross and the other members of the gang had always made "Petey" sound like they were looking down on him. Between that newfound respect and the tequila, it was easy for him to smile and nod and agree to whatever they suggested.

Chuck got the shotgun and gave it to Tomlin, telling him, "You'll just be the distraction, Pete. When you step out and confront the Jensens, they'll be looking at you, so it'll be easier for us to take them from across the street."

"But that's not really the same as outdrawin' 'em, is it?" Tomlin asked with a frown. "It's almost like bushwhackin'."

For a second, anger flickered across the brothers'

faces, then Nate said, "No, it's not the same thing at all. You've got to remember, they'll all be dead and we'll be the only ones left alive to tell the story. So we can tell it any way we want, can't we?"

"Well . . . I reckon that's true . . ."

"As far as the rest of the world's concerned, it'll be a straight-up shootout," Chuck said. "You know, if that's how we wanted to play it, we could take them that way, too. This way is just simpler and quicker, that's all."

Tomlin wasn't sure about that. He had seen the way guns had appeared in the Jensens' hands as if by magic, their movements way too quick for the eye to follow.

He shook his head to get rid of the memory and his uncertainty. Maybe Nate and Chuck were right.

Anyway, it was how Tomlin came to find himself standing in the gathering shadows just inside the mouth of an alley, nervously clutching the shotgun, too late to back out. He had followed the Jensens as they left the hotel, walked a couple blocks to a restaurant for supper, and were on their way back to the hotel. He had thought they might go to one of Taos's saloons and have a drink after they'd eaten, but that didn't appear to be their plan.

As they walked out of the restaurant, Luke took a thin black cheroot from his shirt pocket and put it in his mouth. He didn't set fire to the gasper, just left it there unlit. He was pleasantly full from the meal they had just enjoyed, and while the weather was a little raw, at least it wasn't raining anymore.

Despite that good feeling, he hadn't changed his mind about his future plans, and he figured it was as good a time as any to broach the subject. "I guess you boys will be starting north for Colorado tomorrow."

"We don't mind waiting here until your money comes in, Luke. That shouldn't take more than a few days." Smoke paused, then added, "But that's not what you were talking about, is it?"

Luke chuckled around the cheroot. "Nobody could ever put anything over on you, Kirby, even when you were a kid." He was the only one who used Smoke's given name, and then only when something put him in mind of their childhood back in Missouri.

"What are you getting at, Luke?" Matt asked. "Aren't you coming back to the Sugarloaf with us?"

Luke shook his head. "No, I don't think I am. I believe once my money has come in, I'll head on over into Texas."

"And do what?" Smoke asked. "Look for more outlaws you can bring in dead or alive?"

"That's what I do," Luke replied, his voice a little sharp.

Tomlin saw the four of them a block away, walking at a deliberate pace and talking among themselves as they passed in and out of blocks of light coming from the windows of the buildings they passed.

He used his thumb to cock both of the scattergun's hammers. The Riordan brothers had told him he didn't really have to shoot. They would take care of that, they claimed.

But he wasn't going to let them do everything, he vowed. He wasn't going to threaten the Jensens and spew a lot of bravado. No, he was just going to throw down on them and feed them a double load of buckshot.

Maybe if he did that, he could forget about everything that had happened back in Espantosa. . . .

He swallowed hard, glanced across the street to where Chuck and Nate were hidden behind a parked wagon, and tightened his grip on the shotgun. The Jensens were close enough he could hear them talking. He took a deep breath and steeled himself to step out and start the ball.

"Are you sure you're in good enough shape to be hunting up outlaws?" Smoke asked.

"I'm fine," Luke insisted. "I'll be back up to my fighting weight before you know it."

"Sally won't be too happy if you don't come back with us," Smoke warned him. "She knew we were going off to give you a helping hand, and when I wired her after that whole business was over that you were all right, she replied that I should bring you home with me. She said she'd fatten you up in no time."

Preacher added, "And Miss Sally's bear sign 'll sure do it, too."

"My mouth's watering just thinking about it," Matt put in.

Luke said, "I appreciate all that, but I still think it's time for me to go my own way again. No offense, but I'm used to being by myself—"

He didn't have a chance to say any more. At that moment, a figure scuttled out of the alley mouth ahead of them and swung the menacing twin barrels of a Greener in their direction.

Chapter 7

Instinct took over for all four men. Hands blurred to gun butts. Weapons sprang free of their holsters and roared together in a deafening crash of gun-thunder. Tongues of flame leaped from the muzzles pointed at the shotgun-wielding hombre.

Whoever he was, the fella never had a chance. At least six slugs smashed into his chest, all of them within inches of each other. The bullets tore through his body and burst out his back. He wound up with a hole all the way through him that a man could have almost put a fist through.

The impact of that many bullets tossed him backwards like a rag doll. The Grecner's twin barrels were pointed almost straight up when his finger jerked the triggers and touched off the loads. The blast lit up the street for a split second.

Man and shotgun alike thudded to the dirt street next to each other. Barely three heartbeats had gone by since he had lunged out of the alley to threaten Smoke and the others.

Echoes from the pistol volley and the shotgun's double

discharge still filled the air, but Smoke heard fresh gunfire anyway and was aware of the wind-rip of a bullet as it whipped past his ear. From the corner of his eye he spotted a muzzle flash and whirled in that direction.

The shots were coming from behind a wagon parked across the street. It looked like a bushwhacker was crouched at each end of the vehicle, firing over the side-boards.

Acting out of instinct again, the four men scattered as bullets whined through the air around them. As they split up, they returned the shots, sending a storm of lead at the wagon.

Smoke drifted to his right. Something began striking lightly against his hat and shoulders as he moved, feeling like big drops of rain or small hailstones. After a second, he realized it was the buckshot fired from the Greener, falling back to earth as gravity claimed it.

The buckshot didn't pose a real threat. It was more of an annoyance than anything else. The real danger came from the men behind the wagon, who were still stubbornly spraying bullets across the street.

Smoke dropped to a knee behind a water trough. To his left, Matt had taken cover behind a rain barrel. Preacher had ducked into the alcove of a store's entrance where he was still relatively exposed, but he pressed his whip-like thinness into a small angle, which gave him some protection.

Luke was the only one still out in the open, and he was sliding sideways toward a parked buggy as the Remingtons in his hands spat fire and lead. Suddenly, he stumbled and went down.

Fury filled Smoke at the thought that his older brother might be badly wounded, or even worse.

They hadn't pulled Luke out of that tight spot in

Massacre Canyon only to have him gunned down in the crooked, narrow streets of Taos. Yelling, "Pour it on!" to Matt and Preacher, Smoke sprang up again and dashed toward Luke.

As he approached, he saw Luke struggling to get up, which was a relief of sorts. At least he was still alive. Smoke holstered his guns and grabbed his brother under the arms from behind. As he started dragging him toward the buggy, Luke demanded, "What the hell do you think you're doing? Hunt some cover, Smoke!"

"Not without you," Smoke grunted as he pulled Luke, a big, rangy man, and certainly no lightweight. Smoke's broad shoulders and long arms held enormous strength. He heaved and backed up until both of them sprawled on the ground behind the buggy.

It wasn't the safest place in the world. The would-be killers could still fire through the gaps between the spokes of the buggy wheels. A slug kicked up dust only a couple feet from Smoke as he knelt next to Luke. "How bad are you hit?"

"I'm not hit at all!" Luke answered surprisingly. "One of those guys shot one of my boot heels off!"

That was even more of a relief. Smoke chuckled. "Well, I'm glad you're not about to bleed to death. Since you can't move very well while you're missing a heel, stay here and help Matt and Preacher cover me. I'm going to cross the street so I can come at those varmints from a different direction."

"Let me take my other boot off and I can come with you. I can run in my sock feet."

"Be better if you can make those fellas keep their heads down for a few seconds," Smoke told him. "Reload those Remingtons and let me know when you're ready."

Luke looked like he wanted to argue, but he thumbed

fresh cartridges into the two long-barreled revolvers, then gave Smoke a curt nod. "Go ahead. Matt and Preacher ought to pick up on what you're trying to do."

"We can hope so. Now!" Smoke dashed out from behind the buggy as Luke stood up and began emptying the Remingtons diagonally across the street toward the wagon where the ambushers lurked. Farther along the street, Matt and Preacher followed suit. Bullets chewed into the wagon's frame and threw a shower of splinters into the air.

Smoke was lucky. He didn't step in any holes or slip in any horse manure as he sprinted across the street. When he reached the other side he drew his guns again and angled toward the wagon. The bombardment from Luke, Matt, and Preacher was coming to an end as their weapons began to run dry, but it had served its purpose. Smoke's keen eyes could see the two bushwhackers as they crouched behind the wagon.

They seemed to be aware of the deadly danger in which they suddenly found themselves. They let out alarmed yells as they whirled to face the charging Smoke. He dove forward to the ground as more Colt flame bloomed in the darkness ahead of him. Landing on his belly as bullets tore through the air a couple feet above him, he triggered both Colts.

His shots possessed an uncanny, almost supernatural accuracy. One bushwhacker screamed, dropped his gun, and doubled over as two slugs punched into his guts. The other managed to keep firing, but only for a second longer before a bullet drove deep into his chest and exploded his heart. He dropped straight down, dead even as he collapsed.

The gut-shot man was still alive, writhing on the ground next to the wagon as blood poured between his fingers. Smoke surged up, hurried closer, and kicked the man's gun well out of reach. He holstered his left-hand gun, fished a lucifer from his pocket, and set the match afire with a snap of his iron-hard thumbnail.

The sudden glare revealed the faces of two young men, reasonably handsome and looking enough alike that they had to be related. They were strangers to Smoke. He was sure he had never seen either of them before.

The mortally wounded man was curled up on his side. Smoke toed his shoulder and rolled him onto his back. Keeping the gun trained on the young man, he asked, "Who are you, mister, and why did you try to kill us?"

"Go to . . . hell, Jensen!" the dying man gasped. "We woulda been . . . famous . . ."

That told Smoke all he needed to know as the stranger's final breath rattled in his throat. The gathering pool of dark blood around him told Smoke that one of the bullets must have nicked an artery. The bushwhacker was fortunate to have died quickly. Belly wounds usually meant a slow, agonizing finish, but he had bled to death in moments.

Luke, Matt, and Preacher approached, Luke limping because of the ruined boot on his right foot. As the match burned down and Smoke dropped it in the street, Preacher asked, "Who in tarnation are those fellas?"

"I don't know their names," Smoke said, "but I know what they wanted. They figured on being famous as the men who killed the Jensens."

"And now all they get is a hole in the local graveyard," Matt said. "What about the other one?"

"Let's go take a look," Smoke suggested.

They crossed the street, where he lit another match to reveal the slain gunner's face.

"Petey Tomlin!" Luke exclaimed. "I'd hoped he would have more sense than that."

"Well," Preacher said, "I reckon you can collect the bounty on him, too."

"And that makes it a clean sweep on the Shawcross gang," Matt pointed out. "Ought to be a big enough payday you won't have to work for a while, Luke."

"The money's not the only reason I do what I do," Luke grumbled. "After all these years, it's the only thing I know. And this doesn't change my mind. I'm still not going back to Sugarloaf."

"Sally will be disappointed," Smoke said again as he started reloading his guns. "Things have probably been boring enough on the ranch that she's looking forward to having all of us around again."

Chapter 8

Sally Jensen was perched on the seat of the Sugarloaf's buckboard, giving her a good view of what was going on inside the corral next to it. A part of her would have preferred to climb up on the fence's top rail and sit there, but that wouldn't have been very ladylike. She had hitched up a team and driven over from the barn, instead.

She leaned forward on the seat and called encouragement to the young man seated in the saddle of a wildly plunging and bucking bronc. "Hang on, Cal! You can do it!"

The cowboys gathered along the corral fence cheered young Calvin Woods, too. He wasn't a top hand when it came to bronc busting, but he wasn't bad, either.

The big bay he was on was a particularly salty specimen. From the looks of things, he was about to go flying off the horse's back at any second. Half a dozen times, he had already come within a hairsbreadth of losing his seat.

Sally was so engrossed in Cal's battle with the bay, she didn't notice the rider coming down out of the hills surrounding the ranch headquarters. If she had been looking, she would have seen that he was a tall, lean cowboy with a rugged face and a thick dark mustache touched with gray. At the moment, his face was set in a grim, worried expression.

He reined his paint pony to a halt just as Cal finally lost the war when the bay threw a particularly wicked jump and twist.

He yelled and his arms and legs waved frantically as he sailed into the air. His hat was long since gone, or it would have flown off, too.

Before he ever hit the ground, several of the Sugarloaf hands piled off the top rail and dashed forward. A couple shouted and waved their hats in the air to distract the bay. It pranced away, obviously well-satisfied. Cal crashed to the hard-packed earth with bone-jarring, teeth-rattling force. The other two ran to Cal, caught hold of him under the arms, and hauled him to his feet. They hustled him over to the gate, which another man swung open. The bay didn't have a reputation as a man killer, but there was no point in taking chances.

As soon as the men had Cal outside the corral, the gate was shut again, and the two cowboys who'd been distracting the bay ran for the fence while the horse chased them, clearly not putting much effort into it. As the men scrambled over the fence, the bay turned away and tossed his head arrogantly as if to say that he had showed them.

Sally climbed down from the buckboard seat and hurried over to Cal, who was leaning over with his hands resting on his thighs as he breathed heavily, trying to recover the air that had been knocked out of him by the fall.

"Cal, are you all right?" she asked him.

Without looking up, the young puncher replied, "Yeah, I . . . reckon I am . . . Miss Sally. Just gotta . . . catch my breath."

With a grin, one of the other cowboys said, "By tomorrow he'll have a big ol' bruise where he lit down, but luckily that's where none of us 'll have to look at it!"

"Yeah, he might've been better off if he'd landed on his head," another cowboy gibed. "That's so hard he never woulda felt it!"

"You boys . . . are just too blasted funny . . . for words," Cal panted. He finally lifted his head and glared toward the corral, where the bay was still prancing around proudly. "I'll get that . . . son of a gun . . . next time."

"There's real work to be done first," a harsh voice said.

Sally looked around, finally realizing the newcomer was there. When she saw the expression on his lined and weathered face, she immediately asked, "What's wrong, Pearlie?"

He thumbed his black hat to the back of his head and swung down from the saddle. "Reckon we'd better talk over to the house, Miss Sally."

She felt a chill go through her. Pearlie served as the foreman of the crew that worked the Sugarloaf, and as such, he was a hard worker but usually had a carefree grin on his face.

In earlier times, he had been an outlaw and a gunman, and if things had gone a little differently, Smoke might have wound up killing him instead of hiring him. In moments such as this, when he looked like he was ready for trouble, Sally caught a glimpse of the dangerous hombre Pearlie had been—and still was, when need be.

"All right. That's fine." She glanced over at one of the hands. "Brad, can you take the buckboard back to the barn and tend to the team?"

"Sure thing, Miss Sally," the man said as he lifted a hand and pinched the brim of his hat.

There wasn't a man on Sugarloaf who didn't treat her with the utmost respect. Not only because it would have been dangerous to do otherwise, since her husband was considered one of the deadliest men with a gun on the whole frontier. Quite possibly *the* deadliest. The members of the Sugarloaf crew, which was plenty salty itself, treated Sally Jensen the way they did because they knew she would do to ride the river with. She might have been born back east, but her life as Smoke's wife had taught her how to rope and ride and shoot as well as most men and better than some. Over and above that, she had sand and had proven her courage on more than one occasion. She was smart as a whip, too.

Pearlie handed the paint's reins to one of the other men and walked toward the big ranch house with Sally, his spurs chinking with every step. It was a beautiful day in the high country, but no one would have known that by looking at him.

As they reached the porch, out of earshot of the other men, Sally said, "I can fetch some cold buttermilk and cornbread—"

"Any other time I'd be mighty tempted, ma'am," he interrupted.

That slight breach of manners was enough to tell her just how upset Pearlie really was.

He went on. "Right now, I need to tell you what I just saw up on Lone Pine Ridge."

"Go ahead," she urged.

Pearlie took a deep breath. "Those three fellas I spotted before are back, and I swear to you, Miss Sally, they're up to no good!"

Chapter 9

Sally frowned. "Were you close enough to get a good look at them?"

Pearlie shook his head. "No, they were up on the ridge and I was in the meadow down below, checkin' to see how the winter grass is comin' in. I think they were keepin' an eye on me. My skin got to crawlin' and my back felt like it had a target painted on it, so I'm convinced they were fixin' to bushwhack me if I got any closer to 'em. I drifted on outta there sort of casual-like, so they wouldn't know I'd spotted 'em."

"You did the right thing," Sally said vehemently.

"I ain't so sure about that." Pearlie grimaced. "It felt like runnin' away. Smoke wouldn't have ever done that."

"Smoke wouldn't have risked getting himself killed for no good reason, either," she pointed out.

"Maybe, but I don't like those fellas skulkin' around Sugarloaf without knowin' who they are or what they're doin' here."

Neither did Sally. It wasn't the first time Pearlie had spotted strangers on Sugarloaf range. Some of the other men had reported seeing unknown riders in the past couple weeks, too. Those riders always disappeared whenever anyone got too close to them. It was a worrisome situation.

She was confident that they could handle it, though. She'd had Pearlie and Cal make a survey of the herds and they hadn't found any stock missing, so it didn't appear that the lurkers had rustling in mind.

It was possible the strangers were just hombres passing through the area. In each case, the riders might have been different men.

She had broached that possibility with Pearlie, and he hadn't agreed with the idea.

"Looked like the same horses to me each time," he had said, "and from talkin' to the other fellas who've seen 'em, they agree. We've got three fellas who're lookin' for trouble."

As she paced back and forth on the porch, Sally said, "This has gone on long enough. We need to get to the bottom of it."

"That's the way I see it, too, ma'am. I'll get the crew together and we'll go up to Lone Pine Ridge and roust out those hombres—"

"No," Sally broke in, shaking her head. "If you take all the men up there, those strangers are bound to see you coming. They'll either hide, or more likely they'll clear out before you ever get there."

"Well, if they light a shuck, then we won't have to worry about 'em no more."

"But what's to stop them from coming back later? We need to lay our hands on them and persuade them to answer some questions. A job like that requires more stealth than force."

"So what are you sayin' we ought to do?"

"You can go after them, but you should take a couple people with you—Cal . . . and me."

Pearlie's eyes widened. As he stared at her, he exclaimed, "Aw, he—heck, no, Miss Sally. I don't mind takin' Cal along—the kid ain't near as green as he used to be—but Smoke 'd skin my hide if I was to put you in any danger."

"How do we know any of us will be in any danger? Those men may be harmless."

Pearlie's scornful grunt made it clear just how likely he considered that possibility to be.

"This is my ranch as well as Smoke's. I have a right to know what's happening out on our range."

"I ain't disputin' that, but I can find out and then tell you."

"I'm going along." Sally didn't like giving orders, but sometimes it was necessary. "That's final."

Pearlie looked narrowly at her "How come?"

"How come what?"

"How come you're so dead set on riskin' your life this way? No disrespect intended, ma'am, but it seems to me you're smarter than that."

Sally's face warmed with anger. Her first thought was that Pearlie had no right to speak to her that way, but then she realized he had *every* right. She and Smoke had no more loyal friend than the ex-gunman. He was worried about her, that's all.

And honestly, she didn't have an answer for his question. Maybe she was just feeling the restlessness that came from being stuck at the ranch for a long period of time while Smoke was gone. Their life together had been adventurous, to say the least. On numerous occasions, she had heard the roar of guns close up, smelled the sharp tang of burned powder.

To Smoke, whether he wanted to admit it or not, such things were the breath of life. Sally didn't crave excitement to the same extent, but after a while she began to miss it.

"I don't want to cause trouble," she said. "Pick one more man to come with us. If we get close to those skulkers, I'll hang back and let the three of you round them up. But I want to question them myself."

Pearlie scratched his angular, beard-stubbled jaw. Clearly he didn't care for the idea, but he knew there was only so much he could argue with her. "All right. I reckon we can try it that way, but if it looks like there's gonna be trouble and I tell you to hurry on back here to headquarters, you'll do what I say, right?"

"Of course." Sally paused, then added, "Within reason."

Pearlie sighed. "I got a hunch that last part's gonna be the problem."

Chapter 10

It was too late in the day to start out on their mission, so that gave Pearlie a chance to think about who he wanted to take with him besides Cal.

He settled on a puncher named Ben Hardy, who had been working on the Sugarloaf for a while. He was a quiet, competent, graying man who seemed like he would be coolheaded under fire, although that hadn't really been tested since he'd gone to work for Smoke.

Pearlie hadn't pried into the man's background, either. Such things were seldom done in the West, where every day was a new beginning.

He called Cal and Hardy aside that evening and led them out of the bunkhouse to explain what they were going to do.

When Cal heard that Sally intended to come along, he said, "Aw, shoot, Pearlie, that's not a good idea."

"You ain't tellin' me anything I don't already know, kid," Pearlie replied. "You try arguin' with the lady when she's got her mind made up about somethin'."

Hardy said, "I never heard of a woman getting mixed up in something that could turn out to be gun trouble."

"You ain't never met a woman like Sally Jensen, neither," Pearlie told him. "Things have been pretty quiet around here since you signed on, Ben, but when hell starts to pop, Miss Sally is usually right there in the middle of it. She's loaded guns for us more 'n once durin' a siege, and she'll put a rifle to her shoulder and blow a hole through a varmint that needs ventilatin', too, if need be. She's the finest lady I ever knowed, bar none. Just don't expect her to swoon if things get rough."

"But we're going to do our best to protect her, right?"

"Damn right we are," Pearlie snapped. "Whether she likes it or not."

They were up early the next morning, breakfasting well before dawn. The eastern sky was turning gray when they went into the barn to saddle four horses, including a mare that Sally liked to ride.

She came in while they were doing that. She wore boots, jeans, and an open sheepskin jacket over a man's shirt. Her long, thick dark hair was tucked up under a flat-crowned brown hat.

Some folks would consider it scandalous for a woman to dress like that, but nobody would ever accuse Sally Jensen of impropriety. She had a way of making whatever she did seem perfectly normal and proper.

Besides, the Winchester carbine tucked under her arm went a long way toward discouraging criticism.

With her free hand, she patted the canvas pouch slung over her shoulder. "I packed some sandwiches for us in case we're out all day."

"What kind?" Cal asked, ignoring the frown Pearlie directed toward him.

"Roast beef," Sally replied with a smile.

"And some bear sign?"

"I might have wrapped up some to take along with us."

Cal grinned. "I sort of hope it takes a while to round up those mavericks, then."

"You better tighten that saddle cinch," Pearly told him, "or else you're liable to fall off and land on your head 'fore we get halfway to where we're goin'."

"Haven't you heard? My head's so hard any time I land on it, I don't even feel it."

Pearlie snorted. "You ain't gettin' an argument from me."

Sally slung the pouch from her saddle and slid the carbine into its sheath. She turned to Hardy. "You're coming along with us, Ben?"

"Yes, ma'am."

"You don't think you should argue about a woman getting mixed up in this?"

Hardy said, "It's not my place to argue, ma'am. I ride for the brand."

"That's good to know." Sally turned to Pearlie. "I understand why you're worried about this. You think that if the three of you are having to look after me, it's liable to increase the danger for all of us."

"You said it, ma'am, not me."

"That's why I don't want you looking after me. I can take care of myself."

He nodded. "Sure thing." *None of us believe that for a second, though.*

He and Cal would sacrifice their own lives to keep anything from happening to her. Whether or not Hardy would was still open to question, but Pearlie had a hunch he might.

All in all, he still had plenty of misgivings about it as they all rode out a short time later.

* * *

Lone Pine Ridge was about six miles north of the ranch headquarters. A tall, sandstone bluff, it ran for a mile or more along a bench at the base of a rocky up-thrust that turned into a rugged mountain as it rose. In front of the bluff was a broad pasture that served as part of the winter range for Sugarloaf. One tree, a towering pine, grew at the bluff's edge overlooking the pasture and gave the ridge its name.

A fairly easy trail ran from the pasture up the bluff to the bench, but the approach to it was out in the open where anybody at the top could see who was coming.

A higher trail led around a shoulder of the mountain, but it wasn't as accessible. To get to it, a person had to ride up a steep, rocky slope, then follow a narrow ledge with a forty foot drop-off beside it.

That was the way Pearlie intended for them to reach Lone Pine Ridge.

At the base of the scree-littered slope, he reined in. "We better get down and lead these horses. Less chance of 'em slippin' and takin' a tumble that way."

"You don't have to make it easier for me," Sally said.

"No such thing," Pearlie told her. "I ain't in the mood for a broken neck this mornin'."

"In that case," Sally said with a smile, "it sounds like a good idea to me."

They swung down from their saddles and started up the slope, gripping their mounts' reins. By the time they reached the top, Sally was puffing and blowing, out of breath from the exertion.

"We'll hold up a minute here," Pearlie said.

"I'm . . . all right," she told him. "I can . . . go on . . . any time."

"Soon as the horses rest a mite."

She nodded gratefully.

A few minutes later, they mounted up again.

Pearlie said, "The trail's only wide enough for one horse at a time. I'll take the lead. Cal, you come behind me, then you, Miss Sally. Ben, you'll be bringin' up the rear."

Hardy nodded. "Fine by me."

Pearlie heeled his horse into motion. He had to ride only a short distance before venturing onto the ledge that wrapped around the side of the mountain. The others followed him, one at a time as he had laid out.

The trail angled up steadily, but it wasn't too steep. Pearlie rode with his rifle held across the saddle in front of him, ready for trouble. He didn't expect to run into the strangers as soon as they reached the bench, but there was no guarantee they wouldn't.

Even worse, it was possible they might run into the skulkers on the one-way trail. If that led to a gunfight and any of the horses spooked . . .

The fall wasn't as high as it was in many places in the rugged country, but it was plenty high enough to be fatal. Pearlie sort of held his breath as he rode.

Nothing happened. They reached the end of the trail, where it led out onto the bench on top of the ridge, about half an hour later.

Pearlie held up a hand in a signal for the group to halt. He leaned forward in the saddle and took a good look at the terrain in front of him. The bench was half a mile wide and stretched for a mile, like the bluff. There might be only one lone pine at the edge, but the rest of the bluff was heavily wooded. Some grass grew up there, but not enough to provide good graze, which was why they had never brought any stock up the other trail. It wouldn't have been worth the trouble.

He didn't see any sign of the mysterious riders, but he knew there were hidden clearings among those thick stands of pine. The men could have a camp up in there somewhere.

He said quietly, "Let's stay in the trees where there's some cover. Don't get in a hurry. We don't want to stumble onto those fellers without any warnin'."

They didn't have to ride single file, but the trees made it impossible to spread out much. Pearlie remained in the lead, with Cal and Sally behind him and Hardy still bringing up the rear. They had gone about half a mile along the ridge when Pearlie suddenly halted again.

He lifted his head, took a deep breath, then turned to the others and whispered, "Take a whiff o' that."

Sally smelled the air and whispered, "Wood smoke. And . . . is that coffee?"

"Yep," Pearlie replied. "Tobacco, too. They're up ahead of us, and they ain't far off, neither. We'll get down here."

They dismounted and all four of them took their rifles out. The atmosphere under the pines was tense.

"Miss Sally, you and Hardy stay here and hold the horses," Pearlie said. "Cal and me will see if we can Injun up on those boys and find out what they're doin' here."

"Why don't you leave the kid with Miz Jensen and take me with you?" Hardy suggested.

"Because I've been in some tight spots with the boy before and I know I can count on him. No offense, Ben."

"None taken," Hardy said with a shrug.

"I don't like not going with you," Sally said to Pearlie.

"That was our deal," he pointed out.

"Yes, I suppose it was. The two of you be careful."

"I intend to." Pearlie removed his spurs and motioned for Cal to do likewise. "Come on."

Holding their Winchesters at the ready, they moved off through the trees, silent as Indians.

Chapter 11

During the time Cal had lived on the Sugarloaf, Pearlie had taught the youngster quite a bit about tracking and moving quietly through the woods. Smoke had helped with Cal's education, too. He had even picked up some tips from the old master, Preacher, who in his younger years had been known to slip into Blackfoot villages at night, cut the throats of several of his enemies, and get back out again without his nocturnal vengeance being discovered until morning.

All that tutoring came in handy as Cal cat footed through the trees just as silently as Pearlie, who was impressed by his stealth.

Neither of them said anything. They communicated by hand signals.

Pearlie and Cal had been gone for a few minutes when Ben asked, "You mind if I roll myself a smoke, Miss Sally?"

Sally didn't have to think about it. "Better not, Ben. If

we can smell the tobacco smoke coming from the men we're after, they could smell it coming from us."

"Oh." Hardy grunted. "Yeah, that's true. Pretty smart of you to think of that."

"I guess I've been married to Smoke for long enough that thinking strategically just comes natural to me."

"Yeah, I reckon there's always one ruckus or another going on, isn't there?"

"That certainly seems to be true," Sally said with a smile.

"I didn't mean any offense," Hardy said hastily.

"That's all right," she assured him. "I know trouble seems to follow Smoke around. I knew that when I married him."

As the smell of a campfire grew stronger, Pearlie motioned for Cal to slow down. They crouched lower, practically crawling, until Pearlie reached a point where he could carefully part some brush and peer through the little gap at the hiding place of the three men who had been lurking up there for the past few weeks.

The camp was set up in one of those small clearings he had thought about earlier. A tiny fire crackled merrily inside a ring of stones. Several feet above the flames, the strangers had set up a framework of broken branches. The thickly needled pine boughs dispersed what little smoke came from the fire, so that no one would spot a column of it rising above the trees and be able to track them that way.

The clearing was about fifty feet wide. Three horses were picketed on the far side of it, grazing on what was left of the sparse grass at the edge of the trees. The saddles were on the ground, placed at the heads of three bedrolls to serve as pillows.

The strangers had dragged logs close to the fire where two of them took their ease, smoking quirlies and sipping coffee from tin cups. The old, dented coffeepot was placed at the fire's edge, close enough to keep warm whatever was left inside it.

As Pearlie looked around, he felt worry percolating inside him just like the coffee in that pot. He had seen three men the day before, and three horses were on the other side of the camp, but only two men were in sight. That made him nervous. Where was the third man?

In all likelihood, he was off in the trees tending to some personal business, but Pearlie couldn't know that for sure. As long as the third hombre was unaccounted for, he represented a potential threat, not only to the Sugarloaf ranch hands but also to Miss Sally.

Ben Hardy smiled at Sally. "Sometimes it's hard for me to believe that I'm working for the famous Smoke Jensen."

Sally smiled back. "Some people would say notorious, rather than famous."

"Well, they'd be wrong," Hardy declared. "He's as fine a gent as I've ever met."

"He is, indeed," she agreed.

"How much longer do we have to stay here, Green?" The sudden question from one of the men at the campfire sounded startlingly loud in the stillness of the mountain.

In the bushes, Pearlie frowned and looked at Cal, who frowned right back.

Instead of answering right away, the other man took a long drag on his cigarette. The coal was almost down to the end, so he dropped the butt to the dirt and ground it out with a boot heel. "We stay until the boss shows up and tells us it's all right to leave," the man called Green answered in a harsh voice. "You know that, Joe."

"Yeah, but we've been holed up here too long. You know it ain't safe. Those cowboys are liable to find us—"

"I said we wait until we hear otherwise from the boss," Green snapped. "I don't know about you, but I don't want to get on that hombre's bad side. I've seen some of the things he can do."

Joe looked down at the ground and muttered, "Yeah, that's true. I remember what happened to Lonesome Dan—"

"You just shut up about Lonesome Dan," Green said. "None of us got any business talkin' about that."

A frown creased Pearlie's forehead as he and Cal remained hidden in the brush. The conversation between the two strangers created more questions than it answered.

Who were these men and their mysterious boss who had told them to wait on Lone Pine Ridge? Who was the evidently unfortunate Lonesome Dan, and what had happened to him?

Pearlie didn't have any idea, but he was confident he knew what sort of men the two were. He had seen plenty just like them. Hard-planed faces, beard-stubbled cheeks and jaws, sunken eyes that contained as much warmth and human feeling as a rattlesnake's. They were outlaws and gunmen, plain and simple.

There'd been a time when his face had looked much the same as it stared back at him from a shaving mirror. He had ridden the lonely trails and heard the owl hoot at night with men just like them . . . most of whom were dead. Pearlie knew he probably would be, too, if he hadn't been lucky enough to cross paths with Smoke Jensen.

While they waited for Pearlie and Cal to return, Hardy asked Sally, "When do you think Smoke's going to get back to the ranch?"

"It shouldn't be too much longer. He wired me from Arizona that they weren't going to get in any hurry. His brother Luke had had such a rough time of it and needed to take it easy. Even so, I expect him pretty soon. Maybe another week or two."

"It'll be good to see him again," Hardy said, nodding.

"It certainly will!"

She blushed a little. The thoughts she was having about Smoke's return to Sugarloaf had to be much different from what the ranch hand was thinking.

Joe stared into the dying fire, letting a few minutes of brooding silence go by, then commented. "It seems like Larson's been gone longer than he should have just to check those snares."

The words made sense to Pearlie. The men didn't want to hunt any game because gunshots up on the bench would attract the attention of the Sugarloaf crew. If they had run out of supplies, or just had a craving for fresh meat, the only practical way to get it was by setting snares. He had eaten many a roasted rabbit caught that way, back in the days when he was on the dodge.

Green was in the process of building another smoke and licked the paper to seal the quirly. "It takes a while."

He put the cigarette in his mouth, struck a match, and lit it. After a couple of puffs, he went on. "But you're right. He should've been back by now." Green stood up from the log. "Maybe we'd better go take a look for him."

Pearlie was more worried about their missing companion than they were. Sally and Ben Hardy were back in the trees, a couple hundred yards away. They had no way of knowing that one of the outlaws was wandering around and might come across them at any moment.

Maybe it was time for him and Cal to fade back, Pearlie thought, and rejoin Sally and Hardy. They hadn't found out everything, but at least they knew the three strangers were hardcases and not the sort they wanted lurking around the ranch.

They needed to get back to Sugarloaf headquarters, where Pearlie could gather the rest of the men, come back up, and flush those varmints out, like he'd wanted to do from the first. . . .

Chapter 12

Sally put her hands to her face to cover up her blush and minor embarrassment. "I wonder what Pearlie and Cal found," she mused, changing the subject of Smoke's return.

They didn't have a chance to continue that discussion. At that moment, a man stepped out of the trees nearby, pointed a revolver at them, and snapped, "Both of you freeze right where you are."

Despite that command, Hardy started to reach for his gun and the carbine in Sally's hands rose. Their reactions were instinctive.

"Damn it. I said don't move!" The man's finger was tight on the trigger. His thumb looped over the hammer was the only thing holding it back. He aimed the gun directly at Sally as he told Hardy, "You might kill me, mister, but even if you do, the lady's gonna get a hole blowed through her."

Hardy moved his hand away from his gun butt. "Take it easy. There's no need for anybody to get hurt."

"Reckon I'll be the judge of that," the stranger said as he sneered at them. "You're the ones sneakin' around."

"Not really," Sally said. "We have a right to be up here. This range is part of the Sugarloaf ranch. My husband and I own it."

"Yeah, but this ain't your husband." The man wore a leering grin on his unshaven face. "I know that from listenin' to the two of you talk. What are you doin' up here? Come for a little slap an' tickle on the sly, where the rest of the hands won't know about it?"

Anger that anyone would think such a thing boiled up inside her. She knew the stranger had the drop on them, but her impulse was to swing the carbine up and start blasting anyway—which wouldn't accomplish anything except to get her killed, and possibly Ben Hardy, too, she realized. With an effort, she suppressed the urge to start shooting.

She ignored the man's question and coldly asked one of her own. "What are *you* doing up here? You don't belong on this range."

"Reckon my friends and me go wherever we want," the owlhoot declared. "Now, put that rifle down on the ground, careful-like, and you, rannie, you unbuckle your gun belt and drop it, too."

"Miz Jensen . . . ?" Hardy asked.

Sally sighed. "I suppose we'd better do what he says." She bent over slowly to place the carbine on the ground in front of her, keeping her eyes on the gunman.

Confident that he had them right where he wanted them, he hadn't bothered to lower his revolver and keep it trained on her. It was pointed over her head.

She dived forward and cried, "Now, Ben!" As she landed on her belly, she angled the barrel up and fired the round already levered into the chamber.

At the same time, Hardy grabbed his gun, jerked it

out of its holster, and triggered the Colt twice as he moved quickly to his left, away from Sally.

Before the two men by the campfire or the pair hidden in the brush could do anything, the quiet was shattered by a swift flurry of gunshots.

Pearlie's blood seemed to turn to ice in his veins as he realized the blasts came from the direction where Sally and Hardy waited.

The gunman let the hammer fall as bullets whipped through the air around him. His revolver belched fire. The slug tore through space a good eighteen inches above Sally's head and plowed a furrow in the dirt behind her. She rolled over, levering the carbine again.

The stranger swung his gun toward Hardy and loosed another round. Hardy grunted and stumbled as the bullet thudded into him. Despite being hit, he stayed on his feet and triggered a third shot at the stranger.

From her prone position, Sally fired again. She was rewarded by a spray of blood from the gunman's right arm. He howled in pain. The bullet's impact shattered his elbow, flinging his arm out at his side. The revolver flew from suddenly nerveless fingers.

She worked the Winchester's lever and fired a third time. The stranger was already twisting away, and he dived behind some trees as Sally's bullet whistled past his head.

Somewhere not far away, crashing sounded in the brush.

Someone else was coming, she realized, and she had no way of knowing if it was friend or foe.

Chapter 13

The flurry of gunshots made both Pearlie and Cal stiffen as they crouched in the brush bordering the strangers' camp.

Green was already on his feet. Joe leaped up as well. Startled curses spilled from each man's mouth.

"Damn it. Larson must've run into trouble," Green exclaimed. "Come on!"

Chances were the outlaw called Larson had run across Sally and Ben Hardy, Pearlie knew. Whatever was going on back there, Larson didn't need reinforcements.

"Go help Miss Sally!" Pearlie snapped at Cal. "I'll deal with these two!"

Cal obeyed the order without argument or hesitation, another sign that he wasn't the green kid he had once been. He turned and plunged through the brush toward the sound of shooting.

At the same time, Pearlie drew his gun and sent a couple shots at Green and Joe. The outlaws had started in his direction, but as slugs kicked up dirt at their feet, they stopped short with almost comical suddenness and then dived for cover behind the log where they had been sitting.

"What the hell!" Joe shouted.

"It's an ambush!" Green hollered. "Must be Jensen's men!" He stuck his gun over the log and triggered twice in Pearlie's general direction. The bullets rattled the brush but didn't come very close to the Sugarloaf foreman.

Pearlie fired again. The slug chewed bark and splinters from the fallen tree.

As long as the two outlaws stayed behind the log, he couldn't hit them. The best he could hope for was to keep them pinned down until Cal got back with Sally and Ben.

Pearlie wasn't much of a praying man, but he sent up a plea that all three of his friends would be all right.

One of the outlaws raised up to try a shot. Pearlie was ready and squeezed the trigger. The man yelped as his hat flew off his head. Pearlie hoped the bullet had found more than hat, but judging by the man's renewed cursing, that wasn't the case.

With one ear, Pearlie listened to the other battle that was going on. He heard the heavy boom of pistol shots, mixed in with sharper cracks that probably came from Sally's carbine. She was giving a good account of herself, anyway . . . not that Pearlie would have expected anything else.

A lull fell over the clearing. He took advantage of it to thumb fresh cartridges into the chambers he had emptied.

He heard the two outlaws behind the log talking but couldn't make out any of their words. They were probably planning something, he thought.

A moment later, he found out as one man popped up

and sprayed lead across the area where Pearlie was hidden. He got off only one shot in return before he hit the dirt and hugged the ground for dear life as slugs tore through the brush around him, rattling the branches.

He heard running footsteps and knew the other outlaw was trying to flank him. The varmint was going to be successful. Pearlie couldn't risk raising his head to take aim at him.

If they caught him in a crossfire, he wasn't going to stand a chance.

Cal had his rifle ready as he ran through the trees. Shooting came from both directions, in front of him and behind him. He didn't like being in the middle. He wanted to be in one fight or the other.

He knew Pearlie was right, though. Protecting Miss Sally was always the most important thing, so he continued heading in that direction.

The shooting ahead of him tapered off, just as the other battle seemed to heat up. He heard shot after shot and knew Pearlie might be in bad trouble, but he couldn't turn back to help his friend. He had to do what the foreman had told him.

A shape suddenly burst out of the brush in front of him. Cal didn't have time to stop. He and the stranger ran smack-dab into each other with stunning force.

The collision made them bounce off each other and sprawl on the ground. Cal lost his grip on the rifle and it slid away from him as he landed hard enough to knock the breath out of his lungs.

Gasping for air, he rolled and twisted and reached for the pistol on his hip. He had just closed his hand around it when the other man loomed above him and brought a broken branch crashing down on his shoulder. Cal's right arm went numb.

His attacker raised the branch to strike again.

Cal saw that the man held the branch in his left hand. He was wounded. His right sleeve was bloody from the elbow down, but despite the shock and loss of blood, he still had some fight in him. Lines of rage contorted his face, giving him the strength to battle on.

Cal jerked his head aside as the makeshift club came down. As it slammed into the ground, he felt the branch brush his ear. That glancing blow was enough to make him yelp, but at least it didn't crush his skull.

He jerked his right leg up and kicked the man in the belly. The man grunted and flailed out wildly with the branch. It clipped Cal on the head as he tried to get up and he sprawled backwards again.

Evidently deciding that discretion was the better part of valor, especially considering the shape he was in, the man turned and started to stumble away. Cal scrambled up and dived after him, intending to tackle him around the knees.

The way his head was spinning from the last blow caused him to misjudge his leap. He fell short, made a last grab at the fleeing man, and missed again.

The wounded man plunged through the undergrowth and disappeared among the trees.

Still breathing hard, Cal got his hands and knees under him and pushed himself to his feet. His vision was a little blurry, but he spotted his Winchester lying on the ground a few yards away. He scooped it up and then hesitated, faced with the decision of whether to pursue the man he had fought with or check on Miss Sally and Hardy.

That wasn't a very difficult decision. Cal broke into an unsteady run toward the spot where he and Pearlie had left the other two members of their party.

Chapter 14

The crashing in the brush faded as Sally got to her knees. Whoever had been hurrying toward them had stopped or at least slowed down.

She jumped to her feet and levered the carbine again, then stood there and tracked the barrel back and forth across the trees as she searched for a target. She didn't see anything moving.

A groan from Hardy drew her attention. She turned toward the cowboy and saw him struggling to get up. The front of his shirt was dark with blood. She had known he was hit but hadn't realized it was that bad.

"Ben!" She hurried over to him, dropped to a knee, and held the carbine in one hand as she rested the other on his shoulder. "It's all right. Just lie there and take it easy."

"That . . . son of a . . ." he rasped.

"He's gone. He ran off into the woods."

"He might . . . come back."

"If he does, I'll give him a warm welcome," she said as she gestured slightly with the carbine. She leaned closer. "How bad are you hit?"

"Pretty . . . bad. Feels like . . . he drilled me . . . clean through."

She lifted him just enough to see that he was right. The back of his shirt was bloody, too. And judging from where the bullet hole on the front was located, the bullet couldn't have gone all the way through him without hitting something important.

He coughed. From the bubbling sound of it, Sally was certain he had a hole in one of his lungs. He was drowning in his own blood, and there wasn't a blessed thing she could do about it. He had only minutes to live.

"You better . . . leave me here," he told her. "Go find . . . Pearlie and Cal . . ."

She heard shots in the distance and knew her friends were still in danger. She wanted to go to them, help them, but she wasn't going to abandon Hardy. "I'm not going anywhere." She leaned closer to him. "You hang on."

He took a deep, shuddering breath. She knew from the rattle in his throat as it came back out that he was gone. He stared up sightlessly at the trees. Sunlight flickered through the branches and made the shadows shift on the dead man's face. Sally eased his eyelids down.

She stood, filled with the same sort of anger that Smoke would have felt had he been there. Evil men had come onto Sugarloaf land and had brought death with them. They had to pay for that.

Sally jerked the carbine level as someone came through the trees. Fallen pine needles crunched under the man's boots. Her finger was taut on the trigger as he lunged into view.

"Whoa!" Cal cried as he tried to stop himself. He threw his hands up in front of him as if they would turn aside a bullet. "Miss Sally, don't shoot! It's me!"

Sally held off on the trigger at the last instant. A

tremor went through her as she lowered the weapon. "Cal, I almost shot you!"

"Yeah, I know." He swallowed hard. "Are you all right, Miss Sally?"

"I am, but poor Ben . . ." She looked over at Hardy's still form.

"Dadblast it!" Cal burst out. "I reckon that varmint I tangled with is the one who got him?"

"You fought with one of them?"

"Yeah. Fella who looked like he was shot in the right arm. Are you the one who ventilated him?"

"That doesn't matter now," Sally said. "He's the one who got the drop on us, all right. We managed to turn the tables on him and wound him, but he got away."

Cal grimaced. "He got away from me, too. Even wounded and losing blood like he was, he managed to give me the slip."

"Don't worry about that. At least he didn't try to double back. Where's Pearlie?"

Cal angled his head toward the sound of shooting. "He's trying to keep the other two pinned down, but it sounds like he's got his hands full."

Sally jerked her head in a curt nod. "There's nothing we can do for Ben. Let's go see if we can give Pearlie a hand."

As one of the outlaws tried to get around to his side, Pearlie did the only thing he could. He thrust his Colt out in that direction and started thumbing off shots as fast as he could, firing blindly until he had emptied the revolver.

As that peal of gun thunder ended and the echoes rolled away against the mountainside above him, he shoved the revolver back into its holster and grabbed the Winchester lying on the ground beside him.

He heard a man muttering curses somewhere not far away. Had he hit the varmint trying to flank him? It was possible, he supposed, but it would have been pure luck if he did.

Of course, everybody could use a little good luck now and then.

"Green?" Joe called tentatively. "Green, are you all right?"

"Shut up, you damn fool!" came the harsh reply. Green sounded like he was in pain, no doubt about that. Pearlie was more convinced that he had winged the damn outlaw by accident.

Somebody else was coming. Pearlie heard them crashing through the brush behind him. Might be Cal, might even be Sally or Ben Hardy or all three of them.

Might be the other owlhoot, too. What had they called him? Larson?

Pearlie shifted his grip a little on the rifle and squirmed backwards. He angled to the side and wound up under some thick brush. The branches snagged his clothes and scratched him, but he ignored that minor annoyance.

"Green! Green, don't shoot! It's me! I'm comin' in!"

That was Larson, all right. He staggered past close enough that Pearlie could have thrust out the rifle barrel and tripped him.

He didn't. He was outnumbered three to one and didn't know what had happened to his companions. Giving up on a fight rubbed him the wrong way, but Sally could be hurt bad and need help. The same was true of Cal and Hardy. Finding out what had happened to them had to come before stopping those three hardcases, whether Pearlie liked it or not.

"Damn it. You're shot up." That was Green's voice again. "Joe, get the horses."

Joe whined, "You said we had to stay here until the boss—"

Green exploded. "To hell with the boss! Jensen's men know we're here."

"Listen, Green," Larson babbled. "I . . . I found out something . . ."

That was all Pearlie heard as the men's voices faded. He stayed where he was. A couple minutes later he heard the swift rataplan of hoofbeats as the three outlaws fled.

He had just gotten to his feet with the rifle in his hands when he heard a low call.

"Pearlie!"

That was the kid. Pearlie responded, "Over here, Cal!"

Relief flooded through the foreman when he saw that Sally was with Cal. He looked them both over quickly and didn't see any blood on their clothes.

Sally clutched his arm. "Are you all right, Pearlie?"

"Yeah, I'm fine, I reckon. What about Hardy?"

Sally's face was grim as she shook her head.

Pearlie always tried to watch his language around women, but he grated out, "Damn." He hadn't known Hardy that well, but the puncher had seemed like a decent hombre.

"What about those men?" Cal asked.

Pearlie jerked his head toward the north.

"They lit a shuck outta here. One of 'em had a busted wing, and I think a second one was hit, too. They decided to take off for the tall and uncut while they still could." He grimaced and shook his head. "Sorry I let 'em get away, Miss Sally. I was worried about you and the youngster here."

"Don't be silly," she told him. "I think we all burned enough powder today. We need to get poor Ben back to the ranch and see to it that he's laid to rest properly." She looked in the direction the outlaws had fled. "I'd still like to know who those men were and what they were doing here, but if they don't come back, I suppose it doesn't matter."

"Somebody sent 'em here and told 'em to wait. I know that from listenin' to what they said, so I wouldn't place any bets on 'em not comin' back." Pearlie's mouth was a bleak line under the drooping mustache as he added, "Whatever they were up to, I got a hunch they ain't done yet."

Chapter 15

Men who rode the dark and lonely trails knew the place as Zeke's. No other name was necessary. The two-story log building was the centerpiece of a small community that had no name at all, situated in a winding canyon far from the main trails. Tall and brooding, the canyon walls cast a never-ending shadow over the buildings.

In addition to the big house, the settlement had a barn with an attached blacksmith shop, a small trading post, and a squalid little cabin where a gnarled old man lived. He was a master gunsmith, known far and wide among the men on the wrong side of the law as someone who could repair or modify any gun ever made. His services were usually in demand . . . but not as in demand as the services of those who worked in the big house.

Zeke had three bartenders pouring drinks around the clock as long as there were customers. A frock-coated gambler addicted to laudanum ran a poker game . . . and it was honest. One rule for dealing with outlaws and killers was to play straight with them. They wouldn't stand for anything else.

Busiest of all were the six soiled doves who sometimes worked delivering drinks in the saloon but spent most of their time in the rooms upstairs. Zeke—again, the only name anyone knew him by—made a good living.

He was a tall, thin, gray-haired, gray-faced man who nearly always had an unlit cheroot clenched between his teeth. He wore a gray suit and sat at a table in the corner, taking the cigar out of his mouth now and then so he could sip from a tumbler of whiskey. As a rule, he didn't say much.

He sat up straighter when three newcomers came in. One of them had his right arm in a crude sling. A bloody bandage was wrapped around his elbow. Another man had a crimson-stained rag tied around his left thigh. The third one, who didn't seem to be wounded, helped his companions to a table and then went over to the bar.

"We're lookin' for Jonas Trask," he said to the bartender. "He's supposed to be here."

The bartender glanced past the man and looked across the room at Zeke.

Zeke took the cigar out of his mouth and crooked a finger at one of the doves, who had just set some drinks down at another table. "Go upstairs and tell Mr. Trask some of his boys are here," Zeke said to the woman when she stood at his table.

She was a tall, skinny redhead with fair skin. The scattering of freckles stood out as the order made her turn pale. "I-I hate to disturb him," she stammered.

"Do what I told you," Zeke snapped. He put the

cheroot back in his mouth and clamped his teeth on it as the dove headed hesitantly for the staircase.

He understood her reluctance. Most of the time Jonas Trask was friendly enough, but twice during the time he had been there, somebody had prodded him. In both cases, the other man was a known gunman, but Trask had bested both, wounding them and ending the fight.

What had happened after that was worse. Neither Zeke nor anyone else had tried to stop it. In such a place, a man handled his own problems. If he bit off too big a chunk, no one was going to come to his aid.

Especially when it meant crossing a man like Trask and running the risk of getting the same treatment.

Over at the bar, the man who had asked for Trask said impatiently to the apron, "Well? Didn't you hear me?"

Zeke stood up. Most of the eyes in the room followed him as he sauntered over to the bar. He said in a deceptively mild tone of voice, "Take it easy, my friend. I've sent someone to fetch Mr. Trask."

"Oh." The newcomer looked a little uneasy. "You're the fella who runs this place, ain't you? The one they call Zeke?"

"That's right," Zeke said around the cheroot.

The man wiped his nose with the back of his hand. "Well, I'm sorry for the ruckus. My pards and I have been ridin' hard, and they're hurt."

"Bottle," Zeke said to the bartender.

The man set it on the hardwood.

Zeke used the cheroot as a pointer. "Take that over to your friends. Trask will be down when he's good and ready, I suppose."

The gunman nodded. "Obliged. What do I owe you?"

"If you're one of Trask's men, nothing. He's taking care of it."

"Well, that's, uh, mighty decent of him."

Zeke's mouth quirked a little. He didn't think anybody would use the words *mighty decent* to describe Jonas Trask very often.

As the newcomers passed around the bottle, Zeke returned to his table. Movement on the staircase caught his eye and he looked in that direction. The redhead was hurrying down from the second floor. She was still pale.

Lord knew what she had seen up there in Trask's room.

The man himself sauntered out onto the balcony a moment later and rested his hands on the railing as he looked down and smiled. There was no denying that Jonas Trask was a handsome man with his fine-boned face, his piercing blue eyes, and his shock of black hair. He wore a good suit, a white shirt, and a string tie. The saloon grew quieter as he stood there, and after a few seconds all the noise died away entirely.

In a powerful, resonant voice, he said, "I hear you're looking for me, Joseph."

The gunman who wasn't wounded swallowed. "Uh, yes, sir, I reckon." He waved a hand at his companions. "Green and Larson are wounded—"

"Yes, I can see that," Trask interrupted. "Can they make it upstairs?"

"Yeah, I reckon."

"Come on up, then. I'm sure we have a great deal to talk about." He turned and disappeared back into his room.

Joe and the other two gunmen stood up and went to the stairs. They started up, their tread slow and hesitant.

Zeke had seen men walk that same way when they were climbing the steps to the gallows.

Chapter 16

Halfway up the stairs, Joe Kiley gave serious consideration to turning around, dashing out of the saloon, jumping on his horse, and riding away as fast as he could. Green and Larson could damn well fend for themselves.

Trask had promised all his men a big payoff, though. It was hard for Joe to balance saving his own hide against maybe being a rich man. Rich by his own lights, anyway, which wouldn't take all that much since he'd never really had anything to speak of except a horse, an old saddle, and a gun.

So he kept climbing, with one hand on Green's arm to steady him because of the bad leg. In the two days it had taken to get there, the bullet hole in Green's thigh had started to fester. Green was worried that the leg might have to come off. Joe figured that was a real possibility. He was pretty damn sure Larson's arm was going to have to go. It was beginning to swell and turn black.

The door to Trask's room was open. They were a sorry-looking bunch as they went inside.

The rooms at Zeke's were nothing fancy, but somehow

Jonas Trask made any room he was in seem at least a little elegant. He stood beside a long table with a piece of canvas draped over it, holding a snifter of brandy. He swirled the amber liquid slightly as he smiled again. "Come in, gentlemen. Come in."

Green limped in, followed by Larson.

Joe brought up the rear. *Too late to run now,* he told himself. He remembered his pa reading stories from the Bible when he was a kid . . . especially the one about some hombres who'd found themselves in a lion's den. That was sort of the way he felt.

With his foot, Trask pushed a ladderback chair closer to them. "William, you should get off your feet. Sit down."

Green, whose first name was Bill, shook his head. "I reckon I'm all right, boss. Larson here is in worse shape than I am."

"Well, then, you should sit down, Charles," Trask told Larson. "You do look a bit puny, I must say."

Larson lowered himself onto the chair, being careful of his wounded arm. "I'm feelin' a mite puny, boss, and I don't mind sayin' it."

Trask sipped the brandy but didn't offer them a drink. "I didn't expect to see you gentlemen quite this soon. I was going to send a man to check with you in another day or two and bring you back if you had the information I sent you to get."

Green nodded. He rested a hand on the wall next to him to steady himself. "We've got it, boss. That's why I figured it would be all right to go on and rendezvous with you here, once we'd tangled with Jensen's men."

Trask's voice was sharp as he asked, "But not Jensen himself?"

Green shook his head. "No, sir, he's not there on the

Sugarloaf, just like you thought. They're not expecting him back for another week, maybe two."

"You're certain of that?" Trask looked intensely interested at that news.

Green nodded toward Larson. "Chuck heard Mrs. Jensen talking to one of the hands. She's the one who said it, and I reckon she ought to know."

"Indeed she should," Trask agreed. "What happened? How did the two of you get shot? You were supposed to stay out of sight and not engage Jensen's men."

Green, who had been in charge, explained about the gun battle. Joe was glad to let him do it. There was an old saying about shooting the messenger, and he didn't want that to be him.

Green concluded the story by saying, "I'm sorry, boss. I thought we were bein' plenty careful. I'm not sure how they spotted us. One of those cowboys must have eyes like an eagle."

Trask didn't say anything, just stood there nodding slowly as if considering everything Green had told him.

Nervously, Green went on. "The important thing is that we found out what you wanted to know, right? We've got a pretty good idea of how many men Jensen has riding for him, and we know their routine. And we know that Jensen himself isn't there and won't be for a while."

"You're right. That's very important," Trask agreed.

Green began to look a little less anxious.

"I'd hoped I could gather a large enough force to make our move before Jensen returned from Arizona, and it appears now that I can. Twenty more men are supposed to arrive tomorrow. That will increase our numbers to a hundred." Trask hadn't moved.

Joe wondered how the boss man could afford to pay

that many hired guns, but it was no business of his, he supposed. And to tell the truth, so far, they had gotten more promises than *dinero*.

Trask threw back the rest of the brandy, set the empty snifter on the table, and began to pace back and forth on the Navajo rug. The expression on his lean face became more intense. "Many men have tried to defeat Smoke Jensen in the past and failed. Their mistake was that they'd attacked him directly. I intend to take a more strategic approach and use against him those things that are most precious to him."

Green frowned worriedly. "Should we have tried to grab his wife? I'm not sure we could've gotten our hands on her without getting killed—"

Trask stopped him with an expansive gesture. "No, no, it's actually best that you didn't. Mrs. Jensen is a vital part of my plan . . . but only one part. Other men have kidnapped her and tried to use her to bend her husband to their will, but again, they've always failed. It's like having one ace in a poker hand. That may be the most powerful card, but it can't win the game by itself. What I'm after is a royal flush." Trask punched his right fist into his left palm. "I want everything—Mrs. Jensen, the ranch, the crew, even the town. I've studied Smoke Jensen, and I know he has many friends in the settlement of Big Rock. We'll take it, too, and when Jensen returns he'll find everything he cares about is in my hand!" Trask held up his open right hand and closed the fingers in a tight, convulsive grip. "Everything!"

That sounded like a good plan to Joe Kiley, although he had always been the sort to let somebody else do the thinking for him whenever he could. Trask seemed to be in a pretty good mood, so Joe was bold enough to ask, "We're gonna raid the town first?"

"Exactly. When Big Rock is firmly under our control, we'll use it as our base of operations to take over Sugarloaf."

Green warned, "There'll be a lawman there."

Trask blew out a dismissive breath. "Monte Carson. I've looked into the man's background. A decent sort, a competent lawman, but no match for us. He has a handful of deputies, but they'll be no trouble, either."

"How soon do we ride?"

"As I said, the remainder of our force should be here tomorrow. We'll depart the next day and should arrive in Big Rock approximately three days from now." Trask clucked his tongue and shook his head. "Not you, however, William. With that wounded leg, you're in no shape for a hard ride and a harder fight."

Green sucked in his breath and stood up straight instead of leaning against the wall. He said hurriedly, "I'm fine, boss. This is just a bullet graze. I've been plugged worse."

"I think it's startin' to fester," Joe said.

Green shot him an angry look.

"Is that so?" Trask raised his eyebrows.

"No, it's fine, I tell you—"

Trask held up a hand to stop Green's protests. "I'll take a look at it," he said gently. "It may be there's something we can do to help it heal. There's still some time before we leave." He looked down at Larson, who seemed to have slipped into a half-sleep as he sat in the chair. "Unfortunately, there's no way Charles will be in any shape to aid our cause by then. Even without examining his wound, I can tell by looking at him that he's quite ill. He can be of service in other ways, though."

Trask turned and went over to the small table beside the bed, where a black leather bag sat. He opened it and took out a small bottle with a cork stopper. He took a piece of cloth from the bag, pulled the cork in the bottle, and poured some liquid onto the cloth.

"What are you gonna do, boss?" Green asked.

"Ease his suffering." Trask corked the bottle and replaced it in the bag. He stepped toward Larson with the cloth in his hand, then looked at Joe. "Joseph, if you'd be so kind as to hold Charles's shoulders . . ."

Joe swallowed hard. He didn't want to do it, but he didn't dare refuse the boss's order. He rested his hands on Larson's shoulders from behind, closing them tightly.

Larson startled out of his stupor and raised his head. "Wha—"

Trask moved in and clamped the hand with the cloth in it over Larson's mouth and nose. Larson made a noise through it and tried to get up, but Joe held him down. After just a few seconds of struggling, Larson went limp and his head fell back.

Trask leaned and tossed the cloth onto the other table next to the bag.

"He'll sleep peacefully while I'm conducting my research. Joe, if you'll give me a hand, we'll place him here on this table . . ."

"Sure, Mr. Trask," Joe said.

"Doctor," Trask corrected, smiling serenely. "Never forget. It's *Doctor* Trask."

Chapter 17

Sheriff Monte Carson turned up the collar of his sheepskin jacket as he walked along Big Rock's main street. It was one of those days where the noontime sun was almost too warm for the jacket, especially when a man was out of the wind. The stiff breeze that blew along the street had a bit of a bite to it, though, and the jacket felt good.

Carson wasn't bound for anywhere in particular. He liked to stroll around the settlement he called home, the settlement he had sworn to protect when he pinned on the sheriff's badge. Curley, one of his deputies, was back in the office to handle any complaints that came in.

The hitch racks in front of Longmont's Saloon were full as Carson walked past. No doubt some of the men in the saloon were drinking or gambling, but at that time of day, many of the customers were there to eat lunch. Longmont's served food as well as liquor. Louis Longmont, the French gambler and gunman who owned the place, insisted that it be good food, not just the usual pickled eggs and pig's feet that most saloons served up.

Carson considered stopping for a cup of coffee and a

piece of pie but decided against it and continued on. He'd had a sudden attack of restlessness earlier and wasn't sure what it signified. Maybe he was just getting old.

He'd been the sheriff in Big Rock for a number of years. Pretty exciting years, at that, but every now and then, he remembered what his life had been like before that, when he'd been a drifting gunman, a man to step aside from.

He didn't want to go back to that, not even a little, but Lord help him, part of him missed it. Missed having no real responsibilities beyond the end of his gun. He wouldn't trade what he had, not in a million years, but from time to time, he had to fight the urge to saddle a horse and ride and ride, while he still could. . . .

So he walked around the town and said hello to the friends he passed and pinched the brim of his hat to the ladies and reminded himself why he had settled down there in the first place. Big Rock was a good town, and he was proud to be part of it.

With those thoughts going through his mind, he almost didn't notice the five strangers riding in.

Almost . . . but not quite. His lawman's instincts were always working, and they perked right up at the sight of those men.

One man rode slightly in front of the other four on a very impressive cream-colored horse. He wore a black suit and hat and string tie, like a preacher.

Sensing something about the rider that he wasn't a man of God, Monte Carson started walking a little faster toward the newcomers.

Maybe it was the ivory-handled revolver he wore in a black holster.

The four men behind the black-suited leader were cut from a cloth that Carson recognized right away. They were hardcases, much as the sheriff had been at one time in his life. Maybe worse. While he had never ridden outside the law, those men looked like they were quite familiar with that side of the trail.

It didn't mean they had come to Big Rock looking for trouble. All sorts of people passed through the settlement, most good but some bad. If all they wanted to do was pick up some supplies and move on, he was willing to let that happen. It seemed like that might be the case when the five riders reined to a halt in front of the general store.

However, the only one who dismounted was the man in black. He looped his reins around the hitch rail and turned to greet Carson with a smile. "Sheriff Carson," he said pleasantly. "Good afternoon to you."

"Have we met?" Carson tried not to sound too suspicious, but it wasn't easy.

"No, but I'm familiar with your reputation. Sheriff Monte Carson, the fighting lawman of Big Rock, friend of the illustrious Smoke Jensen."

Carson felt an instinctive dislike for this man, despite his hearty, affable manner.

"My name is Trask. Dr. Jonas Trask." He held out his hand.

With long, slender, supple fingers, it looked like the hand of a surgeon, Carson thought. He shook with Trask and lied, "Pleased to meet you, Doctor. What brings you to Big Rock?"

"I'm here to conduct some important medical research."

"Really?" Carson said as his eyebrows rose in surprise. He couldn't think of any kind of medical research that could be conducted in Big Rock.

"Absolutely." Still smiling, Trask turned his head and

nodded toward the other four riders. "These men are some of my assistants."

Carson was convinced that Trask was having some sport with him. Those hardcases weren't any sort of medical assistants. Carson would have bet any amount of money on that. He didn't like being made fun of, either.

His eyes narrowed in anger. His hand moved closer to the butt of the gun on his hip as he said, "What are you really doing here, Trask?"

"Why, I've told you the truth, Sheriff. I'm here to carry out a very important project that will change the course of medical history. It may well change the course of history itself."

"Maybe you better just move on," Carson snapped. He glanced at the four men still on horseback. They had tensed in their saddles as he talked to their boss. He knew they were ready to slap leather.

If Smoke had been there to back his play, he wouldn't have worried about facing those men. He would be taking them on by himself, though, if it came to that. He was fast on the draw and accurate with his shots, so he would take his chances, but he knew the odds were stacked against him coming out alive.

Even so, he didn't have any backup in him, no matter what the odds.

"I'm afraid we can't leave, Sheriff," Trask said in a deceptively mild tone. "You see, that project of mine has already begun—" With blinding speed, he whipped out the ivory-handled revolver on his hip and smashed it against the side of Monte Carson's head.

Carson had seen Trask's hand start to move, and with the instincts and reactions of a man who had once lived by the gun, he jerked aside, thus avoiding the full force of Trask's blow, but the doctor had hit him hard enough to send his hat flying and knock him to one knee. Though his muscles seemed to act in slow motion, Carson kept trying to pull his Colt from its holster.

Trask kicked him in the face just as he cleared leather. The boot heel exploded against Carson's jaw and he went over backwards, sprawling in the dirt and dropping his gun. He felt around feebly for it but couldn't find it. Consciousness began to slip away from him.

Just before he passed out, he heard Trask shout, "Don't kill any more than you have to!"

Guns roared. People screamed. Hoofbeats thundered. And Monte Carson floated away on a sea of black.

Chapter 18

Several ladies were poking around the merchandise-filled shelves of the general store, but Manager Eli Dawes figured it would be a while yet before any of them were ready to make a purchase. Through the front window, he could see Sheriff Carson talking to a well-dressed stranger.

With that in mind, the middle-aged, apron-wearing Dawes came out from behind the counter and strolled toward the front of the store, thinking the stranger might be a potential customer. Dawes figured he'd greet him with a smile and ask how he could help him.

Then the fella pulled out his gun, pistol-whipped the sheriff, and kicked him in the head. Dawes stood on the other side of the window, watching the violence with his mouth hanging open.

But only for a second. He turned and ran back along the aisle toward the counter where he had a loaded shotgun. As he hurried, he called to his customers, "Ladies! Get to the back of the store! Now!"

Big Rock had seen enough trouble in its time that its citizens knew how to react. The women scurried away from the front of the building in case bullets began to fly and shattered the windows. Dawes wheeled around the end of the counter and grabbed the shotgun from the shelf underneath it.

Just as he swung the weapon toward the door, a man kicked it open. The store's interior wasn't as bright as it was outside, so his eyes had to adjust. He didn't seem to see Dawes right away.

Dawes sure as hell saw the gun in the man's hand, though, and knew the rough-looking stranger meant harm to him and his customers. He brought the shotgun to his shoulder and touched off one barrel.

The boom was painfully loud inside the store. The shotgun kicked so hard against Dawes's shoulder that it made him stagger back a step. As he recovered, he saw that he had missed almost completely. The man in the doorway put his left hand to the drop of blood on his cheek where one piece of buckshot had nicked him. He looked at the crimson in his fingertips and cursed.

Then he thrust out the gun in his other hand and began pulling the trigger. Flame spurted from the revolver's muzzle. Dawes still had one loaded barrel in the shotgun, but with bullets spraying around him, his nerve broke.

He dropped the gun and dived to the floor behind the counter, wishing that the shooting would stop.

Curley was tipped back in the chair behind the desk in the sheriff's office with one foot propped on the desk to balance himself. He wasn't really asleep, but he wasn't fully awake, either. From time to time he dozed off enough to let out a snorting snore. That always woke him up and kept him from descending further into sleep.

That wasn't what had roused him, though. He sat up and shook his head groggily. No, it had been something else . . .

He heard the gunshots and the screams and knew why he was awake.

With a grunt, he lunged to his feet. He jerked open a desk drawer, reached inside, and pulled out a handful of shotgun shells. He snatched a Greener off the rack on the wall behind the desk and broke it open as he ran toward the door. He thumbed a pair of shells into the shotgun and shoved the rest into his pocket.

As he ran outside, Curley heard thundering hoofbeats, gunfire, and shouting from what seemed like all directions at once. It was no simple ruckus that had gotten out of hand. Nor was it confined to one place, like somebody was trying to rob the bank.

Big Rock was under attack—the whole blasted town.

Curley jerked his head from side to side. Strangers on horseback were everywhere. They galloped up and down the street, shooting and yelling. Anybody who got in their way was in danger of being trampled. They didn't seem to be gunning folks down wantonly, but he saw several bodies sprawled in the street and knew citizens were dying.

He bounded off the boardwalk in front of the sheriff's office into the street. One of the invaders was on a circling, rearing horse not far away. Curley dashed closer to him and shouted, "Hey!"

The man twisted toward him and started to swing up a pistol. Curley triggered one barrel. The load of buckshot caught the man in the chest, shredding flesh and smashing bone. It blew him right out of the saddle. He landed in the street in a bloody heap.

Hoofbeats pounded close behind Curley. He whirled around and saw another attacker looming over him. In a fraction of a second that seemed infinitely longer, Curley saw the man point a gun at him. He knew he couldn't bring the shotgun up in time. He was dead. No two ways about it.

Everything lurched into motion again. For some reason, the invader didn't pull the trigger. As he galloped past, he swung the gun at the deputy's head. Curley felt like a stick of dynamite went off inside his skull.

It was the last thing he knew for quite a while.

The battle for Big Rock was over in a surprisingly short amount of time. Sheriff Carson and his deputies were knocked out of action early on, and although the townspeople tried to put up a fight, with no one to rally them, the effort was doomed. Scores of savage, well-armed attackers swept into the settlement from all directions at once and routed the would-be defenders.

Within an hour, Big Rock was like a town conquered by an invading army, solidly under the control of Jonas Trask and his men.

Trask strode along the street and calmly surveyed the death and destruction. He said to the man who walked beside him, "How many men did we lose, Major Pike?"

"Two men killed, two seriously wounded," Pike replied. He wore a brown tweed suit instead of a uniform, but he carried himself with a military bearing. He had a slight limp that didn't seem to trouble him much.

"A few more assorted nicks and scratches. Nothing to worry about."

"Very good," Trask said as he nodded in satisfaction. "And the civilian casualties?"

"Hard to say for sure. I've still got men going through town building by building, cleaning them out. I'd guess maybe a dozen killed, fifteen or twenty wounded."

"The sheriff and his men were all taken alive?"

"Yes, sir, along with the mayor and the men who serve on the town council. We have them all locked up in the jail."

"Excellent. They're all friends of Smoke Jensen. With their lives at risk, he'll think twice about anything he does."

"I hope you're right, Doctor."

Trask gave him a narrow-eyed look. "I'm not in the habit of being wrong, Major."

"No, sir, of course not," Pike agreed hastily.

"What about the other prisoners?"

"We're herding most of them into the church," Pike explained. "We'll likely have to put some of them in the town hall, too, but we have enough men to guard both places." The major hesitated. "There's one man you told us to look for that we haven't located yet. Louis Longmont."

Trask frowned. "The gambler. Jensen's closest friend in Big Rock other than Sheriff Carson."

"Yes, sir. We took over his saloon, just like we did every other business in town. According to the bartenders and the girls who work there, Longmont is out of town. He rode to Denver to sit in on a big poker game there."

"Yes, well, one man really shouldn't make much difference, I suppose. I'd hoped to have Longmont to use as a hostage, too, but with everyone else in town, we'll have plenty. Then, of course, there's the pièce de résistance."

"Sir?"

"Sally Jensen. With her fate in our hands—as well as the fate of nearly everyone else Smoke Jensen cares about—he'll have no choice but to surrender and do exactly as we say." Trask took a deep, triumphant breath. "Finish things up here as quickly and efficiently as you can, Major. Tonight we're riding to the Sugarloaf!"

Chapter 19

Monte Carson felt like a hundred Indians were jumping up and down on his head and walloping it with tomahawks. The sensation got even worse when he tried to lift his head and open his eyes. He groaned and let his head slump down against whatever he was lying on.

"Sheriff? Sheriff, you awake?"

Carson winced as somebody shouted in his ear. Then he realized whoever had spoken wasn't yelling. It just sounded that way because his head was in such bad shape.

"Blast it, Sheriff, I wish you'd wake up. I don't know what to do here."

Carson recognized the voice. It belonged to Deputy Curley. The realization made other memories lurch by fits and starts into his brain. The strangers riding into Big Rock . . . the well-dressed but somehow sinister man who had introduced himself as Dr. Jonas Trask . . . being buffaloed by Trask and then kicked in the jaw . . .

Carson forced his eyes all the way open, despite the fresh wave of pain inside his skull caused by the light hitting them. He blinked a couple times and tried to focus on the blurred face that swam into view above him.

"C-Curley . . . ?" he rasped through lips that felt like dried-out corn husks.

"Yeah. Lemme help you sit up, boss."

Carson wanted to tell him not to do that, but it was too late. Curley looped an arm around the sheriff's shoulders and lifted him into a sitting position.

The world spun madly in the wrong direction for what seemed like an eternity. When it settled down a few seconds later, Carson looked around and saw that he was in a jail cell.

One of the cells in his own jail, no doubt.

He sat with his back propped against the stone wall. He and Curley weren't by themselves in the cell. Four other men were crowded in there with them, including Eli Dawes from the general store and Stan Virdon, the butcher.

The three other cells behind the sheriff's office were full of prisoners, too, all of them leading citizens and businessmen of Big Rock.

"What the . . . hell is goin' on here?" Carson muttered.

Curley's face was grim. He had a bloody gash on his forehead where somebody had hit him, probably with a gun. "They've taken over the town, Sheriff."

"Who?"

"Damned if I know. A bunch of outlaws, from what I could tell. Must've been a hundred or more of 'em. They came from every which way. I blew one of 'em out of his saddle, but then another one pistol-whipped me and knocked me out. I come to as they was draggin' me in here."

"There was a man named . . . Trask . . ."

"Handsome but mean-lookin' fella in a black suit?" Curley asked.

"That's . . . him."

"Yeah, he came in here a while ago to take a look at us. Actually, it was more like he was gloatin'. He was talkin' to a fella who was with him. Trask called him Major Pike, but he wasn't wearin' no uniform. The major was tellin' Trask that he had assigned patrols to ride around the town and grab anybody who tries to get in or out."

"What about . . . the railroad?"

Curley shook his head dispiritedly. "They blew up the rails with dynamite a few miles away on one side of us, and they caused an avalanche and blocked the tracks in one of the passes the other way. Won't be no trains comin' to Big Rock for a week or more. It'll take that long to fix all the damage."

The pain in Carson's head was beginning to fade to a dull, throbbing ache. He could live with that if he had to. He could even focus his thoughts a little better. "Why? Who in the Sam Hill are they, and why attack Big Rock?"

"Well, I don't know for sure . . . but judgin' by some of the things that fella Trask said to the major, I think it's got somethin' to do with Smoke Jensen."

"Smoke?" Carson repeated. That made sense, he supposed. Smoke had made plenty of enemies over the years. He had spoiled the plans of numerous outlaws and put an uncountable number of them under the ground. Not just run-of-the-mill owlhoots, either. Plenty of men in high places—politicians and business tycoons, even European aristocracy—had sworn vengeance on Smoke Jensen.

As far as the sheriff knew, Smoke was nowhere

around. He had gone off to Arizona on a desperate mission to rescue his brother Luke. That had gone well, according to what Sally had told him the last time she was in town, but Smoke wasn't expected back for a while yet.

Carson sighed. He couldn't fathom the invaders' motivations, but he supposed it didn't really matter. He, Curley, and most of the town's leading citizens were locked up. The sheriff knew better than most that breaking out of the solidly constructed jail was well nigh impossible.

All they could do for the moment was wait and hope for a break in the situation.

"You reckon they're gonna attack Sugarloaf next?" Curley asked.

"Could be," Carson said. "But if they do, even with Smoke not there . . . they won't have an easy time of it."

Chapter 20

According to the members of the crew who had known him the best, Ben Hardy had no close family in Colorado. Some cousins in Missouri were his closest relatives. So it had made sense to lay him to rest in the cemetery on Sugarloaf.

Following that, Sally had told Pearlie to increase the number of men riding the range, especially in the area of Lone Pine Ridge. She thought it was unlikely that the three intruders would come back, especially considering the damage that had been done to them, but no one could rule it out. The crew would need to be extra vigilant for a while.

Almost a week had passed with no sign of any more trouble. Despite that, she thought it was best not to let down their guard. Smoke would be home soon, and he could decide what to do. He might want to try trailing the three men, although too much time might have passed for that to be feasible.

She was in the study in the big ranch house, reading by lamplight. She had always been an avid reader, mostly of the classics, although now and then she indulged herself with a lurid, yellow-backed dime novel, mostly just to see how ridiculous it could be. Smoke had been featured in a number of those tales. He liked to make fun of them, saying that they were all written by Hudson River cowboys, since none of the authors seemed to have been any farther west than that in their lives.

Wrapped in a thick robe, she sat in a comfortable armchair and read a novel by a Frenchman named Jules Verne. It was a fantastic story about a ship that could travel under the sea, as well as the insane genius who captained it. Sally had an adventurous streak in her—she had to in order to have married a man like Smoke Jensen—and as she read she thought how exciting it would be to travel in a vessel like that.

Out in the bunkhouse, a poker game was going on among several of the hands. Payday was a ways off yet, so they were using matches as the stakes. Some men were cleaning their guns or awkwardly darning socks. One plucked idly at the strings of a guitar. A few had already turned in and were snoring in their bunks even though the lamps hadn't been blown out yet.

Pearlie was trimming his toenails with a bowie knife.

Cal watched him and grinned. "Better be careful. One slip and you'll lop a toe clean off."

Pearlie grunted. "It's been a long time since I lopped off anything I didn't intend to."

"I'm just saying that knife's mighty sharp."

"A dull knife ain't much good for anything, is it?"

"Well, no, I guess not."

"All right, then, hush up. This is delicate work. A man don't need to be distracted while he's doin' it."

Cal threw his hands in the air and exclaimed, "That's what I was just saying!"

Pearlie grinned and went on with what he was doing.

Out on the range, half a dozen men rode nighthawk, watching over the herds and keeping an eye out for trouble. One of them, a cowboy named Walt Miller, was riding near a stand of trees when he though he heard something. He reined his horse in that direction and put his hand on the butt of the gun at his hip as he called, "Hey, is somebody over there?"

A three-quarter moon floated in the Colorado sky. Its silvery illumination flickered on something. Miller barely saw it before he felt an impact against his chest as if someone had lightly punched him.

He looked down to see the handle of a knife sticking out from his shirt front. As pain erupted inside him, he realized that almost the entire length of the blade attached to that bone handle was buried in his chest.

The crippling agony made him hunch over in the saddle. He clawed at his gun, desperate to get it out and start pulling the trigger. He had no illusions that such an act would save his life. He already knew he was a dead man. But a burst of gunfire would warn the other nighthawks that something was wrong.

A rope settled around Miller's shoulders, closed tight, and jerked him out of the saddle. He hit the ground before he could draw his gun and died seconds later without raising the alarm.

Around Sugarloaf, similar scenes were being repeated. One guard was knifed in the back; another had his throat cut. As one of the nighthawks rode under a thick tree limb, the man hidden in shadow on top of it dropped a loop around the cowboy's neck and hauled hard on the rope, lifting the luckless man out of the saddle and choking him to death before he could make a sound.

In the wake of these killings came men on horseback, closing in relentlessly on the ranch headquarters.

The poker game in the bunkhouse broke up with a cowboy named Cunningham the big winner. He looked at the pile of matchsticks in front of him and grinned. He would probably lose most of them back to his pards before payday rolled around, but for tonight he was triumphant.

On the other side of the long room, a puncher threw a boot at the man with the guitar. "Quit pluckin' on that twanger, you dang frog-faced galoot!"

The man with the guitar took offense, naturally enough, and heaved the boot back at its owner. A fight likely would have ensued if Pearlie hadn't stepped in. He had finished trimming his toenails, but he still held the bowie knife. No man with a lick of sense would have argued with him.

A few minutes later, the lamps were all blown out, and peace descended on the bunkhouse along with darkness.

That lasted for ten minutes, just about long enough for most of the men to doze off, before hell broke loose outside.

Pearlie bolted up off his bunk as shots roared. He wore only his long underwear and a pair of socks, but that didn't stop him from grabbing his rifle and racing toward the bunkhouse door.

It wasn't just a few isolated shots shattering the peaceful night. A nearly continuous rolling wave of gunfire swept over the Sugarloaf's headquarters.

Pearlie's first thoughts were of Sally Jensen. She was alone in the house. Whatever was going on out there, he needed to reach her side and make sure she was safe.

The bunkhouse had only a few windows. Before he could reach the door, each of those windows shattered as a rock was thrown through it. Hard on the heels of those rocks came balls of fire that sailed through the broken windows and landed on bunks or rolled across the floor, spreading their flames.

Pearlie had seen such things before and knew they had to be balls of pitch-soaked cloth wrapped around rocks and set ablaze just before they were heaved through the windows. They caused instant chaos in the bunkhouse as startled cowboys tried to put out the fires. A few of the men were on fire, or at least their clothes were. They hopped around, yelling frantically.

Pearlie bellowed, "Grab guns, you ranahans! Some of you fight them fires, and the rest come with me!" He didn't wait to see if the others did as he said. He flung the door open and started to dash out.

At the last second, he realized that was just what the attackers wanted him and the rest of the crew to do. Rifles were already trained on that door, and as it flew back they opened fire. Pearlie skidded to a halt and threw himself backwards and down as fast as he could.

Slugs whistled through the air around him as he hit the rough floor. Somewhere behind him a man yelled in pain. Pearlie knew at least some of that flying lead had found a target. He sprayed three shots out at the night, levering the Winchester as fast as he could between shots, then rolled to the side, lifted a leg, and kicked the door shut. "Somebody drop that bar!" he shouted.

Cal grunted with effort as he lifted the thick beam that leaned against the wall beside the door. He dropped the beam in the brackets built for it on either side of the entrance. It would take a battering ram to get that door open until the bar was removed.

The bunkhouse was built sturdy on purpose, so it could resist an attack. The log walls would stop most bullets. The windows represented a danger. As soon as the door was closed and barred, the attackers began concentrating their fire on the broken windows.

"Keep your heads down!" Pearlie called. He knelt beside one of the windows, thrust the rifle barrel past the jagged glass, and triggered several rounds at the muzzle flashes he saw winking in the darkness like deadly fireflies.

At the other windows, men began mounting a defense. The air quickly filled not only with smoke from the little fires scattered around the room but with powder smoke, as well.

"Get those fires put out!" Pearlie yelled over his shoulder. He saw that the men were getting the blazes under control, slapping them out with blankets from the bunks. "Cal!"

"I'm here, Pearlie," the youngster said as he appeared at Pearlie's side.

"This repeater of mine is about to run dry. Stay low and get that box of .44-40s from my war bag."

Cal nodded. Crouching, he ran across the room to Pearlie's bunk and reached underneath it to get the box of cartridges.

He came back with the ammunition and his own Winchester. He set the open box of bullets between them and took up a post on the other side of the window. While Pearlie reloaded, Cal leaned out and cranked off five rounds as fast as he could before return fire forced him to duck back out of sight.

"They've got us pinned down," Cal said as he panted a little.

"Yeah," Pearlie agreed grimly. "They sure do."

Things didn't look good for him and the rest of the crew—however, that wasn't his main worry.

Sally was still alone in the house.

Or maybe she wasn't—and that thought was even worse.

Chapter 21

Sally was still engrossed in the story of the *Nautilus*, Captain Nemo, and Professor Aronnax, when she heard the dull boom of gunshots outside, interspersed with the sharper cracking of rifle fire. Reacting instantly, she bolted up from the comfortable chair. The leather-bound volume fell to the floor at her feet, already forgotten. She lunged across the room to a gun rack mounted on the wall.

The rack held several different types of long arms: shotguns, Winchester repeaters, an old Henry, an even older Sharps .50 caliber buffalo rifle, and a couple shorter-barreled Winchester carbines she always carried with her as a saddle gun whenever she went riding.

The weapons were all loaded, although the Winchesters and the Henry usually didn't have a round in the chamber. She remedied that in the carbine she took down and worked the lever with practiced ease. The carbine was ready to fire.

She ran out of the study and along the hall toward the front of the house, knowing better than to rush outside blindly. That was a good way to run smack-dab into a bullet. Hurrying into the darkened parlor, she pushed a curtain aside, and looked out.

She was in time to see a man wearing thick gloves to protect his hands throw some sort of burning object through a broken window into the bunkhouse. Other men on horseback galloped back and forth, firing handguns and rifles toward the windows. Sally caught her breath as an orange glare shot up inside the building. Those crude incendiary bombs had started fires inside the bunkhouse.

She saw at least twenty attackers, and from the sound of all the shooting going on, at least that many more were joining the assault on the Sugarloaf's headquarters. Even without proof, there was no doubt in her mind that it was connected somehow to the three men who'd been lurking around the place earlier. Her instincts told her it was true.

One group of riders peeled off from the others and charged toward the house. Knowing that she was probably in great danger, Sally didn't hesitate to break out the window glass with the carbine's barrel. She brought the weapon to her shoulder and began to fire through the opening. She aimed at the charging horsemen and cranked off five rounds.

One man went backwards off his horse like he'd been slapped out of the saddle by a giant hand. Another reeled to the side, obviously wounded, and would have fallen if he hadn't dropped his gun and grabbed the saddle horn.

That left three of them. As they reached the house, they vaulted from their saddles and leaped onto the porch. She tried to angle the carbine to fire at them, but they were too close to the wall. She heard one of them kicking at the door.

They weren't going to get in very easily that way.

Smoke had built the house to be defended. The door was thick and barred, and a man could kick it all day without busting it down.

Unfortunately, the same thing couldn't be said of the windows. They were secure enough when the shutters were closed, but she hadn't had time to do that. She gasped as she heard glass crash in another room and knew she had to keep a cool head.

The lamps in the front room weren't lit. The only light came from the hallway, and that originated in the study so it wasn't very bright.

Sally glided toward the closest corner where thick shadows lay and let the darkness wrap itself around her. With the carbine ready for action, she stood with her back pressed against the wall and waited.

She heard stealthy sounds from the hall. The men were trying to move silently, but they were a little too clumsy.

Shadows moved near the entrance to the front room. She brought the carbine to her shoulder and aimed it in that direction.

A moment later a man said in a harsh whisper, "Be careful! We don't know who-all's in here."

"Somebody is," another man replied, "and he blew Johnny Clark right outta his saddle!"

Sally smiled grimly. They assumed that because whoever was in the house had gunned down one of their companions, that person had to be a man. If they gave her a chance, they would soon discover that a woman could be a good shot, too.

The second man went on. "Duke, you and Corbin go upstairs and have a look around. The Jensen woman's probably up there hidin'. Remember, whatever you do, don't hurt her."

"Not even a little bit, Nichols?"

"No more than you have to," the gunman replied. "Pike said the doctor was mighty clear about that."

That brief exchange told Sally quite a bit. They had attacked the Sugarloaf because they were looking for her. The fact that they wanted to take her alive indicated that they intended to use her for leverage against Smoke. His enemies had tried that before, always to their great regret.

Most of the time it had been their *last* regret.

The mention of a doctor was puzzling. She couldn't recall any physician who had a grudge against her husband. Maybe the men meant a professor, although that seemed unlikely. Most of the time out on the frontier, anybody who used the word *doctor* was talking about a sawbones.

None of that mattered, Sally reminded herself. What was important was that she was in danger, regardless of the motive or the source, and that men who worked for her and Smoke, their friends as well as their employees, might well be dying trying to fight off the unexpected invasion.

That thought reminded her of the men who had killed Ben Hardy. Evidently, they had been the advance scouts. The whole thing smacked of a military operation, and she realized if the attacking force was big enough, she and the crew couldn't fight it off. She had to start thinking in terms of escape.

With dozens of ruthless, well-armed invaders right outside the house—and some of them inside—that wasn't going to be easy.

One of those shadows from the hall suddenly loomed blackly in the entrance to the front room. The man whispered to his companions, "I'm pretty sure those shots were coming from in here."

"Why don't we just spray the whole place with lead?" another man asked.

"Because Mrs. Jensen might be in here, you damn fool!" Nichols snapped. He raised his voice. "Mrs. Jensen. Sally Jensen. Are you in here?"

Sally held her breath. She didn't say anything, didn't move. Her finger was taut on the trigger.

Nichols cursed and told his companions, "Get ready, I'm gonna strike a match—"

Sally heard the rasp of a lucifer being struck. She knew she couldn't hide anymore, so there was no point in further stealth. As sparks began to spurt from the match, she aimed a short distance above it and fired the carbine.

Chapter 22

The muzzle flash lit up the room. In that shaved heartbeat of brightness, she saw that the man with the match was holding it out well away from his body. The bullet from her carbine smacked harmlessly into the wallpaper. He'd been trying to draw her fire, she realized. He had meant for her to hear what he was saying.

"Rush her now!" the man shouted as he dropped the match.

Desperately, Sally worked the carbine's lever as footsteps pounded across the room toward her. She pulled the trigger again. The weapon blasted, and a man screamed.

Somebody grabbed the carbine's barrel and wrenched it to the side. Sally cried out as the man tore it from her grasp.

That wasn't the only way she could fight back. She was in her own home, and her familiarity with it came in handy. As the man loomed up in front of her, she grabbed a vase off a side table and swung it at his head. The vase shattered with a huge crash. The man groaned, stumbled, and fell.

The carbine clattered on the floor.

"Grab her!" Nichols yelled.

Sally dived for the carbine. It was too dark in the room to see anything, so all she could aim for was the sound she had heard as it fell.

Her hand struck the weapon and it slid across the floor. Booted feet stomped heavily around her as she scrambled after the carbine on hands and knees. In the back of her mind was the knowledge that she couldn't win the fight—there were just too many of them—but she didn't have it in her to surrender. Smoke never gave up hope, no matter how bad the odds against him were, and she wasn't going to, either. One of the things she had learned from him was to always keep fighting.

She wrapped her hands around the carbine just as somebody grabbed her robe from behind and started to pull her backwards. The man yelled, "Here she is! I got her!"

Sally twisted and lashed out with the carbine's barrel, sweeping it through the air above her. It thudded solidly against something, and the man holding her robe let go. She rolled onto her bottom and scooted backwards on the floor, pushing hard with her feet.

She bumped into a pair of legs. A hand swiped at her and tangled in her hair for a second. When it came loose, so did a few strands of her hair. Pain made her yelp. It also made her angry. She worked the carbine's lever.

The hardcases who had invaded the ranch knew that sound. A man shouted, "Look out! She's gonna—"

His words were drowned out by shots smashing from the carbine. She didn't worry about shooting anybody who didn't have it coming. She swung the barrel from left to right and kept firing as she scooted until her back hit the wall.

She didn't know how many of the men she had hit, if any. She pushed herself up, heard someone charging her again, and pulled the trigger. The carbine's hammer clicked on an empty chamber. She was out of bullets.

She threw the carbine in front of her as hard as she could and heard it hit something. A man grunted in pain. She hoped she had broken his nose or even his skull. She twisted away and lunged through the shadows.

She had to get out of the house.

It was her only chance. As long as she was confined in there, sooner or later, they would overwhelm her by sheer force of numbers, if nothing else. By all rights, they should have captured her already. She had been lucky—and they probably hadn't expected her to put up such a fierce fight.

They should have expected it, she thought. She was married to Smoke Jensen, wasn't she?

Her feet were bare, so she moved without making much noise. She saw the glow that marked the doorway with the light coming from the study. Flitting like a phantom, she darted into the hallway.

A man yelled behind her, "There she goes! She's headed for the back of the house!"

She knew how steep the odds against her were, but she hoped that if she could get out of the house, she might be able to reach the trees and then make her way into the mountains. Unarmed, barefoot, dressed only in a robe and nightdress, spending a chilly night in the mountains wasn't an appealing prospect at all, but it sure beat being captured by men who had to be up to no good.

Some of the hands might get away, too. The battle was still going on. She heard the furious gunfire from the direction of the bunkhouse. If she could join forces with Pearlie and Cal, they could still make a fight of it . . .

She ran past the study door and on into the kitchen. It was dark, but she knew where everything was. She found a meat cleaver and clutched its wooden handle tightly. At close quarters, it would be a vicious weapon.

Men blundered around elsewhere in the house, searching for her. She heard footsteps upstairs, too. She wasn't sure what they were looking for up there, since it should have been obvious to all of them that she was downstairs. Maybe they thought there were some back stairs and wanted to keep her from slipping up them.

Getting trapped on the second floor was the last thing she wanted. She wanted *out*, out where she would have the freedom to move around. She edged toward the back door, feeling her way along.

It opened before she could get there. Dark shapes filled the doorway, silhouetted by the light from the moon and stars.

"Get that lantern lit, damn it," a man growled.

She didn't wait for them to be able to see what they were doing. She let out a bloodcurdling scream— Preacher had told her that would make almost any man jump and think twice about what he was doing—and charged among them, slashing back and forth with the cleaver.

Men yelled in surprise and pain. Sally kept her head down and rammed into a man with her shoulder. Under normal circumstances she might not have been able to budge him, but he wasn't braced for the impact and went over backwards with a startled shout.

She bounded through the door and into the clear.

It was a matter of outrunning the pursuit, reaching the trees, and giving the men the slip as she worked her way up the thickly wooded slopes behind Sugarloaf's headquarters. She raced like the wind.

Hoofbeats thundered to her right. Sally tried to shy away from them, but it was too late. A man on horseback loomed up out of the night. He turned his mount so that it came alongside her, leaned down from the saddle, wrapped his arm around her waist, and jerked her off the ground.

She cried out and tried to twist so she could strike at him with the cleaver. He was a good rider, though, and seemed to be controlling the horse with his knees, leaving both hands free. One arm was tight around her and the other hand caught hold of her wrist as she tried to wield the cleaver. A vicious twist made her gasp in pain and drop it.

With that threat disposed of, the man grasped his reins again and slowed the horse. His arm was like an iron band around her, holding her in front of him on the horse and pressing her tightly against him. "You put up a good fight, Mrs. Jensen, but it's over." He turned the horse.

"My husband will kill you," she said through clenched teeth. "That's if I don't get a chance to do it first."

He laughed and sounded genuinely amused. "Smoke Jensen won't do anything but what we tell him to, as long as he wants to keep his wife, his crew, and all his friends in Big Rock from dying."

Sally's heart sank. They had attacked Big Rock, too? Had they taken over the town? How many people had been killed?

"So just take it easy, stop fighting, and make it easier on all of us," her captor went on. "It's time you met the doctor."

Chapter 23

Out in the bunkhouse, things were starting to get desperate.

All the fires were out, so the place wasn't in danger of burning down anymore, but the flying lead had killed a couple men and several more were badly wounded. Pearlie and Cal had come through unscathed so far, but they knew that couldn't last much longer.

"Kid," Pearlie said as he thumbed fresh cartridges into his Winchester, "we gotta make a break for it."

"How are we gonna do that?" Cal asked. "There are too many of them out there!"

"We're gonna turn their own tactics against 'em. Keep fightin'. I'll be back in a minute."

Staying low because bullets were still coming through the broken windows, he made his way to a small closet at the far end of the bunkhouse and felt around inside its darkened interior until he found what he wanted—the jug of kerosene they used to fill the lanterns.

On his way back to the window with the jug, he stopped at his bunk to pull on his clothes, stomp into his boots, and buckle on his gun belt. He told the other men to take turns doing the same thing while continuing to battle the invaders.

"Are we gettin' out of here, Pearlie?" one of the cowboys asked.

"We dang sure are," Pearlie said, adding under his breath, "one way or the other."

Back to the window where he had left Cal, he told the youngster to go get dressed. "Don't waste no time about it, neither," Pearlie warned. "I got a hunch those hombres out there might be gettin' tired of this. They're liable to launch an all-out attack any time now."

"I understand."

While Cal was dressing, Pearlie cut a strip of cloth off the tail of his flannel shirt and stuffed one end of it into the neck of the kerosene jug, which was nearly new and almost full.

Cal was as good as his words, making it back to the window in only a few moments, dressed in boots, jeans, and a buckskin shirt. His gun belt was strapped around his lean hips. He exclaimed, "You're making a bomb!"

"Yep. Don't know if it'll be enough to turn the tables on those varmints, but I reckon it's just about our only chance."

"What do we do?"

"You stay here and keep an eye on 'em. I'm gonna unbar that door and wait for them to charge us again. When they do, I intend to pitch that jug right in amongst 'em. If it explodes like I hope, it'll blow some of 'em to hell and distract the others enough for us to go out shootin'. Once we're out, everybody scatter. With any luck, some of us will get away and can keep on fightin'."

Cal nodded again, then said wistfully, "I sure wish Smoke was here."

Pearlie sighed. "So do I, kid. So do I."

Satisfied that the strip of flannel had soaked up enough kerosene to serve as a makeshift fuse, Pearlie went around the room explaining the plan to the rest of the defenders, all of whom nodded in grim-faced understanding. Even if Pearlie's plan didn't work, they would go out fighting. Most of those tough, veteran cowboys wouldn't ask for anything else.

Pearlie unbarred the door, then held the jug in one hand and a lucifer in the other as he looked toward the window where Cal stood vigil and fired an occasional shot.

After a few minutes, Cal called, "Looks like they're forming up for a charge, Pearlie!"

"I knew it," Pearlie said. "They got us outnumbered, and they never set out to have no siege."

"Here they come!"

Pearlie used his thumbnail to snap the match to life. He held the flame to the kerosene-soaked rag, which caught instantly. He had to move fast to keep the jug from exploding in his hand. He dropped the match, jerked the door open, and pitched the jug toward the attackers as hard as he could.

The group of riders had just surged forward, shooting as they came, when the jug sailed among them and erupted in a huge ball of flame.

The explosion engulfed several men and horses and seared some of the other mounts enough to make them jump around wildly. In the blink of an eye, a well-coordinated attack turned into wild chaos.

"Come on!" Pearlie yelled as he burst out of the bunkhouse. He'd grabbed his rifle from where he had leaned it against the wall beside the door, and the Winchester spurted fire and lead as his shots raked the invaders.

Cal and the rest of the crew were close behind him.

Rifles and pistols roared as they spread out. Their bullets tore through several of the attackers and knocked them off their out-of-control horses.

But there were just too many gunmen. Reinforcements closed in from all sides. Sugarloaf cowboys were gunned down and ridden down. The battle quickly began to turn into a slaughter.

Pearlie was headed for the barn. He thought maybe if he could get in there, he might be able to slip out the back and then circle around toward the house. He was still worried about Sally. Some of the invaders had charged the house, and although he had seen muzzle flashes from one of the windows and knew that Sally was fighting back, he had no idea how that part of the fracas had turned out.

Most Western men, even the most hardened outlaws, wouldn't harm a decent woman on purpose—but a bullet had no mind of its own, and a hell of a lot of them were flying around.

Even over the gun thunder filling the air, Pearlie heard hoofbeats pounding toward him. He pivoted to his right, dropped to one knee, and fired the Winchester at the man trying to ride him down.

Unfortunately, the man's horse chose that moment to rear up. Pearlie's shot caught it in the throat. Mortally wounded, the horse collapsed. Its rider kicked his feet free of the stirrups, sailed over the dying animal's head, and crashed into Pearlie. The impact drove him over onto his back, jolted the rifle out of his hands, and knocked the breath out of his lungs.

The hardcase who'd rammed into him wasn't in much better shape. He lost the six-shooter he'd been holding, so he stuck a knee into Pearlie's belly and grabbed for his throat. The outlaw's fingers locked around Pearlie's windpipe and tightened ruthlessly.

Caught without much breath in his body to start with, the lack of air quickly began to affect the foreman. A red haze settled over his eyes and his muscles seemed to have lost most of their strength. He tried to buck upward and throw the attacker off, but he couldn't manage it.

He felt consciousness start to slip away and knew that if he passed out, chances were good he'd never wake up again. He was about to make a last-ditch effort to break free when the man suddenly let go of his throat and toppled to the side.

Cal stood over Pearlie and urged, "Come on! Let's see if we can make it to the barn!"

As Pearlie sat up, he glanced over and saw that the back of the attacker's head was bloody and misshapen. Cal held the Winchester he'd brought from the bunkhouse. Pearlie knew the youngster had used the rifle's butt to stove in the hombre's skull.

"I'm . . . obliged to you . . . kid," he panted as he got to his feet. "Reckon you . . . saved my life."

"Shoot, you've saved my life plenty of times," Cal said. "I'm glad I got a chance to return the favor."

Pearlie picked up the Winchester he had dropped and dashed toward the barn again with Cal at his side.

Another of the invaders on horseback tried to cut them off. Both rifles cracked at the same time, and the bullets hammered the man out of the saddle and dropped him limp and lifeless to the ground. Pearlie and Cal made it to the barn, where Pearlie pulled one of the big double doors open and they slipped inside. He didn't know if any more of the outlaws had noticed them.

"Let's head for the back," he told Cal. "I want to get around behind the house."

"I'm worried about Miss Sally, too. I don't reckon we can get there by going straight across, though."

"Naw, it's the next thing to hell out there," Pearlie said.

The barn's interior was in utter darkness, but having spent so much time in there, the two of them were able to make their way around. Horses in the stalls were making a racket. The shooting and yelling outside had spooked them.

Pearlie found the small rear door and started to open it, then hesitated. Gunmen could be waiting to open up on them as soon as they stepped out.

But they couldn't stay in the barn. Pearlie was under no illusions that the crew of the Sugarloaf would win the battle. They had done a lot of damage to the invaders, but in the end, those on the ranch were simply too outnumbered to prevail. Eventually, the victors would send men to search the barn and all the other buildings and root out any survivors. Pearlie didn't want him and Cal to be there when that happened.

He took a deep breath, then pulled the latch string and opened the door.

No shots blasted. Pearlie and Cal stepped out, and the only gunfire continued to come from the front of the big building.

"Head for the trees," Pearlie rasped. He took off at a run for those sheltering shadows with Cal right beside him.

Chapter 24

On the other side of the main house, Sally had stopped struggling against the man who held her. She was just wasting her strength. Better to conserve it and bide her time until she had more of a chance to get away.

Her captor rode to the back of the house where several men waited. One of them held a lantern.

The light revealed a lean, handsome man in a dark suit and string tie standing slightly in front of his companions as if he were in charge. He had an unmistakable air of command about him, in fact. "Ah, Major Pike!" he said in a resonant voice as the man rode up with her. "I see you obtained our main objective."

So the man who had grabbed her was a major, or at least had been at one time, Sally thought. That agreed with her impression that the attack had seemed like a military operation. The men weren't soldiers, though, she decided. None of them were in uniform. They looked like the same sort of hardcases Smoke had battled many times in the past.

"Whatever you're up to, you're going to regret it, mister," she said coldly to the man in the black suit. "You can't use me against my husband. He'll see to it that you pay for what you've done, all of you."

"On the contrary, Mrs. Jensen—and by the way, thank you for not bothering to deny who you are. I've seen pictures of you, and I would never fail to recognize such a beautiful woman, but as I was saying, despite your bravado, your husband will do exactly as he's told or I won't be able to guarantee the safety of you, the members of your crew who survive this battle, or the citizens of Big Rock. Surely Smoke Jensen wouldn't want the blood of so many people on his hands."

"It won't be on his hands," Sally snapped. "It'll be on yours. Who are you, anyway?"

The man didn't answer the question right away, gesturing instead. "Put the lady down, Major. There's nowhere she can run. She's intelligent enough to know how futile that would be."

Pike lowered Sally to the ground. "You'd better listen to the doctor, ma'am. Don't make this any harder on yourself than it has to be."

Sally straightened her robe, pulled it a little tighter around herself, and ignored how much her bare feet hurt from running on the ground. She lifted her head defiantly as she glared at the man in the black suit. "So you're the mysterious doctor."

"Indeed," he said with a self-satisfied smile as he lifted a slender, supple finger to the brim of his hat. "Dr. Jonas Trask, at your service."

"If you were really at my service, you'd take that fancy gun you're wearing and blow your own brains out."

"I assure you, that's not going to happen. Now that I'm finally so close to the object of my quest, I won't allow anything to keep me from it."

His quest? What in blazes did that mean? In the past,

evil men had gone after Smoke because they wanted vengeance or out of greed when he stood in the way of some lawless scheme of theirs, but she wasn't sure she had ever heard such fervor in the voice of an enemy.

Trask's motivations didn't really matter, only his actions, which were already bad enough to have earned him a bullet a dozen times over. He wasn't finished. He snapped his fingers and ordered, "Take her back into the house and make her comfortable. From the sound of it, the resistance is almost finished."

Sally's heart sank when she realized that was true. The shooting was a lot more sporadic, and that could only mean that most of the Sugarloaf hands had been killed, wounded, or captured. The enemies' overwhelming numbers, as well as their ruthless nature, had been enough to carry them to a bloody victory.

There isn't going to be any last-minute rescue. . . .

Just as that thought went through her head, shots rang out from the nearby trees, the ones Sally had been trying to reach when she fled from the house earlier. Pike yelled in pain and slumped forward in his saddle. As his startled horse reared, he hung on and shouted, "Get the doctor inside!"

A rider burst from the woods, firing a pistol as he charged toward the house. He bent low to make himself a smaller target. Rifle fire continued from the trees. One of the hardcases doubled over and collapsed as a slug punched into his guts. The others had to scramble for cover as bullets kicked up dirt around them.

One of the men grabbed Trask's arm and hauled him toward the back door of the house.

No one had hold of Sally. Her captors had been so confident of their triumph that they hadn't bothered to restrain her. She turned and sprinted toward the onrushing horseman. Pike cursed, fought his spooked mount back under control, and wheeled the horse around to gallop after her. Sally glanced over her shoulder at him. He might be wounded, but he wasn't giving up. She knew he would be able to catch her before her rescuer—whoever he was—arrived.

Another shot came from the trees and Pike's horse screamed as its forelegs buckled. The major went down with the horse and didn't move. Sally hated to see animals harmed, but in this case, it couldn't be avoided.

"Miss Sally!"

The shout came from the man racing toward her. Pearlie! She recognized his voice. He slowed the horse, leaned toward her, and held out his hand. They grabbed each other, clasping wrists, and he swung her up in front of him as he whirled the horse, shielding her with his own body as they galloped toward the trees.

With expert control, Pearlie guided the lunging horse between the trunks of the pines. He called, "Head down!" as low-hanging branches threatened to sweep them from the animal's back. They reached a clearing, and another rider fell in alongside them. Sally couldn't see him, but she had a pretty good idea who he was.

"Cal!" she gasped.

"Right here, Miss Sally," the young man confirmed. "Are you all right?"

"I am now. Let's light a shuck out of here!"

"That's just what I reckoned we'd do," Pearlie said.

Dark fury filled Jonas Trask as he stood in the parlor of the ranch and watched one of the men clean and bandage the deep bullet graze in Pike's upper left arm. Trask could have done a better job of the medical attention, of course, but he was too angry at the moment to deal with such trivial details.

Outside, an ominous quiet lay over the ranch. The survivors from the Sugarloaf's crew, most of them wounded, were back in the bunkhouse and under heavy guard.

One of the gunmen came in and talked quietly to Pike for a few minutes, then left. Pike's deeply tanned face was bleak from more than the pain of his wounded arm.

"What was that about?" Trask snapped.

"Casualty report," Pike said. "Eleven of our men were killed. More than a dozen wounded, and some of them probably won't make it."

"I would say that the losses were worth it," Trask replied with an angry, bitter edge in his voice, "if not for the fact that the person we were really after got away!" He shook his head and blew out his breath. "How could they snatch her out of our grasp, when we were so close to total victory?"

"I thought they were all done for," Pike said. "But that's no excuse. I know that, Doctor." With his arm bandaged, he shrugged back into his coat, wincing a little. "We'll get her back. They can't have gotten very far. I've already sent out search parties. You'll have Mrs. Jensen in your hands again before you know it."

"I had better," Trask said. "I had damn well better."

The men in the room were all hard-bitten killers, but every one of them paled a bit at the threat in the doctor's voice.

Chapter 25

Fleeing from the ranch with Pearlie and Cal, Sally found herself climbing higher and higher into the mountains. She rode double with Pearlie, perched behind him on the horse's back with her arms around his waist. Riding that way was a little easier on both of them.

"These aren't Sugarloaf horses, are they?" she asked. "Where did you get them?"

"We ran into a couple of those fellas and, uh, borrowed 'em," Pearlie replied.

She figured the *borrowing* had involved some gunplay and didn't press him on the matter. When you were fighting for your life and the lives of your friends, you did whatever was necessary to survive.

"Where are we going?" She was very aware that she was unarmed and not exactly dressed for life as a fugitive.

"Headed for a line shack I know of, up in the high country," Pearlie explained. "It's as far away from ranch headquarters as you can get and still be on Sugarloaf range. Seems like a good place to lay low for a spell."

She was more than happy to trust him about that. Other than Smoke, he knew the ranch better than anyone else. If he said a line shack was up there, it would be up there.

They had ridden on for a few minutes, before she summoned up her courage and asked, "Were we . . . were we the only ones who got out?"

"As far as I could tell, we were," Pearlie answered solemnly. "Of course, it was pretty doggone hectic. Might be some of the other fellas slipped away without me noticin'."

"I didn't see anybody else get away, either," Cal added in a glum voice.

Sally frowned. "So as far as we know, it's just the three of us. Three people against a small army."

"You got any idea who those varmints are and why they attacked the Sugarloaf?" Pearlie asked.

"The man who captured me was called Major Pike. I don't think he was an actual major, though. Maybe once." She paused. "He wasn't really in charge, though. He answers to a man named Jonas Trask. I was talking to him when you showed up to get me out of there, Pearlie. Trask calls himself a doctor."

Pearlie glanced back over his shoulder. "You don't reckon he's a real doctor?"

"He may well be, for all I know, but if he is, he's like no doctor I've ever seen. He seems devoted to taking lives, rather than saving them."

"A doctor of death," Pearlie said with a grunt.

"Yes. That's a very good description of him."

They rode on. The night grew colder. The first snows of the season wouldn't be blowing in for a good while yet, but at that elevation the nights were almost always chilly.

The terrain was more rugged, too. The horses had to labor up steep slopes. Sally wasn't sure she had ever been on that part of their range before. The Sugarloaf was vast, and while Smoke knew every foot of it, she didn't. "Do we graze cattle up this high?"

"Yes, ma'am, in the summer we do," Pearlie replied. "Lately we've started movin' 'em back down to the winter range." His voice hardened. "That job may not get done, with those no-good polecats takin' over the ranch."

"They may have control of Sugarloaf right now," Sally said, "but they won't keep it. We'll see to that." It was a bold claim, but she intended to follow through on it. She had been born with a fighting spirit, and her time as Smoke Jensen's wife had only increased her natural resolve.

Of course, they were overwhelmingly outnumbered, she reminded herself, and had only a few guns between them. But they could worry about that later, once they had reached the line shack, started a fire, and warmed up a little.

She had to do something about clothes, too. She couldn't fight outlaws in a nightdress and robe. That just wouldn't be ladylike at all, she thought with a grim smile.

A short time later, the slope leveled out. A broad, grassy meadow stretched in front of them, visible in the light from the moon and stars. A rugged ridge lay on the other side of the meadow.

"Line shack's over at the foot of that ridge," Pearlie explained as he and Cal reined in. "If you want to slide down, Miss Sally, I'll ride over there and check it out. Should be empty this time o' year, but I don't reckon we ought to ride up bold as brass without makin' sure of that."

Sally let go of him and dropped off the horse to the

ground. Cal dismounted, too, and stood beside her as Pearlie heeled his mount into motion again.

"Be careful," Cal called after him.

"I intend to be," Pearlie said over his shoulder. He rode with the reins in his left hand and the Winchester in the right.

Sally said worriedly, "Those men who attacked the ranch shouldn't know anything about this line shack, should they?"

"I sure wouldn't think so," Cal replied. "Who knows how long they were sneaking around, though, before they made their move? I think those three fellas we ran off, the ones who killed Ben Hardy, must've been some of the same bunch."

Sally nodded. "The same thing occurred to me."

They fell into a tense silence as they watched Pearlie cross the meadow. The light was bright enough for them to follow his progress, but they couldn't make out any details.

Pearlie didn't get in any hurry. Sally expected at any moment to see the flash from a gun's muzzle or hear the crash of a shot.

Neither happened. He made it to the line shack without incident, dismounted, and moved toward the shack with the rifle held ready

Sally couldn't see him anymore. "Did he go inside?"

"I reckon he must have." Cal's voice was edged with worry.

A few moments later, light flared on the other side of the meadow, but it wasn't a muzzle flash. After a second's glare, it settled down to a steady yellow glow.

"He must've lit a lamp or a candle," Cal said. "That must mean everything's all right."

A shadow crossed in front of the light, and then they heard the distant sound of hoofbeats. Pearlie was returning, moving at a brisk pace instead of his earlier deliberate approach.

He drew rein and reported, "The place is empty. I had a good look around. Nobody's been there for weeks. Found something that's gonna come in handy, too."

"A Gatling gun?" Cal guessed.

"What? No. What in tarnation makes you think there's a Gatling gun in that line shack?"

"I didn't think there was," Cal said with a shrug. "But you've got to admit, it would have come in handy."

Pearlie muttered something under his breath that Sally couldn't make out, then said, "One of the fellas who was up here over the summer left a change o' clothes behind. It's just a pair o' pants and an old shirt and some socks, but that's better than nothin', I reckon."

"It certainly is," Sally said gratefully.

"I warn you, they'll be a mite big on you."

"Don't worry. I'll make them work."

Pearlie extended his hand and she grasped it. He helped her up behind him again, and the three of them started across the meadow toward the line shack.

"You know," she said, "the Gatling gun would have been nice, too."

Chapter 26

The day after taking over the town, Trask sent Pike into the church and the town hall to talk to the people of Big Rock and explain to them that they would be allowed to return to their homes and businesses, but only under certain conditions. Closely guarded and kept overnight as they'd been, he figured they'd stewed in their fear so they wouldn't get any ideas about resisting.

"We're gathering up all the guns and knives and anything else that can be used as a weapon," Pike warned them. "Anybody who's caught with a weapon or anybody who tries to harm any of my men, with or without one, will be executed on the spot. No exceptions and no mercy."

Some angry muttering came from the prisoners, but no one spoke up in objection to Pike's edicts.

"There will be a curfew," he went on. "No one is to be on the streets except during daylight hours. If you're caught outside your house after dark, you'll be shot then and there. Try to leave town any time of the day or night, and you'll be shot. Other than that, you're free to go on about your business. We control all the ways in and out of Big Rock. We control the telegraph office. The railroad is blocked on both sides. For the time being, Big Rock is ours. Don't interfere with us, and you'll come out of this alive. Cause us any trouble, and you're dead. Man, woman, child, it doesn't matter. Disobey, and you're dead. Simple as that."

A few of the townspeople still wore looks of defiance, but they didn't say anything. For the most part, the population of Big Rock was completely cowed.

Once they were released, they went back to their homes, their stores, their saloons, livery stables, and blacksmith shops, shuffling along under the watchful gazes of the leering, heavily armed killers. Nobody cared about business at the moment, but they needed something to do. They couldn't just sit around all day being terrified.

They had the nights for that.

Inside the jail, Monte Carson fumed. He had gotten over being knocked out, and as his headache eased and his strength returned, his anger grew. He had sworn to protect the town, but he hadn't been able to prevent its takeover by ruthless gunmen.

He stood at the cell door for long hours, his hands gripping the bars.

"You can't blame yourself, Sheriff," Curley told him. "Hell, they way outnumbered us. We put up a fight, but we couldn't hope to win against those odds."

"*You* put up a fight," Carson said bitterly. "You even gunned one down. I didn't do a damn thing except get pistol-whipped by Trask."

"I reckon anybody can get taken by surprise, Sheriff.

Even Smoke Jensen." Curley paused. "Speakin' of which . . . he was on his way back here, wasn't he?"

Carson nodded. He knew why his deputy asked that question. Curley thought that when Smoke showed up, he would put everything right. Folks had confidence in Smoke's near-mystical ability to overcome any odds and defeat any enemy. They had a right to feel that way, given his history.

At the same time, it was a little galling, Carson thought. He had once had a reputation of his own as a pretty tough hombre.

All he wanted was a chance to prove he still could be one.

While Major Pike was laying down the law in the settlement, Dr. Jonas Trask rode to Sugarloaf. He was a bit like an ancient Greek king, he thought, riding at the head of his army to claim the palace of a vanquished foe. Instead of spear-carrying centurions, he had hard-faced gunmen packing iron.

He was moving his headquarters from the hotel to the ranch, where he would remain until he had what he wanted. All his equipment was loaded on a large wagon with an enclosed bed. It had arrived late the previous day, along with the hardcases escorting it.

A large man rode on the wagon seat and handled the reins attached to the mule team pulling it. Powerful muscles in his arms, shoulders, and chest bulged under the shirt he wore. His body seemed filled with strength and vitality.

The broad face under the brim of his hat, though, was utterly vacant. Eyes that should have been bright were dull and almost lifeless. His mouth hung open slightly as he swayed back and forth on the wagon seat. He was aware enough of his surroundings to keep the team moving, but that was all.

As they came in sight of the ranch house, Trask felt excitement quicken inside him. It would be the site of his greatest triumph, he thought. That was where his work would finally reach its culmination.

But he didn't need to get ahead of himself. He still needed to get his hands on the final piece needed to complete his grand design—Smoke Jensen.

Trask reined his horse to the side and fell back a little to ride next to the wagon. He pointed to the house and said to the driver, "That's where you're going to take the wagon. Do you understand, Dan?"

"Yes, Doctor," the man said heavily. His voice was as dull as his eyes.

"Carry all the crates inside and put them in the dining room. That will be my surgery. And be careful with them. Some of the instruments are quite delicate."

"Yes, Doctor," Dan said again. His powerful muscles would make short work of toting the heavy crates.

Trask knew he could work all day and never seem to get tired.

A rider galloped out from the ranch headquarters to meet the newcomers. Trask recognized him as Eli Putnam, who he had left in charge the night before when he and Major Pike had returned to Big Rock.

Putnam lifted a hand in greeting. "Howdy, Doctor. We got everything moved around and ready for you in the house, the way you wanted it."

"Very good," Trask said briskly. "Have you found Mrs. Jensen?"

Putnam grimaced slightly. "No, sir, I'm afraid we haven't. Not yet. But several search parties are out lookin' for her and those fellas she rode off with, so it's only a matter of time until we locate 'em."

"Time is one thing we don't have an abundance of," Trask said as they moved to the side so the wagon and the other riders could go on past. His voice was sharp with irritation. "I've let it be known in Big Rock that Sally Jensen is my prisoner. It's vital to my plans that that claim be true by the time her husband shows up."

"Yes, sir." Putnam frowned. "But it seems to me that as long as Smoke Jensen *believes* that you're holding his wife prisoner, that's as good as actually havin' her, ain't it?"

"A bluff is only successful as long as you don't have to produce what the other man thinks you have. There may well come a time when Jensen will have to lay eyes on his wife in order to believe that her life is actually in danger."

Putnam nodded. "Yeah, I reckon that makes sense."

"Of course it does." Trask's words were like a whip-lash. "Do you think I'm stupid, Putnam?"

"Uh, no, sir!" the gunman responded hastily. His eyes had gone wide with fear. "No, sir, that's not what I think at all. Everybody knows you're the smartest fella around these parts or any other."

"All right. Find Mrs. Jensen."

"Yes, sir!"

Trask heeled his horse into motion and rode on to the ranch house. As soon as he dismounted, a man was there to take his horse and lead it toward the barn. He knew the mount would be well cared for. None of his men would dare do any less.

As he strode into the house, he pulled off the black gloves he wore for riding and dropped them on a small table in the parlor. He looked around. A sneer gradually appeared on his face.

The house was furnished in simple, comfortable style, although everything was of top quality. Smoke Jensen was rumored to be a rich man. Not only was his ranch quite successful, but there was also something in his past about a lost gold mine or some such thing. Trask hadn't investigated that matter thoroughly, since it wasn't important to his overall plans.

Jensen wasn't really special, though. He was just another frontier bumpkin. Except for one thing.

One secret that he possessed.

A secret that Jonas Trask intended to make his own.

All the furniture had been moved out of the dining room except the long table, over which pieces of canvas had been draped. While Trask looked around, Dan carried in the crates from the wagon and placed them along the wall. Trask would open them and remove all the equipment later. Some of it was so delicate he didn't trust anyone except himself to handle it.

After setting down one of the crates, Dan straightened and asked, "Who lives here, Doctor?"

The question took Trask by surprise. He swung around to look at his assistant. He wondered if Dan had begun to regain more of what he had lost. It had been a long time since the big man had asked a question or shown any real interest in his surroundings. For a while, he hadn't even been able to speak or take care of his personal needs. He had been little more than a giant infant.

Something had prompted Trask to keep him around, and he had seen Dan make slow progress until he was capable of being a servant. "I live here now, Dan. This house used to belong to a man named Smoke Jensen."

Dan just grunted, turned away, and lumbered out to

continue unloading the wagon. Trask watched him go and smiled. Whatever brief spark of intelligence had surfaced in the big man's brain, it had flickered out after only seconds.

But what was science, after all, but one long chain of such sparks, springing to life, burning brightly, then dying, until finally a flame of new knowledge was born?

Jonas Trask rubbed his hands together lightly. He couldn't wait to get started on the momentous events that would transpire.

All he needed was Smoke Jensen.

BOOK TWO

Chapter 27

Smoke, Matt, and Preacher stopped in Raton, New Mexico Territory, near the Colorado border, for several days. Preacher's horse had gone lame. Smoke, an expert on horseflesh, told them the animal, the latest in a long line of big gray stallions Preacher never called anything except Horse, would be fine after a few days' rest.

He sent a wire to Sally in care of the telegraph office in Big Rock saying that he would be delayed briefly but not explaining why. He got a reply back the next morning declaring that she would be happy to see him when he arrived but telling him that he should take however much time he needed getting home.

Something about the wire from Sally seemed a little off to him, but it was hard to read too much into a few words printed on a yellow telegraph flimsy. It was possible she might be just a little under the weather.

He was a mite out of sorts himself. Luke had followed through on his decision to go his own way again, and he had parted company from the other three men in Taos.

He had every right to do so, of course. Smoke wasn't

denying that, but he had gone way too many years believing that Luke was dead and hadn't laid eyes on him during all that time. Since learning differently, he saw his older brother only occasionally, one or two times a year, and he missed Luke whenever he wasn't around. Family ties were powerful as far as Smoke was concerned, and such ties extended to those who weren't blood relatives but were just as close that they might as well have been. Those like Matt and Preacher.

Once Horse had recuperated and was able to travel again, the three men set off northward, climbing through Raton Pass with its spectacular view, soon finding themselves across the border, crossing the plains and rolling hills of south-central Colorado with the snowcapped Sangre de Cristos looming to the west.

Not wanting to push the gray stallion too hard, they continued their slow but steady pace for several days. Eventually they angled northwest, through another pass, and headed straight for the Sugarloaf. They would reach Big Rock first, where Smoke planned to stop and say hello to Monte Carson—but only briefly. He was eager to get home and be reunited with Sally.

As the terrain grew more rugged, they could have followed the roads to Big Rock, including a last stretch that paralleled the railroad tracks, but there wasn't a shortcut anywhere in that part of Colorado that the three men didn't know.

For that matter, there weren't many trails anywhere in the West that at least one of them hadn't traveled a time or two.

They came to find themselves riding along a wooded slope about two hundred yards above the wagon road parallel to the steel rails of the Denver and Rio Grande that twisted back and forth considerably as they followed the course of a fast-flowing stream. The way Smoke, Matt, and Preacher were going was much straighter and would cut half an hour or more off the trip. Big Rock was only a mile or two ahead of them.

Smoke felt his anticipation growing. Reaching Big Rock meant he was that much closer to home—and Sally.

Maybe that was the reason he wasn't quite as alert as he might have been.

Preacher was the one who said in a low voice, "Hold on a minute, boys. Might be some trouble down there. I don't much like what I'm seein'."

All three men reined in. Smoke asked, "Whereabouts, Preacher?" His thoughts of home had vanished. He had complete faith in the old mountain man, and if Preacher suspected trouble might be lurking in the vicinity, Smoke wanted to know what it was.

"Look in that thick stand of trees down yonder, be-tween the railroad and the creek," Preacher said. "Just to the right o' that rock that's sittin' next to the trail."

Smoke and Matt watched closely the area Preacher had indicated.

After a moment Matt said, "There's somebody in there on horseback."

"More than one somebody," Smoke said. "I make it three men. How about you, Preacher?"

"Yup," Preacher agreed. "Three it is. And there ain't no reason for 'em to be sittin' there all hidey-holed up like that unless they're up to no good."

"Maybe they just stopped to roll quirlies and let their horses rest," Matt suggested.

Smoke shook his head. "If that's all they were doing,

likely they'd just move over to the side of the road and stay out in the open. It looks to me like they're hiding."

"Bunch o' dang bushwhackers, if you ask me," Preacher said.

Matt nodded. "Could be. What are we going to do about it?"

"You know it's probably not any of our business," Smoke pointed out.

Matt grinned at the comment. "Since when did that ever keep us from poking around?"

Smoke had to admit that Matt had a point.

Preacher rested his hands on his saddle horn. "Listen, you go to pokin' at a beehive with a stick and you're liable to get stung less 'n you've smoked it first. Reckon that's what we'd better do. You boys ride back a ways, work your way down to the road, and then ride along it like you don't have a care in the world. That might draw them varmints out."

"Yeah, and it might just paint targets on us," Matt pointed out. "What do you plan to be doing while Smoke and I are doing that?"

Preacher pointed with his beard-stubbled chin. "Figured Dog and me would circle around and come up behind those boys. Maybe they'll be talkin' and let slip what they're up to."

"And if they do open fire on us . . . ?" Smoke asked.

Preacher patted the butts of his revolvers. "Then I'll be right there to blow holes in 'em."

Smoke didn't doubt that the old mountain man could do it. Age had neither dimmed Preacher's vision nor slowed his reflexes. Oh, he might be a hair less quick on the draw, but that meant Preacher was still faster with a gun than nine out of ten men.

He was about as stealthy in the woods as ever, too. He could get behind the men lurking in the trees without them knowing he was there. The Blackfeet hadn't nicknamed him Ghost Killer without a good reason.

"Gimme twenty minutes or so," Preacher went on, "then you fellas commence to ridin' along that road like it's a Sunday afternoon and you ain't got nothin' better to do."

"*Is* it Sunday afternoon?" Matt asked. "I think I've lost track."

"No, I believe it's Tuesday." Smoke lifted his horse's reins and turned the animal back in the direction they had come. "Come on."

Chapter 28

Smoke and Matt went one way, Preacher the other. The old mountain man had confidence in the plan he had come up with. He had turned the tables on numerous bushwhackers during the adventurous life he'd led.

Of course, it was possible that Matt was right and the men hiding in the trees didn't have anything bad in mind. Preacher didn't believe it, though. Trouble had a habit of finding the three of them when they were apart; put them together and it was almost inevitable that hell would pop.

It had been almost a week since anybody had shot at them. Preacher didn't like that. He sometimes figured that dodging bullets was what kept him young.

With Dog padding along with him, he rode on well past the spot where the mysterious hombres were lurking. He was pretty sure he recalled a place where the railroad tracks and the road made a bend around a fairly sharp curve. That ought to shield him from the hidden watchers' view. When he felt like he had passed it, he worked his way down the slope until he reached the edge of the trees and brush.

Preacher brought Horse to a stop and swung down

from the saddle. He took off his hat and stuck his head out to take a look. Right away, he saw that he had guessed right. He was past the curve and could cross the road and the steel rails without being seen.

That is, if nobody else was skulking around. Preacher stood still for a long moment, eyes squinted, head cocked a little to the side as he listened intently and sniffed the air. He didn't hear anything except small animals moving around, didn't smell human sweat or horseflesh or tobacco smoke. His senses told him he was alone, and his instincts agreed with them.

He clapped the old brown hat back on his head and led Horse across the road and the tracks.

Once he had the stallion well hidden in the trees again, he tied the reins loosely around a sapling and said quietly, "You and Dog just stay here, Horse. I best go afoot from here on out. If I need you, I'll whistle, and you two come arunnin'."

Horse tossed his head up and down, almost like he was nodding. Preacher grinned and patted him lightly on the shoulder. Dog whined, clearly not happy with Preacher's decision not to include him, but he would follow orders. As far back as the old mountain man could remember, he'd had an uncanny, almost supernatural ability to communicate with animals, especially horses and dogs.

Preacher faded into the brush and started back toward the spot where the men were hidden.

He heard them talking well before he got there. Whatever they were up to, being quiet obviously wasn't part of it. When he was close, he parted some brush to make a tiny gap and peered through it.

The three men had dismounted, but their horses stood with reins dangling, ready to ride again at a moment's notice. It didn't appear that the men had even loosened the saddle cinches.

One of them was smoking a stogie. They passed around a silver flask. It was all Preacher could do not to snort in disgust at their lackadaisical attitude. If they were bushwhackers, they were doing a piss-poor job of it.

But he supposed that when it came to ambushes, the proof was in the killing. As long as they gunned down who they were supposed to, nothing else mattered.

Question was, who were they gunning for?

Preacher had taken one look at the men and known they were killers. He had seen hundreds of their stripe over the years. *Stripe* was the right word, he mused. He knew skunks when he saw 'em.

Listening to their conversation for the next few minutes did nothing but confirm his initial impression of them. In the crudest possible terms, they talked about women they had known, most of them saloon girls. They talked about bank robberies and train and stagecoach holdups. They talked about killings they had witnessed— and some they had participated in. No matter how sordid or violent, they seemed to find all the stories amusing.

A bitter taste filled Preacher's mouth. He wished Smoke and Matt would go ahead and ride up the road, so maybe these varmints would shut up their filthy talk.

Then one of them said something that made the old mountain man's ears perk up.

"I've heard a lot of men say Smoke Jensen's the fastest hombre who ever buckled on a gun belt," the man declared.

The one smoking the stogie puffed on it and laughed. "I reckon he's fast, all right, but there's only one way of finding out who's the fastest, isn't there?"

The third man said, "Well, it's not you, Dalby, that's

for damn sure. I swear, I could count to ten in the time it takes you to pull that hogleg."

"That's a damn lie," Dalby said, scowling. He tossed the cigar butt aside and straightened. "Any time you want to give me a try, Vinton—"

"Hold on, hold on," the first man said sharply. "The major sent us out here to watch the road and make sure nobody gets in or out of town, not to shoot each other."

Preacher's jaw tightened. He didn't like the sound of what he had just heard. He didn't like it at all. He didn't know who the so-called major was—not a real military man, surely, or he wouldn't be giving orders to owlhoot scum like these fellas—but evidently the man had taken over Big Rock. That was the only reason he would want to keep folks from leaving.

"What if Smoke Jensen himself comes along, Harkness?" Dalby asked the first man. "What are we supposed to do then, if he really is that fast?"

It's Smoke they're after. That revelation came as no surprise to Preacher. Smoke had made enough enemies over the years for a dozen regular men. Maybe two dozen.

Harkness said, "Jensen's not going to throw down on us. Not if he wants—" He stopped short and lifted a hand. "Listen. I hear horses on the road."

That would be Smoke and Matt, thought Preacher as he bit back a curse. He'd been in a hurry for them to get there and shut up the dirty-talkin' varmints, but he'd changed his mind, wishing they were coming along a few minutes later. If they were, the men might have inadvertently spilled everything that was going on. He shrugged. Nothing could be done about that.

The men swung into their saddles and moved quickly toward the road.

Maybe with any luck, he and Smoke and Matt wouldn't have to kill all three of them, Preacher told himself. If they could get their hands on a prisoner, he could convince the hombre to talk. He was sure of that.

For the moment, all he could do was glide through the trees after them.

Smoke and Matt had taken their time, making sure that Preacher had the chance to get in position. As they approached the spot where they had seen the men lurking in the trees, neither of them doubted that the old mountain man was right where he was supposed to be.

"I'm starting to feel a mite antsy," Matt commented as they walked their horses along side by side. "Like somebody's looking at me over the barrel of a gun right now."

"Could be they are," Smoke said with a faint smile. "Wouldn't be the first time, would it?"

"Well, no, not hardly. But don't tell me you've gotten used to the feeling."

Smoke shook his head slightly. "You never do."

His eyes moved constantly, seeking out signs of danger. Every sense was on high alert. He was expecting it when three men on horseback suddenly burst out of the brush and blocked the road.

"Let them start the ball," Smoke quietly told his adopted brother. "We want to find out as much as we can."

One of the men called, "Hold it right there!"

The outlaws hadn't drawn their weapons, but their hands hovered close to gun butts.

Smoke and Matt reined in.

Smoke asked in a deceptively mild tone of voice, "What's this all about, mister?"

"We'll ask the questions," the man snapped. "Where are you two headed?"

Smoke nodded down the road. "On into Big Rock."

"Got business there, do you?"

"That's right."

"Well, you don't anymore. The town's off-limits, and our orders are to arrest anybody who tries to ride in."

"Arrest?" Smoke repeated. "You're lawmen?"

"That's right. Now, are you comin' along peacefully?"

Smoke didn't believe for one second that the men were officers of the law. He had seen too many hard-cases not to recognize that sort when he saw them. They were gunmen, pure and simple, hired killers more than likely . . . but they wanted to take Smoke and Matt into Big Rock, and that was where they wanted to go.

"Follow my lead," he said to Matt from the corner of his mouth. Then he raised his voice. "Take it easy, deputy. We're not looking for trouble. If you want us to come with you—".

"Damn it, Harkness, I've seen that hombre before! *That's Smoke Jensen!*" Dalby clawed at the gun on his hip.

Chapter 29

Harkness yelled, "Damn it, Dalby, don't—" but it was too late.

Dalby's gun was already in his fist.

Smoke and Matt were on the move instantly, as soon as Dalby reached for his gun. Smoke yanked his horse to the right while Matt went to the left. Spreading out in the face of danger was pure instinct for them.

Dalby's bullet whipped through the air between them as they separated. He didn't get a chance to fire again. His shot had barely sounded when two shots crashed from Matt's Colt. The bullets slammed into Dalby's chest and slapped him backwards, out of the saddle. His right foot hung in the stirrup as his horse bolted. The spooked horse dragged the dead man along the road as it galloped between Smoke and Matt.

On the other side of the wagon road, Smoke had palmed out both revolvers. The hardcase called Harkness may not have wanted a fight, but it had gone too far to stop and all the men knew it.

Harkness yanked his gun from its holster, but he

didn't get a shot off. Smoke's right-hand Colt boomed. The bullet tore through Harkness's throat. As he bent backwards from the impact, blood fountained from the torn arteries in his neck.

The third outlaw screamed like a madman and kicked his horse into a run just as Preacher emerged from the trees behind him and fired both guns. The unexpected move threw off the old mountain man's aim and both slugs whistled through the air.

The hardcase thundered toward Smoke and Matt, spraying lead at them as fast as he could jerk the trigger. From the looks of it, he was trying to blast his way past them so he could flee.

The tactic might have worked if he hadn't been facing enemies as coolheaded under fire as Smoke and Matt Jensen.

As it was, they fired at the same time. Their bullets tore through the man at different angles and corkscrewed him out of the saddle. He thudded facedown to the ground.

Preacher hurried forward and exclaimed, "Dadgum it! I wanted to take one of them varmints alive."

"No way for us to know that," Matt said. "And once the shooting started, there wasn't time to do anything fancy."

The horse dragging Dalby had vanished around the bend. Harkness was clearly dead with blood pooling darkly around his head where he lay after toppling off his mount.

Preacher hooked a boot toe under the shoulder of the third man and rolled him onto his back. His bloody chest still rose and fell, and they could hear his harsh breaths as he struggled to draw air into his lungs.

Smoke dismounted and joined Preacher at the wounded man's side.

Preacher hunkered on his heels. "Son, you ain't got far to go 'fore you cross the divide. How come you and those other fellas were waitin' out here for Smoke Jensen?"

Smoke frowned as he heard that question.

The dying man rasped, "You . . . you go to . . . hell . . . old man! . . . The major . . . he'll see to it . . . the doctor . . . the devil . . . Ahhh!"

The man's back arched and his boot heels drummed briefly on the hard-packed dirt. Then he slumped as his final gasp rattled in his throat.

Preacher stood and thumbed his hat back. "Well, if that don't beat all. What'd he mean by the devil? And who're the major and the doctor?"

"What did you overhear, Preacher?" Smoke asked. "Did they give you any hint as to what's going on here?"

"A hint's all they did give me," Preacher replied. "From the sound of it, their bunch has taken over Big Rock."

Matt said, "We got the same idea when they started talking about arresting us."

Preacher let out a disgusted snort. "These varmints weren't real deputies. Monte Carson never would've pinned badges on owlhoot scum like them."

"You're right about that," Smoke agreed. A grim feeling began to grow inside him. "That means Monte must be their prisoner—or worse."

"Yeah," Preacher said with a nod. "It's you they was really after, Smoke. They were supposed to capture you, not kill you. They acted like they had somethin' they could hold over you, to make you do whatever they wanted."

"Like hostages in town," Matt suggested.

"Yep. That fella Dalby lost his head and went for his gun. That was all the spark it took."

Smoke's heart slugged harder in his chest at the mention of hostages. His enemies had tried that before. "Did they mention anything about Sally or the ranch?"

Preacher shook his head. "Not a dang word. The same thing occurred to me, Smoke, but there ain't no reason to think Sally's in danger."

"There's no reason to think she's not, either."

Preacher just shrugged. He couldn't argue with Smoke's logic.

Matt said, "It might be a good idea to hash this all out somewhere else. We're close enough to town that somebody could have heard those shots, and if these fellas' friends are running things in Big Rock now, they might send somebody to see what the commotion was all about."

Smoke's face wore a bleak expression as he nodded. "You're right. Let's move higher in the hills where it'll be harder to find us."

"What about these carcasses?" Preacher asked.

"Might as well leave them where they fell. I suppose we could hide them, but even if they vanish, their friends will still know that something happened out here."

"That'll make 'em be on the lookout for trouble," Preacher warned.

Smoke nodded. "Good. Because trouble's on the way."

Chapter 30

Half an hour later, Preacher, Smoke, and Matt stopped in a clearing high enough that in the distance, they could see the steeple on the church in Big Rock, along with the roofs of a few buildings. They dismounted.

Smoke propped a foot on a fallen tree and peered intently at the distant settlement. "If the owlhoots are guarding the roads into town, they're liable to have patrols out, too, but it's not very likely any of them will come this high."

Matt asked, "Who do you think they are, Smoke?"

"I don't have any idea." Smoke shook his head. "I've got plenty of enemies, I suppose."

Preacher grunted. "Not that many who are still alive and kickin'."

Smoke smiled humorlessly. "I suppose that's true, but most of the men I've had to kill are bound to have friends and relatives."

"What about the major and the doctor?" Matt asked. "Either of those ring any bells?"

Smoke shook his head again. "Not really. Those men

we shot it out with weren't regular army, any more than they were deputies."

"I'd say that's right," Preacher agreed.

Smoke frowned in thought for a moment, then asked, "When you were eavesdropping on them, Preacher, did they happen to mention you or Matt?"

The mountain man pursed his lips as he considered the question. "Nope, I don't believe they did. I'm sure of it. They didn't."

Smoke rubbed his chin. "Then maybe they don't know the two of you are with me. Maybe they think I was coming into Big Rock alone."

"What difference does that make?" Matt asked, clearly puzzled.

"It means they won't be looking for the two of you."

"They're grabbin' ever'body who tries to get into town," Preacher pointed out.

"That's right. And they don't know who you are." Smoke looked back and forth between his two companions. "With all three of those men dead, the others have no way of knowing that there's any connection between the two of you and me."

Matt let out a low whistle. "So there's nothing stopping us from getting into town and finding out exactly what's going on."

Smoke nodded. "That's the way it looks to me."

Preacher said, "Problem with that idea is that we'd be prisoners. Wouldn't be able to do nothin' to help matters."

"I might be able to slip in without them knowing I'm there," Matt said.

"And I know dang well I could," Preacher added.

Smoke agreed. "That's what I was thinking. The two of you find out exactly what sort of odds we're facing, and we can rendezvous later to figure out what to do about them."

"Where should we meet?" Matt asked.

Smoke considered the question for a moment, then said, "How about Knob Hill? It's closer to Big Rock than Sugarloaf, but it's pretty handy to both of them."

Matt and Preacher nodded. They knew where the rocky hill was located.

"Where'll you be in the meantime?" Preacher asked.

"I'm heading for Sugarloaf," Smoke declared. "I'm not going to do anything else until I'm sure that Sally is all right."

Chapter 31

Pearlie sat motionless in the sun with his back against a rock. He was at the top of the ridge above the line shack, having climbed there earlier to relieve Cal. For the past two days, one of them had been up there all the time during daylight hours, keeping an eye on the valley hundreds of feet below and the lower slopes that led up.

If any of Trask's men started poking around in the vicinity, the fugitives wanted as much warning as they could get.

Down below, a thin tendril of smoke curled from the shack's stone chimney. Sally kept the fire small, just enough to boil coffee, fry salt pork, and bake biscuits from the small cache of supplies left in the line shack. They were trying to make those provisions last as long as possible.

Pearlie was careful to keep his rifle and pistol where the sun couldn't hit them. A reflection of sunlight off metal from the ridge would be a dead giveaway that a man with a gun was up there. A pair of field glasses might have come in handy, but he wouldn't have risked using those, either. His eyesight was good, so he was willing to rely on it.

Inside the line shack, Sally poured herself another cup of coffee while Cal dozed in one of the bunks. The men took turns standing guard at night, as well as watching from the ridge during the day, so they grabbed what sleep they could, when they could.

The shack had only two bunks. Cal and Pearlie traded off in one of them and Sally had the other.

Some people would consider it scandalous that a married woman was sharing the crude cabin with two men, neither of whom was her husband, but she had long since stopped caring about narrow-minded folks and their hidebound notions of propriety. If somebody wasn't brave enough to say to her face what they thought, she didn't care about their opinions.

She sat down at the rough-hewn table. She wore the flannel shirt and denim trousers that one of the ranch hands had left behind, along with a pair of thick socks. The shirtsleeves and trouser legs were rolled up quite a bit, but the socks fit surprisingly well. The puncher who had left the clothes must have rather small feet, she had thought when she'd first pulled on the socks.

They were all right as long as she was at the line shack, but if she was going to be riding or moving around much, she needed a pair of boots. She didn't know where she would get them.

She wished she had her carbine, too. Cal's Winchester lay on the table and she could use it if she needed to, but a weapon with a shorter barrel was easier for her to handle. She was more accurate with a carbine, too.

She had just taken a sip of coffee when three thuds sounded in rapid succession on the shack's roof. Her head came up sharply.

That was the signal for trouble. Pearlie had pitched down three small rocks from the top of the ridge, one after the other, aiming them at the roof. They had agreed on that when the men first started standing watch, but it was the first time any of them had used the signal.

"Cal!" Sally said as she leaped to her feet. "Pearlie's spotted something."

The cowboy came out of the blankets thrashing and sputtering, got his wits about him quickly, and snatched the Winchester from the table. "He gave the signal?"

"Three rocks landed on the roof, one right after the other," Sally confirmed.

"Dang it! That means trouble, all right." He hurried over to the door and eased it open a crack. The line shack didn't have any windows, although there were loopholes in all four walls where folks inside could fire rifles if they were forced to defend the place.

Cal put his eye to the narrow opening and peered out. After a moment he said, "I can't see anything. Maybe I better go out there and take a look around." He drew his Colt from its holster and half-turned to extend it toward Sally. "Here, Miss Sally. You hang on to this, in case you need it."

She took the gun from him. "Be careful, Cal."

"I wish there was some way for Pearlie to let us know what he saw from up yonder. If we stay here for very long, we're gonna have to work on that."

On that hopeful note, Cal slowly opened the door wider. In the wild country, movement was what attracted the eye, so he continued to take it slow and easy as he slid out of the line shack.

Sally didn't realize she was holding her breath. When she finally had to take a breath, it was shallow and quiet as if she worried that whoever was outside might hear it.

She jumped a little as a figure appeared in the door, but it was only Cal coming back. He said excitedly, "I saw a rider on the other side of the meadow coming this way."

"Just one man?"

"Yeah." Cal hurried to the fireplace. The fire had burned down to embers and was barely putting out any smoke. "Maybe he didn't see that, and the wind's from the wrong direction for him to smell the fire. Maybe he'll ride up without knowing that anybody's here, and we can get the drop on him."

"You're sure it's one of Trask's men?"

"Who else would it be? As far as we know, they're running this whole part of the country now."

He was right about that, Sally thought. Trask was bound to have searchers out looking for her, and the rider was probably one of them.

The horses they had ridden were in a shed at the back of the line shack. The stranger wouldn't be able to see them as he approached. Cal had pulled the door closed when he came in, so from outside the shack ought to look like it was deserted. The man would want to have a look inside it anyway, just to make sure his quarry wasn't hiding there.

"We need to grab him if we can," Cal went on. "He'll have guns, ammunition, maybe a few supplies. And he's got a horse. We need a mount for you, Miss Sally."

"And boots. Maybe I'd be able to wear his boots."

"Yeah, we'll get you outfitted." Cal hesitated. "If he's one of those gun-wolves who work for Trask, chances are he's not gonna give up without a fight."

Sally's hand tightened on the revolver. "Then we'll just have to give him one."

Chapter 32

Sally and Cal flanked the doorway with their backs pressed against the rough log wall. At Cal's insistence, she stood where the open door would shield her, so the stranger wouldn't be able to see her right away.

"I can shoot him as soon as he comes in," Cal suggested.

"We're not certain he works for Trask," Sally pointed out. "He could be some innocent cowboy riding the grub line. We can't risk that."

"Not likely he is, but I'll hold my fire unless I have to shoot. Maybe I can knock him out, so we can tie him up and then find out who he is."

That sounded like a workable idea to Sally. She said as much, then added, "Just be careful. I don't want anything happening to you."

"Me, neither," Cal said with a grin.

Sally figured that up on the ridge, Pearlie was going crazy because he couldn't get down to help them. If he moved from his hiding place, the approaching rider was bound to see him and know that something was wrong. That would ruin their chances of capturing the man.

The few minutes it took for him to cross the meadow seemed to last forever. Finally, Sally and Cal heard hoof-beats outside. They stopped as the rider reined to a halt in front of the line shack.

A moment later, spurs *ching*ed softly as the man approached the door. They heard a little thump, and the door swung open. The barrel of the stranger's rifle came into view, and Sally knew he had used it to push the door open. That was what they had heard.

He didn't come the rest of the way in. He was being careful. He called, "Hey, anybody in there? I don't mean any harm. Not lookin' for any trouble."

Sally and Cal didn't respond. They stood absolutely motionless and silent, not even breathing.

"Just seen this line shack," the man went on. "Figured I might stay here a spell and rest my hoss. Don't want to intrude on nobody, though."

The voice wasn't familiar to her at all. The man really was a stranger, and that meant in all likelihood he was one of Jonas Trask's hired guns.

But they still couldn't be a hundred percent certain, so she waited and hoped Cal would do the same.

The rifle barrel poked farther into the shack. The man's footsteps were heavy as he advanced warily. The light was considerably dimmer inside than it was outside, so he had to wait for his eyes to adjust.

Cal decided that he had waited long enough.

Sally heard him spring forward. She held the revolver in both hands and kicked the door out of the way in time to see him try to slam the Winchester's butt against the back of the stranger's head.

Unfortunately, the man either heard Cal or instinctively sensed what was about to happen and reacted with the speed of a striking snake, twisting aside so the rifle butt struck his left shoulder. The blow staggered him, but it didn't make him fall down or drop his rifle.

He swung the barrel toward Cal and pulled the trigger. The shot was ear-numbingly loud in the line shack's close confines.

With the man between her and Cal, she couldn't see if the youngster was hit. She couldn't blaze away with the Colt in her hands, either. If she missed she might shoot Cal herself.

She leaped toward the stranger and chopped at his head with the revolver. The blow landed with a solid thud and knocked the man forward. He dropped to his knees. Relieved to see that Cal was still on his feet and didn't seem to be hurt, it was evident the man's shot had missed him.

Cal moved in and landed a solid stroke to the jaw with the Winchester's stock. The blow knocked the man sprawling on the puncheon floor. He managed to hang on to his rifle, though, and as he rolled over, he worked the lever. Flame spat from the muzzle as another sharp crack rang out.

Cal launched himself in a dive at Sally at the same time, yelling, "Look out, Miss Sally!" He crashed into her and knocked her off her feet. The slug whipped through the air beside her head, narrowly missing her.

Sally hit the floor hard. The impact jolted the gun out of her hands and it clattered away from her. Cal rolled, trying to get up, whirl around, and defend them.

A few feet away, the stranger struggled up to his knees and shook his head groggily. He yelled, "You nearly stove my head in! If Trask didn't want you alive, you'd pay for that, by God!" He turned the rifle toward Cal and snarled, "But you, kid. Nobody cares if you live or die!"

He was about to fire again and send a bullet ripping through Cal when a shot blasted thunderously from the doorway. The slug punched into his chest and knocked him over backwards. The rifle flew out of his hands.

Breathless, Sally looked at the door and saw Pearlie standing there. Smoke curled from the muzzle of the Winchester he held. He levered the weapon and said coldly, "You're wrong. *I* care."

"And so do I, Pearlie," Sally said. "You got here just in time."

"Aw, I woulda had him," Cal muttered, but all three of them knew that wasn't true. The youngster wore a look of profound gratitude on his face as he nodded to Pearlie, who returned the nod in a moment of silent communication that was all the two friends needed.

Pearlie came into the shack and covered the fallen gunman as he approached.

Sally asked, "Is he dead?"

"Yep," Pearlie replied. "One of Trask's men, I reckon?"

"Yes. I didn't recognize him, but he said something about Trask wanting me to be taken alive, so that's proof enough as far as I'm concerned."

"Me, too," Pearlie agreed. "Sorry I didn't get here sooner. I started climbin' down as soon as he got to where he couldn't see me."

"You made it in time," Sally told him. "That's all that really matters."

Pearlie finally lowered the rifle. "Now we've got another problem. The shack walls probably muffled those shots some, but sound carries a long way in this thin air. There are bound to be more of Trask's men not far off, and there's a good chance they heard the shootin'. They'll come arunnin' to find out what it's about."

Cal said, "So we need to saddle up and get out of here while we've got the chance."

"Yeah. Hate to lose this hideout, but I don't think we have a choice. At least we've got this fella's horse now, so all three of us can have a mount."

"And I'm taking his boots." Sally steeled herself to carry out the unpleasant task of removing them from the dead man's feet.

Pearlie sensed what she was feeling. "I'll do that for you, Miss Sally. Kid, grab this jasper's horse and make sure it don't get away, then throw the saddles on the other two."

"You bet, Pearlie." Cal hurried to carry out the orders.

Pearlie bent to take off the dead man's boots. "Miss Sally, if you'll get his rifle while I'm doin' this . . ."

"Of course." She picked up the fallen rifle and retrieved the Colt she had dropped.

Pearlie traded the boots for the guns. He tucked the extra revolver behind his belt.

Sally sat down on one of the bunks to pull the boots on her feet. The thought that they had come from a dead man—one of their enemies—made a little shiver go through her, but she wasn't going to let that stop her from wearing them.

"How do they fit?" Pearlie asked as she stood up and stomped her feet down in them.

"They're too big. If I had a couple extra pairs of socks, they wouldn't be too bad, but they'll do for now. They're a lot better than nothing."

"That's the way life is, all right. Make do with what you can get. And right now we got to get—"

Cal burst through the open door and yelled, "Too late! Here they come!"

As if to confirm his warning, guns cracked and

boomed outside, and bullets began to whistle through the door as Cal yelped and dived out of the line of fire.

Pearlie grabbed Sally and swung her away from the door. He kicked it shut and told Cal, "Bar it!"

Cal scrambled to his feet and dropped the bar over the door. It wasn't nearly as sturdy as the one in the bunkhouse, but it would keep intruders out for a while.

Pearlie handed Sally the rifle he had taken from her only a few minutes earlier.

Cal had already put his eye to one of the loopholes to study the situation outside. "Looks like half a dozen of 'em," he reported. "It's a flat-out charge across the meadow."

Bullets thudded into the door and the thick walls of the line shack but didn't penetrate.

Pearlie slid the barrel of his Winchester through another loophole. "Let's make 'em think twice about that."

Sally joined them at the wall and thrust the barrel of the dead man's rifle through another opening. "We'll give them a warm welcome."

"Not warm," Pearlie said. "Hot. Hot lead all the way."

The three of them proceeded to do just that as they opened fire and gun thunder filled the inside of the line shack.

But even as they fought valiantly, they knew how desperate their predicament was. They were outnumbered, outgunned, and pinned down. They could make the enemy pay a price, but they couldn't win.

Unless something happened to change the odds, by the time it was over, they would all be prisoners—or dead.

Chapter 33

Smoke hauled back on the reins as he heard a pair of muffled booms in the distance. The shots were separated by a minute or so. He thought they came from a rifle. "What do you think, Dog?"

Preacher had sent the big cur with him, thinking it would be easier to sneak into Big Rock without Dog along. The varmint hadn't been happy about being separated from his trail partner, but he had gone along with what Preacher had told him.

With the fur on his neck bristling, Dog looked up the wooded slope in the direction the shots had come from and growled.

"Yeah, that's what I was thinking." Smoke turned his horse and sent the animal up the slope. The shots had come from somewhere above him, and he wanted to find out what they meant.

Also, this was *his* range, and if somebody was shooting up there, he had a right to know what the ruckus was about.

After leaving Matt and Preacher on the road outside Big Rock, he had circled wide around the settlement, using his extensive knowledge of the area to figure out the quickest way to reach Sugarloaf. He had considered riding straight to the ranch headquarters, then decided against that idea and circled again, even though that delayed him more.

If anyone was lying in wait for him, it was better to approach from the direction opposite what they would expect. A big part of winning any battle was being where the enemy didn't think you would be.

He'd heard those shots and was getting farther from the ranch headquarters, rather than closer. Anxious to see Sally again and make sure she was all right, the postponement chafed at him. He climbed a couple hundred feet, hoping it wouldn't take him long to check out the gunfire.

As the slope began to level out, he recognized the landscape. He was approaching a big meadow used for summer graze. One of the more isolated line shacks was located up here.

Suddenly, more shots roared and shattered the high country stillness. It was a full-fledged volley, and it wasn't far away. Smoke pulled his rifle from its saddle scabbard and urged his horse to move faster.

He reached the edge of the trees bordering the meadow and saw half a dozen men on horseback riding away from him. They galloped toward the line shack visible in the distance, all of them blasting away with rifles and pistols as they charged.

Puffs of powder smoke came from the loopholes in the shack's front wall. From the looks of it, several people were holed up in there defending themselves.

From his angle he couldn't tell much about the men attacking the shack. At first glance, none of their horses looked familiar, but that didn't mean all that much.

Based on what Preacher had overheard, it seemed likely the men were part of the same bunch that had taken over Big Rock. Worried that they would move in on Sugarloaf, Smoke guessed that some of his men were holed up in the shack.

Even if he wasn't sure exactly what was going on, he knew he had to take a hand in it. He couldn't sit by and do nothing.

He heeled his horse into motion again and galloped after the attackers.

Firing from the saddle, he sent a couple rounds whistling over their heads to see what they would do. Two of the men immediately split off from the others and wheeled around to meet the new threat. Smoke grabbed the reins and slowed his horse. His eyes were keen enough that he could make out the men's faces. He had never seen either of them before.

They didn't hesitate. They opened fire on him.

So be it, thought Smoke. They had called the tune. They could dance to it.

Once again, he lifted the Winchester to his shoulder and started shooting. His movements were sure and smooth as he worked the rifle's lever between rounds. Five shots erupted from the Winchester while he ignored the wildly aimed slugs that whined around him. Both men pitched from their saddles and landed in limp, bullet-riddled heaps.

Smoke switched his attention back to the others. One of the remaining four was down, he saw, doubtless knocked off his horse by a shot from inside the line shack. The other three slowed their charge and began to mill around. They suddenly realized they had gone from having the advantage to being in deep trouble in the blink of an eye. They were caught in a crossfire, and as

Smoke drilled another man, the two who hadn't been hit yet yanked their horses around and raced away at an angle, taking off for the tall and uncut.

One of the racing horses stumbled and fell, sending its rider sailing over its head. Smoke aimed at the lone remaining rider and fired again. The man kept going for about twenty yards before slowly toppling out of the saddle. He bounced once when he hit the ground, then didn't move again.

Smoke rode hard toward the man who had been thrown when his horse went down. He wanted a prisoner to question, and that hombre had the best chance of still being alive.

The fallen man was alive, all right. In fact, he leaped up and muzzle flame spouted from the gun in his fist. Smoke aimed for his right shoulder, but the man shifted just as Smoke squeezed the trigger. The bullet caught him in the throat, tore all the way through, and exploded out the back of his neck. He dropped like a rag doll.

Smoke grimaced as he lowered the rifle and slowed his horse again. His shot had been aimed true. There was nothing he could do about where it had ended up.

Maybe one of the others was still alive after all.

As Smoke began checking, the line shack door swung open. A man carrying a rifle stepped out, waved the weapon over his head, and shouted, "Smoke!"

That was his foreman Pearlie, Smoke realized as his heart suddenly thudded harder in his chest. It wasn't unusual to find Pearlie anywhere on Sugarloaf range, but Smoke had thought he would be down at the ranch headquarters, several miles away and hundreds of feet lower.

Smoke didn't let that thought distract him from the task at hand. He rode quickly from body to body, looking for one of the attackers still breathing and able to answer questions.

All of them were dead, victims of the accurate shooting by Smoke, Pearlie, and whoever else was in the line shack.

Smoke's desire to resolve that question made him turn his horse and urge it into a trot toward the primitive structure.

Another man had emerged from the shack, and Smoke wasn't surprised to recognize young Calvin Woods. Cal and Pearlie were best friends, and most of the time they weren't going to be very far apart.

A third figure stepped out, shorter than the other two, clad in a flannel shirt and denim trousers and carrying a rifle like Pearlie and Cal. At first glance Smoke figured it was another of the Sugarloaf hands.

Then he realized something was different about the defender. The slender but curved shape, the thick mass of dark hair . . .

"Sally!" The name burst from his lips.

He kicked the horse into a gallop and thundered the rest of the way across the meadow. She ran out to meet him, and as he swung down from the saddle while the horse was still moving, she came into his arms, grabbed him around the neck, and pressed her lips to his in an urgent, passionate kiss.

Smoke wasn't sure exactly what was going on, but finding out could wait. He had his wife in his arms again after weeks of being apart from her, and that was all that mattered.

Chapter 34

After Smoke had ridden off, Matt and Preacher stayed in the clearing for a few minutes, talking about how they were going to proceed.

"I was thinking I might circle around the town and come in from the other direction," Matt said.

"And I'll go back down to the road and mosey at it from this side," Preacher said. "Wouldn't do to stay too close together. That way if one of us gets nabbed, the other one will still have a chance of gettin' into town without them fellers knowin' about it."

"They're not going to catch me," Matt said.

"Well, they sure as hell ain't gonna catch me," the old mountain man declared. "I don't get caught less 'n I want to." He tapped a finger against his temple. "I'm sneaky that way."

"We need to figure out somewhere we can rendezvous so we can compare notes and figure out what to do next. Maybe Louis Longmont's saloon?"

"If those varmints got the whole settlement treed, the saloon and the other businesses may not be open," Preacher pointed out.

Matt rubbed his chin and frowned. "Yeah, you're right about that. How about the school? It's on the edge of town, and those gun-wolves probably won't be keeping too close an eye on it."

Preacher nodded. "Reckon that'll do. Good luck to you, youngster."

"Same to you, old-timer."

They rode out of the clearing, headed in different directions.

Preacher went back to the spot where they'd had the shoot-out with the three sentries. He wanted to see if the bodies had been discovered yet.

The dead gunmen still lay where they had fallen. Their horses cropped grass nearby at the edge of the road. From the looks of things, no one had come along since he and Smoke and Matt had ridden off earlier.

That probably wouldn't hold true for much longer. The men who had taken over the town were bound to have patrols out, as well as posting guards on the roads.

It might be a good idea, Preacher decided, to drag the bodies into the woods, unsaddle the horses, and let them wander off. The dead men would be discovered sooner or later, but it wouldn't hurt to delay that process.

He had just swung down from the stallion's back when he heard some odd noises from back up the road, the way he and Smoke and Matt had come. Something was clattering and clanging, as if a bunch of metal objects were bumping against each other.

Tensing, Preacher turned in that direction and dropped his right hand to the butt of the Colt holstered on that side. He closed his fingers around the smooth walnut grips.

A wagon came into view, pulled by a team of four mules. It wasn't a buckboard or a ranch wagon or an immigrant wagon with a canvas-covered bed. It had a square wooden compartment on its back, and its sides were covered with hooks from which were suspended a variety of pots, pans, silverware, tools, farm implements, and other things Preacher couldn't identify right offhand. They swayed back and forth as the wagon rocked, banging together to create the racket he had heard. The noise had a strange sort of musical quality about it.

The man on the seat handling the reins was so fat and round that he bore a distinct resemblance to a ball. His squarish head reminded Preacher of a block of granite with a thatch of white hair on top of it. He wore a brown tweed suit and a darker brown derby was pushed to the back of his head. Rimless spectacles perched on his nose. They were tied to a ribbon looped around a vest button.

A saddle horse was tied to the back of the wagon. Draped over its back and lashed in place was the body of a dead man.

Preacher was so surprised by everything he saw that he hadn't thought to move into cover.

The fat man didn't seem threatening, though. He kept the team moving until he was about twenty feet from Preacher, then he hauled back on the reins and brought the wagon to a halt. "I suppose you're responsible for this carnage, eh?" he said in a rather high-pitched voice that held what sounded like some sort of European accent.

"You mean these fellers?" The old mountain man gestured toward the dead men in the road with his left hand. He kept his right hand on the Colt, just in case. Appearances could be bald-faced liars.

The fat man jerked a thumb over his shoulder. "And this one I came across, back up the road a piece."

Preacher knew the third corpse had to be the gunman who'd been dragged off when his horse stampeded. The fat man must have gotten his foot loose from the stirrup and thrown him over the saddle.

"Shoot, no, I ain't responsible for them," Preacher answered. Until he knew who the fat man was and what he was doing there, he wasn't going to admit anything. "I was just ridin' along and seen 'em alayin' here, so I got off my horse to see if there was anything I could do for 'em."

"Both dead, eh?"

"Dead as they can be," Preacher confirmed.

The fat man clucked his tongue and shook his head. "Terrible, just terrible. I sometimes wonder if this country out here will ever become civilized."

"I wonder the same thing," Preacher said, "but I'm usually hopin' it won't. Not too much, anyway. Those of us who seen it back when it was new and wild sort of miss them days."

A shudder went through the fat man, which made all three of his chins jiggle. "Not me. I've seen enough trouble in my time. I came to this country to get away from the tsar's Cossacks, and what do I find? Men even wilder and more savage! Why, if I could, I'd turn right around and go back to New York!"

Preacher wasn't sure what the hombre was talking about, so he let that pass. He squinted at all the wares hanging on the wagon. "Peddler, are you?"

"And a tinker as well," the fat man said. "I can mend or repair just about anything, and I sharpen knives, scissors, axes, anything with an edge. Isaac Herschkowitz is the name." He turned on the seat and pointed. Sure enough, the name was painted on the front of the wagon, with the legend TRAVELING ENTREPRENEUR underneath it.

"They call me Art." Preacher hadn't used his given name in a long time, but an idea had suddenly popped into the back of his head.

"I'd say I'm pleased to meet you, but under the circumstances . . ." Isaac Herschkowitz shrugged his shoulders eloquently. "What are we going to do with these unfortunate gentlemen? We can't just leave them lying in the road. It wouldn't be decent!"

"No, I reckon not," Preacher agreed. "I think there's a town up yonder a ways. I suppose we could load 'em in your wagon and tote 'em on in to the undertaker."

"In my wagon?" Herschkowitz shuddered again. "I think not. Those are their horses over there, correct? We can put the bodies on them, the way I did with the other one."

"Yeah." Preacher scratched his jaw and frowned as if in thought, although he had already made up his mind what he was going to do. "But hold on there, Ike. I just got to thinkin' . . . I been lookin' to go into business for myself, maybe buy an outfit like you've got there. How'd you feel about sellin' it to me, lock, stock, and barrel?"

The fat man's eyes widened in surprise. "Sell everything to you? Why, I'd like nothing better! As I said, I've seen enough of this barbaric country. But forgive me, my friend, you don't appear to be a man who's overly flush."

"Don't believe everything you see," Preacher said with a grin. He'd been fairly well-to-do ever since he and Smoke had uncovered that vein of gold many years earlier. For the most part, Preacher didn't have much use for money other than buying supplies and ammunition for his wanderings, but he generally had a decent amount with him in case he needed it. "I'll give you, say, three hundred dollars for the lot."

Herschkowitz's eyes bulged. "Three hundred dollars." Most men had to work six months or more to make that kind of money. A wandering peddler like him might not make that much in a year. But doubt appeared on his face, and he frowned. "You expect me to believe that you have three hundred dollars?"

"I ain't askin' you to take my word for it. I'm talkin' about gold double eagles. You can put 'em in your pocket and ride away."

"On what?"

Preacher nodded toward the grazing horses. "These fellers don't need those mounts no more. You can take one of 'em, saddle and all. We'll throw the extra carcass over the back o' my stallion. Ol' Horse, he won't like it none, but he'll do what I ask of him."

"This . . . this is an astonishing turn of events!" Herschkowitz said. "You really propose to buy my wagon and my goods?"

"And them mules. Wagon ain't no good without a team to pull it."

"Yes, of course, the mules, too. For three hundred dollars." Herschkowitz sounded like he still couldn't believe it.

"Feller with that much money in his pocket could ride on back to Denver, buy hisself a train ticket for New York City, and have plenty left over to get set up good once he gets there. What do you say, Ike?"

"You want to trade . . . whatever it is you do . . . for life as an itinerant peddler and tinker?"

"I dang sure do," Preacher lied.

The fat man spread his hands and shrugged. "Well,

who am I to stand in the way of a man's dreams? I accept your proposition, Arthur."

Preacher walked over to the wagon and held up his hand. "We'll shake on it."

"Indeed we will." Herschkowitz clasped the old mountain man's hand.

Preacher took a buckskin pouch from one of his saddlebags and counted out fifteen double eagles. He let them run through his fingers into the palms of Herschkowitz's outstretched hands.

With the deal concluded, they loaded the two corpses on the horses. As Preacher had predicted, the stallion snorted and gave him a look when they draped the grisly burden over the saddle, but Preacher said, "Settle down there, Horse. You won't have to put up with it for very long."

"I have some personal items in the back of the wagon," Herschkowitz said. "I suppose you'll allow me to take them with me. I didn't intend for them to be part of the deal."

"Sure. I wouldn't ask a feller to part with his personal belongin's." Preacher cocked his head to the side and squinted. "Howsomever, if you was to throw that derby hat in on the deal, I'd admire to have it."

"My hat?" Herschkowitz took it off and held it between his pudgy fingers. "For the amount you paid me, my friend, I can certainly afford to part with a hat!" He held it out. "Here you go."

Preacher took off his old, high-crowned hat and clapped the derby on his head. With a grin, he cocked it at a jaunty angle and asked, "How do I look?"

"Positively distinguished!" Herschkowitz said.

Chapter 35

Preacher climbed onto the seat of peddler's wagon and picked up the reins. He still wore his denim trousers, but he had replaced his buckskin shirt with a gray wool one he used as a spare, although he hardly ever wore it. He had donned a jacket as well, first shaking the dust off it since he hadn't worn it in a couple years. The derby perched on his head.

His clothes weren't all that was different. Preacher was clean-shaven. He had used his seldom-employed razor and a mirror hanging on the side of the wagon and scraped the thick silvery bristle from his face. He had taken off his gun belt and stowed it in the back of the wagon, although one of the Colts was tucked in the waistband of his trousers where the jacket concealed it.

None of the changes were major, but taken altogether, they created an effect that would make it difficult for most folks to recognize him as the gun-fighting old mountain man he was. At least, he hoped that was true.

He clucked to the team and flicked the reins against their backs, then slapped the lines a little harder when the stolid mules failed to move. Finally, they got going and pulled against their harness. The wagon lurched into motion. Tied behind it trailed the gray stallion and the other two horses, carrying the dead men.

Preacher chuckled to himself as he wondered what Smoke and Matt would think if they could see him. For that matter, he wondered how some of his old friends from the fur trapping days would react. Audie would no doubt have plenty to say. Nighthawk would just look at him, shake his head, and say, "Ummm."

It was a crazy idea, and Preacher knew it. As a rule, he didn't give in to such wild notions . . . but every now and then, a hunch came over him, and he played it.

Although he was confident he could have snuck into Big Rock without getting caught, fate had presented him with a way to ride into town as bold as brass and not have the men who had taken over suspect who he was or why he was there. It was a daring plan. Some of the townspeople might recognize him, despite his effort to change his appearance, and accidentally give away his identity, but if he could carry out the masquerade successfully, it might shorten the time needed to find out what was going on in Big Rock.

As he drove toward the settlement, he considered the story he would tell. He didn't figure anybody would believe that his name was really Isaac Herschkowitz, so he would tell people that was the name of the wagon's previous owner. It wouldn't be a lie for him to say that he had bought the wagon from Herschkowitz. That was exactly what had happened.

The rest of the story also had some elements of truth in it. He would claim that he had come across the horse that had dragged the dead man along the road—which had actually happened to ol' Isaac—then found the other two dead men as he drove toward town.

The friends of the dead gunnies likely would know that Horse hadn't belonged to any of them, but that couldn't be helped. Preacher hadn't been willing to part with the stallion, even though it might have helped his plan succeed if he had let Herschkowitz ride off on the stallion.

He would just have to plead ignorance on the matter of the horses. Nobody would be able to prove otherwise.

Of course, all of it depended on the invaders not shooting him as soon as they laid eyes on him. If they tried that, they would get a surprise. Preacher had six rounds in the Colt he carried, and he would make them all count.

But maybe it wouldn't come to that, he told himself. He looked like a harmless old man. Surely nobody would try to shoot him.

He came in sight of the town without encountering anybody else. As he kept the team moving, he surveyed what he could see of Big Rock. The settlement looked almost deserted. A few people were moving around, but not nearly as many as would have been on a normal day.

As he reached the edge of town and started along the main street, several men strolled out of a saloon. The moving wagon and the jangling noise it made had drawn their attention, and they turned sharply toward it.

One of them exclaimed, "Hey! Who the hell's that?"

Preacher couldn't hear what the other men responded, but their reaction was swift enough. They leaped down from the boardwalk in front of the saloon, ran to the hitch rack, threw themselves into saddles, and thundered toward the wagon, drawing their guns as they charged.

Chapter 36

Matt didn't know the area around Big Rock as well as Smoke did, but he had been there often enough that he was confident he could find his way around to the other side of the settlement.

He avoided trails and struck out cross-country, figuring he'd be less likely to run into any patrols that way. As he rode, he wondered who would be foolish enough to come with armed men and try to take over. According to what Preacher had heard, it sounded like they were after Smoke. Was "the major" an old enemy or somebody new?

And what about "the doctor"? What would a sawbones want with Smoke?

It didn't make sense to Matt . . . but that was why he was on his way into town, he reminded himself. It was his job to find out what was going on.

Sure he had circled completely around Big Rock, he turned his horse and headed for the settlement. He hadn't seen anyone, hostile or otherwise, and he hoped that luck held.

He rolled his shoulders and shifted in the saddle.

Actually, an odd feeling hung over that whole part of the state. It was like everybody was hunkered down holding their breath, just waiting for something bad to happen.

Matt had sensed that in other times, other places . . . and always, without fail, sooner or later hell had broken loose.

His instincts led him unerringly to the schoolhouse. He reached the edge of some trees and reined in to look across an open field at the back of the big, whitewashed building. The schoolkids played in that field every day during their free time.

He frowned. No children were in sight. Maybe they were all inside. Or maybe the school was closed during the time of emergency. If gunmen had taken over the town, parents would want their youngsters close by, to keep them safe.

Matt thought it the safest way to slip into town, as well as meet Preacher there later. The invaders wouldn't likely think a threat would come from the vicinity of the school—a nonthreatening place.

Matt dismounted and took off his gun belt. In a town taken over by armed outsiders, nothing would draw attention faster than the sight of a man wearing a gun. He was sure one of the first things the invaders had done was disarm everybody.

He drew his Colt and stuck it in the waistband of his trousers at the small of his back, then put on a buckskin jacket he took from one of his saddlebags. The jacket would conceal the gun, at least from casual discovery. He coiled the gun belt and hung it from the saddle horn.

"You're going to have to stay back here in the trees where nobody will see you," he told his horse. "There's enough graze, and I'll tie you loosely enough you can get free if I don't come back for you. But don't worry. I'm coming back."

With that vow made, he went to the edge of the growth and paused to study everything he could see. No one was moving anywhere. The town seemed to be locked down tight.

The school was about fifty yards from where he was and an equal distance from the nearest building. If he headed straight for the back of the school, the building and the trees that grew around it, would make it difficult for anyone to spot him. He was just about to step out and make a run for it when motion off to the right caught his eye.

A woman was walking toward the school with a determined stride. Matt didn't recognize her, but he didn't really know many people in Big Rock other than Monte Carson and a couple sheriff's deputies.

Matt hoped that Carson was all right. The sheriff and Smoke were old friends.

Two men came into view as they followed the woman. Swaggering was more like it, Matt thought. One of them called something after her. He couldn't make out the words. Both men laughed, so he figured it had been something crude that they found amusing.

The woman didn't look back. She kept walking. In fact, she walked a little faster. Clearly, she was bound for the schoolhouse. There was nowhere else to go in the direction she was headed.

She reached the front corner of the school and disappeared from his view.

The two men following her did the same. They wore guns, Matt noted, proof they were part of the occupying force.

Whatever they wanted from the woman, it wasn't

likely to be anything good. Maybe they were just hoorawing her and didn't mean her any harm, but he didn't want to take that chance. He took his hat off, held it in his left hand, drew in a deep breath, and broke out of the woods to sprint toward the school.

The fifty-yard run took less than ten seconds, but it seemed much longer. He reached the building without incident, and stopped to press his back against the rear wall while he caught his breath.

Like most Western men, he considered a job that couldn't be done from horseback as something not worth doing, so he wasn't used to running. Nor were the riding boots he wore made for it.

He'd made it to the back of the building and nobody was yelling in alarm, so he was satisfied. After a moment, he put his hat back on and moved to the corner, edging his head around for a look. Nothing.

He heard footsteps inside the building, figured the woman and the two men had to be in there, and cat footed along the wall. Although the windows on the side of the building were closed in the cool weather, a quick glance through one confirmed that all the student desks and benches were empty.

As he neared the front of the school, he was able to look along the street. He spotted a few armed men here and there, but none seemed all that alert. Likely, they felt they had everyone in the town cowed and that no one would dare oppose them.

As far as Matt could see, they were right.

But they didn't know somebody new was in town.

Through the school's open front door he heard voices coming from inside. Mostly it was the men who were speaking, but from time to time the woman would say something. He still couldn't make out the words. One of the men laughed. It was an ugly sound.

The smart thing to do, Matt told himself, would be to slip around behind the school again, wait until everybody left, and then sneak into town. He needed to find somebody who could tell him exactly what was going on.

Maybe he wouldn't have to go to that much trouble, he realized. The woman might be able to tell him everything he needed to know. Surely she wasn't part of the force commanded by the major. She was probably the teacher, even though she didn't have any students at the moment.

If the two gunmen left and the woman stayed, he could talk to her and find out what she knew. It was a good plan. He turned to slide along the wall until he reached the rear of the building again.

The plan might have worked . . . if the woman hadn't chosen that moment to let out a frightened scream.

Chapter 37

Matt straightened from his crouch to look through the nearest window. The woman was struggling with one of the men while the other hombre stood by chuckling and leering. The one wrestling with the woman pawed at her dress.

So much for my plan, Matt thought. He knew there was no way he could stand by and watch a woman being assaulted.

His mind worked at breakneck speed as he considered his options. He could draw the Colt at the small of his back, burst in, and ventilate those two skunks before they knew what was going on.

And those shots would draw at least a dozen more heavily armed killers who would rush to the school to find out what was going on. Matt didn't mind when the odds were against him, but those odds were overwhelming. He'd wind up dead, and in the fracas the woman might get hurt, too.

Those thoughts flashed through his mind in a heartbeat. His hand flew to the gun and placed it behind one of the stone blocks that formed the school's foundation.

They were set several feet apart, and he had no trouble reaching behind a block and dropping the gun.

He could always come back and retrieve it later. With that taken care of, he turned and raced for the front of the school.

The door stood ajar, and he simply burst in, lunged toward the struggling figures, grabbed the shoulder of the hombre manhandling the woman, and jerked him around. Matt's fist crashed against the man's jaw with enough force to lift him off his feet and send him toppling over one of the desks in an ungainly sprawl.

"What the hell?" the second man exclaimed.

Matt heard the rush of feet as the man charged him and turned to meet the attack. At least the fella hadn't slapped leather and tried to gun him down.

Yet.

Matt ducked under the wild roundhouse punch the man threw and stepped closer to hook two swift punches, a right and a left, to his belly. The man grunted in pain and bent forward, which put his chin in perfect position for the right uppercut Matt brought whistling from his knees.

The man's jaw clicked together with tooth-cracking force as his head went back. His knees buckled. As he fell, he reached out to grab Matt's jacket in a weak grip.

It was enough to prevent Matt from stepping back and getting ready for more trouble. He heard the woman say, "Look out!"—then something rammed into him from behind and drove him forward.

He tripped over the man he had just knocked down. Both he and his tackler landed on one of the desks. Its legs cracked under their weight and they fell as the desk broke beneath them.

Matt drove an elbow back into his opponent's belly.

The man grunted as he looped an arm around Matt's neck, trying to crush his windpipe. With only a second to grab a breath of air before the man's forearm tightened cruelly across his throat, Matt knew that breath wouldn't last long.

He got his hands and knees under him and bucked his body upward, failing to dislodge the man choking him. Matt threw himself to the side and rolled over a couple times, but that didn't break the man's grip, either.

Matt's hand fell on a piece of broken wood from the desk. He snatched it up and jabbed up and back, aiming at the man's face. The man yelled and jerked away, loosening his chokehold enough for Matt to writhe out of it.

Matt twisted around on the floor and struck up at the man's face, which was bleeding where the jagged wood had scratched him. The punch was short but packed a lot of power. It landed solidly and knocked the man off him.

Clambering to his feet, Matt turned toward the woman to make sure she was all right. He got just a glimpse of a frightened but lovely face surrounded by a thick mass of chestnut hair before the other man grabbed her from behind and pressed a gun barrel to her head. She gasped in surprise and terror but didn't try to pull away. She looked like she was too terrified to move.

Reflex made Matt take a step toward them, but he stopped short as the man threatened, "Hold it right there or I'll blow her brains out!"

A little breathless from the fight, Matt said, "Take it easy, mister. Nobody needs to get shot."

"I ain't so sure about that!" the man raged. "My jaw feels like you damn near broke it!"

Matt hadn't expected him to recover quite so quickly. Obviously, he had a lot of stamina. Also, he was angry. That was fueling him, too.

Matt heard boot leather scrape the floor behind him, followed by a curse. He turned a little and saw that the man had picked up one of the broken legs from the desk and was poised to swing it at his head.

"Wait a minute, Dixon," snapped the man holding the woman at gunpoint. "I want to find out who this is before we stomp him to death."

"Please!" the woman cried. "Please don't hurt him! He . . . he's my brother Charles."

Matt drew in a deep breath. If that was the way she wanted to play it, fine. He was willing to go along with it. He had no idea what her name was, so he said, "Don't worry, sis. These men aren't going to hurt you."

Dixon, the one with the desk leg, sneered. "That's mighty big talk for a man who's gonna be dead in a few minutes."

The other one asked, "So you're the schoolteacher's brother?"

"That's right," she put in before Matt had a chance to answer. Her voice quivered, which was understandable since she had a gun muzzle pressed to her head. "He's Charles Morton. Who else would he be?"

"I don't know. I don't recall seein' him around town the past couple days."

"That's because he's been staying inside our house. We both have, as much as possible. He . . . he didn't want me to come here today. But I had to make sure the school was all right, that you men hadn't done any damage to it."

Matt said, "And I was right to tell you to stay inside, wasn't I, sis? You just wound up getting us both in trouble."

She glared at him. "Well, I didn't ask you to come along and help me, now, did I?"

Matt hoped that sounded enough like a spat between siblings to be convincing.

Evidently it did, because the man with the gun took the weapon away from her head and pushed her toward one of the benches. "Sit down," he growled. "We'll deal with your brother."

"Please don't hurt him," the woman said again. Instead of sitting down, she stood with her hands clasped together in front of her.

She was young, in her early twenties. And undeniably lovely, a fact he was aware of even in the perilous circumstances. He wondered what her name was . . . and hoped he would get the chance to find out.

The man pointed the gun at Matt. "You heard what the major told the whole town the other day. Anybody who gives us any trouble dies. Plain and simple."

"But . . . but no one has to know what happened here," the woman argued. "And if the two of you spare Charles's life, no one else has to know about that, either."

Dixon leered at her. "You gonna make it worth our while to do you a favor like that, missy?"

The woman drew in a deep breath, which made her breasts lift under the plain gray dress she wore. Her chin had a defiant tilt as she said, "If I have to."

"The hell with that." Matt's sudden anger wasn't feigned. "I won't let you do that—"

"It's not really your decision, is it?" she interrupted. "You think I'm going to stand by and watch someone die when there's something I can do to prevent it?"

Matt understood that. He had risked his own life plenty of times to help people who needed a hand.

But it wasn't her life she was talking about.

"Here's something else you men should think about before you kill my brother or molest me." Her voice had taken on a tone of cool determination. "You probably wouldn't want your friends or your employer to know how one unarmed man thrashed the two of you. But that's what will happen if you hurt either of us. I'll spread the story all over town. People will believe me. I have a reputation for honesty. And it'll get back to the rest of your . . . your gang. You know it will."

Both men scowled at her.

Dixon said, "Maybe we ought to just kill you, too."

"That would look good. Two men murdering a defenseless woman. I thought it was against some sort of Western code to harm a decent woman."

The man with the gun suddenly muttered a curse and shoved the iron back into its holster. "Come on, Dixon, let's get out of here. These two are more trouble than they're worth."

Disappointment showed on Dixon's face. "But Bracken, they could still talk—"

"Not if they got any sense, they won't. The schoolma'am is smarter than that. Aren't you, honey?"

"If you leave us alone, we won't have any reason to cause trouble for you," she said.

Dixon pointed to the scratch on his face. "What about this?"

"You could say you ran into a tree branch," the woman suggested.

Clearly, Dixon still didn't like it, but Bracken was the one in charge. He jerked his head toward the door, and they began to back off. He pointed a finger at Matt. "You better just lie low, mister. If I see your face again, I'm liable to put a bullet in it just on general principles."

"I understand," Matt said. Lying low and not drawing the attention of the invaders had been his intention all along. Things just hadn't quite worked out that way.

Dixon muttered a few more curses, and then the men were gone

Matt turned toward the woman and was surprised when she threw her arms around him and hugged him tightly.

But that was what a brother and sister who'd just had a narrow brush with death would do, wasn't it? He returned the hug, lowered his head so his mouth was close to her ear, and whispered, "What's your name, anyway?"

"Lorena," she whispered back. "Lorena Morton."

"Pleased to meet you, Miss Morton. I seem to be your brother Charles."

Chapter 38

Leaving Smoke and Sally alone for a while so they could enjoy their reunion, the Sugarloaf foreman and the young cowboy greeted Dog—an old friend of theirs—rounded up the horses belonging to Trask's men, and dragged the bodies of the fallen outlaws into a grisly heap off to one side of the line shack.

Smoke and Sally walked off under some trees, so Pearlie took advantage of the opportunity to haul the dead man out of the shack and add his carcass to the pile.

"What are we gonna do with 'em, Pearlie?" Cal asked. "It'd take a mighty big grave to hold all those polecats."

"Yeah, and I don't feel like doin' that much diggin'," Pearlie responded. "I was thinkin' we'd tie the varmints over their saddles and send the horses trottin' back down the mountain. Chances are they'll go back where they came from."

"And Trask will know he's lost seven more men. We're whittling 'em down, aren't we?"

"Yeah," Pearlie said as he rubbed his chin. "Problem is, there was a whole passel of 'em to start with. At this rate, they're liable to outlast us."

"You can't be happy about anything, can you, you sour old cuss?"

"Reckon I'll be happy when we've got all those owlhoots off the Sugarloaf and things get back to normal around here," Pearlie said.

"I thought finding ourselves in a whole mess of trouble *was* normal around here."

Pearlie squinted. "If I had my hat with me, I'd take it off and wallop you with it, youngster."

Smoke and Sally walked up in time to hear the good-natured squabbling. Even though he knew the gibes didn't mean anything, he said, "Save your hostility for the enemy, you two. And keep an eye out. Somebody else might have heard all the shooting that went on earlier and come to investigate it."

Pearlie nodded. "I been watchin' the slopes lower down. Ain't seen anything movin' yet."

"We're a long way from ranch headquarters. I doubt if they heard it down there. We don't have any way of knowing where Trask's other patrols might be, though."

Pearlie looked at Sally. "You told Smoke about that fella who calls hisself a doctor?"

"Of course I did. You didn't think we were over there under the trees just whispering sweet nothings in each other's ears, did you?" She blushed a little, which in Smoke's eyes just made her prettier.

"We might've done a little of that," Smoke said with a grin, then he grew more serious. "But yes, Sally told me about Dr. Trask and his men."

"You know who he is, Smoke?" Cal asked. "Is he an old enemy of yours?"

Smoke shook his head. "I never heard of the man until just now, unless he was using some other name when I knew him. Sally described him to me, though, and he doesn't sound that familiar. Could be a lot of men in the world who look something like that."

A little shiver went through Sally. "You wouldn't believe that if you'd seen him close up like I did, Smoke. Once you'd looked in his eyes, I don't think you'd ever forget him. You can see the madness in him."

"A fella's got to be crazy if he thinks he can just waltz in and take over the Sugarloaf like that, not to mention Big Rock," Pearlie said.

"That seems to be just what he's done," Smoke pointed out. "I don't know why, don't know what he intends to gain by it, but that doesn't really matter. The important thing is figuring out how we're going to stop him."

"I don't mind sayin', I feel a whole heap better about things now that you're back, Smoke," Pearlie said. "But that don't change the fact that there's four of us and dang near a hundred o' those hardcases."

"Fewer than that now," Cal said, "after the fight at the ranch and what happened here. I'll bet we've done for at least a dozen of them, maybe more."

Pearlie frowned. "All right. So the odds are only twenty to one, instead of twenty-five. That still don't bode well for our chances, kid."

"It's not quite that bad," Smoke said with a faint smile.

"You're talking about Matt and Preacher and Luke, aren't you?" Sally asked him.

"Luke didn't come back with us, I wish he had. He wanted to get back to his bounty hunting, or so he claimed. I think mostly he's just not real comfortable being around people he cares about. He's not used to it." Smoke paused. "But Matt and Preacher were with me when we ran into some of Trask's men on the road the other side of Big Rock, and they've gone on into town to see if they can find out what's behind all this. That's why I brought Dog with me."

Sally wore a worried frown as she said, "I'm sure Trask left plenty of men in Big Rock to keep things under control there. Matt and Preacher are liable to be riding right into trouble."

"Maybe," Smoke said. "Or maybe not. Those two are tricky enough I'm not sure trouble could find them unless they wanted it to."

Chapter 39

Preacher's instincts told him to grab the gun in his waistband and blaze away at the men charging toward him on horseback, but that wasn't what a traveling tinker and peddler would do, so he suppressed the impulse.

At least, he would as long as the men didn't open fire. If they commenced to burning powder, all bets were off.

They didn't shoot, but they did surround the wagon, the mule team, and the three horses tied on behind the vehicle.

One of the riders leaned over, grasped the hair on a head that hung limp in death, and lifted it. "Damn!" he yelled. "It's Dalby!"

"The other two are Harkness and Jenkins," a second man reported. "They were on guard duty out along the road that follows the railroad tracks into town."

"And that's where I found 'em," Preacher said, raising his voice so he could be heard clearly. "They'd been gunned down. I couldn't just leave 'em alayin' there in the road, so I rounded up their horses and loaded 'em up. Figured I'd turn 'em over to the sheriff in town."

One of the men covering him grunted. "You can

forget about that. There's no law in Big Rock anymore except us."

Preacher squinted and cocked his head to the side. "So it's like that, is it? Well, that don't make no never mind to me. If you fellas are friends of these boys and want to take 'em off my hands, that's all I'm worried about. Just untie them reins and I'll be amoseyin' on my way—"

"You can forget about that, you old pelican," snapped the man he'd been talking to. "You're not going anywhere."

"Now, hold on just a cotton-pickin' minute—"

"Who the hell are you, anyway?"

Preacher jerked a thumb at all the goods hanging from the wagon and said with a note of pride in his voice, "Can't you tell? I'm a peddler . . . and a tinker, to boot. If you got anything needs fixin', chances are I can fix it."

One of the other men leaned forward in his saddle and sounded out the name painted on the wagon. "Isaac . . . Hersch . . . ko . . . witz. What kind of a name is that, Cully?"

"One that doesn't look like it fits this old coot," the spokesman said.

Preacher frowned. "I'm liable to take offense, you keep callin' me *old* that way."

Cully let out a harsh bark of laughter, then demanded, "What's your name?"

"They call me Art," Preacher said. "I bought this wagon from Ike Herschkowitz, as he'd be happy to tell you if he was here."

"Art what?"

Preacher scratched his jaw. "You know, it's been so

long since I used my full handle, I sort of disremember. Just call me Art. That'll do."

"And you're just a traveling peddler?"

"Yep."

"We're going to search this wagon, you know. If we find anything that tells us you're lying, you'll be sorry."

Preacher waved a hand. "Search all you want. You won't find nothin' but the finest trade goods west o' St. Louis." He hoped that was true. He hadn't thought to look in the back of the wagon.

One of the other men dismounted and opened the door at the back of the wagon compartment. Preacher felt the vehicle shift under the man's weight as he climbed in. A couple tense minutes went by, then the man stepped down from the wagon. "Looks like a load of junk to me. I don't reckon we have to worry about this old geezer, Cully."

"There you go with that *old* business again," Preacher complained.

"Shut up," Cully said. "Did you see anybody else out there on the road where you found these bodies?"

"Do you want me to shut up or do you want me to answer your questions?"

Cully raised his gun, looped his thumb over the hammer, and eared it back.

Preacher raised a hand. "All right. Take it easy. I didn't see nobody. Didn't hear no shootin', neither, so the fracas that laid those fellas low musta happened a while 'fore I come along."

One of the men who had been looking at the bodies rode forward. "Cully, Harkness's horse is missing. I never saw that big ugly gray stallion before."

Cully eased the hammer down on his gun and lowered the weapon. "One of the damn owlhoots who shot it out with them must've gotten unhorsed during the fight. Maybe he grabbed Harkness's mount to ride off." Cully looked at Preacher. "You happen to know anything about that?"

"Not a blessed thing," Preacher declared with utter sincerity. It had been decades since he'd learned how to tell a convincing lie, and he hadn't forgotten in all that time.

"You believe him?" a man asked Cully.

After a moment's thought, Cully nodded. "Yeah, I think I do."

Preacher lifted the reins a little. "I can go on about my business, then."

"If anybody in this town wants to buy that junk of yours, that's fine," Cully said. "But you're not going anywhere."

"You mean I got to stay here?"

"That's exactly what I mean." Cully waved a hand at the other men, who holstered their guns and began to disperse, riding back down the street toward the saloon they had come from. "Just stay out of trouble and you won't be hurt."

"How long am I gonna be stuck here?" Preacher whined.

"Until we're finished with the business that brought us to Big Rock."

"What might that be?"

Cully glared. "Asking questions is a good way to get yourself killed."

"Sorry," Preacher muttered. "Didn't mean no offense."

"But I'll say this," Cully went on. "It all depends on a man named Smoke Jensen. Heard of him?"

"Seems like I have," Preacher said. Just about everybody in that part of the country had heard of Smoke, no matter who they were, so it wouldn't do to pretend ignorance.

"The sooner he cooperates with us, the sooner this is all over," Cully said. "And since our boss is holding his wife prisoner, Jensen better play along if he ever wants to see her again."

It took an effort, but Preacher kept his face emotionless. The varmints had Sally! Smoke had been worried about that, and rightly so, it seemed.

But the outlaws had made the worst mistake of their life. Smoke would see to it that they got what they had coming, and Preacher and Matt would give him a hand.

That thought made the old mountain man glance along the street. He didn't see any sign of Matt, which wasn't all that surprising.

He wondered if the young fella had made it into town yet. Where was he?

Chapter 40

Lorena Morton picked up one of the pieces of broken desk and sighed.

"Let me clean that up for you," Matt offered. "It's kind of my fault it's busted."

"It's not at all your fault. You were just trying to help me . . . Charles."

He knew why she called him that. She was trying to get in the habit. Now that she had established the lie with the men who had taken over Big Rock, she had to keep up the pretense of being his sister.

In whispers, so he wouldn't be overheard from outside, he had explained to her who he really was and what he was doing there. She had been stunned to hear that he was Smoke Jensen's brother.

"That's who they're really after," she had told him, keeping her voice down. "There's a rumor going around town that their boss, a man named Trask, is holding Mrs. Jensen hostage out at Sugarloaf."

That news made a jolt of anger go through Matt. He knew how deeply Smoke loved Sally, and he had visited in their home enough that he loved her, too. The thought of her being in the hands of a bunch of ruthless hardcases made him furious.

He knew he needed to keep his emotions under control if he was going to carry out the mission. He explained to Lorena how he and Smoke and Preacher had run into the guards a couple miles on the other side of town and then split up to find out what the situation was.

Matt already had a lot of the information he had come for, thanks to Lorena and her quick thinking. Her nimble wits had salvaged things after he'd come bulling in.

Of course, he had saved her from being molested, so they were sort of square on that score, he thought.

A faint note of warning sounded in the back of his mind as he spilled everything to her. He had no way of knowing that she wouldn't run to Trask's men and betray him. He didn't consider that very likely, but he couldn't rule it out.

Sometimes, though, a fella just had to put his faith in his instincts . . . and they'd told him he could trust Lorena Morton.

"Do you even have a brother?" he had asked her.

"No. All my family is dead. That's why I . . . I left my home back in Missouri and came out here to teach school. This is my first year in Big Rock."

Once everything was out in the open, he helped her clean up the damage from the fight and put the desks and benches back in order.

"You're going to have to come home with me, you know. They're liable to be watching, and I've already told them that you live with me."

"Are you sure that's all right?" Matt asked. "I don't want to do anything to compromise a lady's reputation."

Lorena smiled. "There's nothing improper about a brother and a sister sharing a house, is there?"

"No, I reckon not," Matt said as he put his hat on.

Of course, the feelings that he had when he looked at Lorena weren't exactly brotherly. . . . "I'll have to come back here later, though."

"Why?"

"I'm supposed to meet my friend Preacher here, once we've both had a chance to look around and see what's going on." Matt shrugged. "Then we'll have to get out of town and find Smoke so we can tell him about it."

Lorena nodded. "I see. Well, you do whatever it is you need to do, and I'll help you any way I can."

"I'm obliged to you."

"Not at all. Whatever those terrible men are planning, they have to be stopped. Just . . . be careful, Charles. I . . . I wouldn't want anything to happen to you."

He thought he detected a husky quality in her voice that didn't exactly sound sisterly.

Chapter 41

Although Albert Pike rode out to Sugarloaf every day to check in with Trask, his job was to see that the settlement remained firmly under the control of him and his men. He had established his headquarters in the Big Rock town hall and sat at one of the tables, going over the guard and patrol schedules he had drawn up.

He had never forgotten the first time he'd laid eyes on Jonas Trask. He never would. It had been in a hospital tent, late in the war, with the sound of artillery and rifle fire not far off as Union and Confederate troops clashed in the savage battle of the Wilderness.

He rubbed his eyes, remembering that time.

A major in a Union regiment, he was commanding his troops in the midst of the carnage when a Rebel minié ball tore through the muscles of his left thigh. The wound was bad enough that he was thrown on a stretcher and carried off the field of battle to the hospital tent.

He had no illusions about what was going to happen to him. Some bloody-handed butcher of a so-called

*surgeon was about to cut off his leg and throw it on a
pile with hundreds of other maimed, discarded limbs.
Pike would either die right then and there from the shock
of the amputation or he would die an even more miserable death from blood poisoning in four or five days.*

*But one way or another, he would die. He would never
go home to his family.*

*Lying on a table with trenches cut in it so the blood
could run off and add to the pools already soaking into
the ground, he saw a man lean over him and smile.*

*"You're going to be all right, Major. I'll see to that,"
the man said.*

"My . . . my leg." Pike gasped. "You'll take it—"

*"Only as a last resort," the man assured him. He was
pale, and drops of splattered blood stood out on his face
like freckles. His hands and the sleeves of his white coat
were red to the elbows. His deep-set eyes burned with a
fire unlike any Pike had ever seen before. "The bullet appears to have missed the bone, so I think I can save it.
I'll do my best, Major. I'm Dr. Jonas Trask."*

Pike smiled. He had been devoted to the man ever
since.

Despite all the odds, Trask had saved Pike's leg. It was
still stiff from the injury and always would be, giving
him a slight limp, but his leg was there and he could use
it. And he hadn't died screaming in that hellhole. He
owed his survival to Trask, who had come to see him in
a hospital in Washington, D.C., months later, after the
war was over.

"You'll be released from here soon, Major," Trask had
said, "and then you'll be mustered out of the army. How
would you like to come and work for me?"

"I don't know what you've got in mind, Doctor," Pike had said as he lifted his hand from where it lay on the sheet beside him, "but whatever it is, I'm in."

They'd shaken hands, sealing the partnership, and had been together ever since.

Although Pike had been surprised when he found out that Trask planned to put together a gang of criminals, he hadn't objected. He owed his life to the doctor, so whatever Trask wanted was all right with him.

Anyway, he soon came to see that the petty rules of normal men didn't apply to Trask. The doctor was a genius, well beyond such things as laws. Over the past decade and a half, the crimes carried out by Pike and the gang he had put together had paid for Trask's research. Pike didn't know exactly what that research was all about, but it didn't matter. He was sure that eventually Trask's brilliance would pay off and transform the world for the better.

That was why, even though it bothered Pike a little whenever innocent folks had to die, he never lost faith in the doctor. As Trask sometimes said, no progress ever came without a price.

Cully Martin came into the room. Since most of the men hadn't served in the army, the major had never insisted on military discipline among the gang, but Cully held himself almost like he was standing at attention. "Something's happened, Major. An old peddler just drove his wagon into town."

Pike looked up with a frown. "He came in alone? None of the guards brought him in?"

"*He* brought the guards. He had the bodies of Harkness, Dalby, and Jenkins with him."

Pike shot to his feet in anger. "What the hell happened?" he demanded.

"According to the old man, he found the bodies on the road a couple miles outside of town. He said he didn't hear any shots, so the fight must have taken place a while earlier. He put the bodies on their horses and brought them in." Cully grunted in grim amusement. "He said he figured on turning them over to the sheriff. He didn't know Carson's locked up in his own jail."

"You're sure of that?" Pike asked sharply. "You believe this peddler's story?"

"He seems like a harmless old man," Cully said with a shrug. "There's no way in hell he could've downed three tough hombres like Harkness, Dalby, and Jenkins. Anyway, if he had anything to do with their deaths, he wouldn't have brought their bodies into town as bold as brass like that, would he?"

"You wouldn't think so," Pike said, frowning. "Unless he's a lot trickier than you're giving him credit for."

Cully shook his head. "Not that old pelican, Major. I'd bet a hat that he's harmless."

"You'd better be right. Where is he now?"

"I don't know. Probably in one of the saloons soaking up some beer. I told him he couldn't leave town, and he promised he wouldn't cause any trouble."

Pike just grunted.

Cully thumbed his hat back and went on. "One thing was a little strange. One of the horses he used to bring in the bodies doesn't belong, and Harkness's horse is gone."

"The killers switched one of the horses for some reason. That's the only explanation that makes any sense."

"Yeah, but why would they do that?"

"I don't know." Pike's voice hardened. "We'll ask them when we catch them."

"You're sending men after whoever it was?"

"That's right," Pike said with a decisive nod. "Round up the best trackers in the gang and get out there where it happened. See if you can pick up the trail or at least find something that might tell us who killed those men."

"Are you gonna tell the doctor about this?" As Cully asked that question, he sounded a little nervous for the first time during the conversation.

"Not yet," Pike said after a moment's consideration. "Not until I have something more solid to report to him."

"I'll get those boys and start out right away," Cully promised.

"See that you do."

As Cully left the town hall, Pike sat down again. He leaned back in his chair and frowned, no longer seeing the papers spread on the desk in front of him.

Losing three men was an annoyance. Losing three men under mysterious circumstances was worse. He didn't like it when things happened with no explanation.

Maybe he would hunt up that old peddler and ask him some questions. The whole matter might turn out to be nothing important, but Pike wasn't going to take that chance.

Chapter 42

Everything in the big ranch house was set up to Dr. Jonas Trask's satisfaction. He needed only one more thing in order to complete his research.

Smoke Jensen.

Trask tried to curb the impatience he felt. He had no way of knowing exactly when Jensen would arrive in the area, but it was bound to be soon. The doctor's agents in Arizona had wired him when Jensen left in the company of three other men. Even if Jensen had been taking his time on the return trip, he ought to show up any time in Big Rock or at the ranch.

Trask wondered who those other three men were, but he didn't consider the matter of any real importance. No doubt they were friends of Jensen's, but they were of no interest to Trask.

Only Smoke Jensen, the so-called fastest gun in the West, held the secret Trask desired to make his own.

Major Pike was under orders to make it known in Big Rock that Sally Jensen was a prisoner on the ranch. All the men who had come to the Sugarloaf with Trask had similar orders. No matter who Jensen encountered first upon his return to the area, he would receive the news that his wife was a captive and the only way for him to save her life was to surrender.

As long as he didn't discover that Sally had escaped, her safety was the only leverage Trask needed to get what he wanted. Of course, it was always possible that she would be recaptured soon. Plenty of capable men were searching for her.

He sat in a comfortable leather armchair in Jensen's office, reading what was supposed to be a scholarly tome by a German scientist named Von Junzt. Actually, it was filled with all sorts of mystical claptrap. Still, Trask found it contained a few nuggets of useful information, if one could wade through all the nonsense.

The massive, dull-faced servant called Dan stood nearby, waiting stolidly for orders. He would stand there without moving all day if necessary and never complain.

Dan's hair had grown back out to conceal most of the huge scar on his head, but Trask knew it was there. He had very few regrets in life. A brilliant mind had no need for regrets; what lesser intellects would regard as mistakes were only opportunities that had not yet borne fruit, he knew.

If there was one thing he might have done differently, Dan was the living representation of it. Lonesome Dan Sloane had been a superb member of the organization, a valued subordinate to Major Pike. He had been eager to take part in the doctor's research . . . and just look at him.

Well, he still played his part the best he could under the circumstances, Trask thought with a sigh as he turned his attention back to the German's fevered scribblings.

Hurried footsteps sounded in the hall. One of the men, McCoy, stuck his head in the open door. "Doctor,

I hate to bother you, but there's something out here you need to see."

"What is it?" Trask asked impatiently as he marked his place in the book with a finger. "Don't be deliberately obtuse, man." He saw McCoy grimace and figured he didn't know what the word meant. Surely he could figure it out from the context, Trask thought.

"There's some dead men," McCoy explained.

Well, that held the promise of being at least somewhat interesting. Trask removed his finger from the page and replaced it with the ribbon marker attached to the book. He set the volume aside and stood up. "Come along, Dan."

Without a word or any change of expression, Lonesome Dan followed Trask out of the room.

"They came in tied over the saddles of their own horses," McCoy babbled. "I don't know what to make of it, boss."

"How many men are you talking about?" Trask asked as they reached the front door.

McCoy waved as they stepped out onto the porch. "Four right now. I sent some of the boys out to have a look around and make sure there's not any more."

Trask stopped short at the sight of the four horses standing there, each with a dead man draped over the saddle and tied into place, as reported. Men stood holding the reins to keep the skittish horses from spooking more. From the looks of it, they didn't care for the grim burdens they carried.

"You say they came in on their own?" Trask asked.

"Yes, sir. Just wandered up. Horses'll do that, you know, when they're loose and have got their heads.

They'll nearly always go back where they came from. But here's the funny thing—"

"I don't think there's anything amusing about these men being killed," Trask snapped.

"No, sir, you're right," McCoy agreed quickly. "I mean it's odd. I know these fellas and their horses, and some of 'em . . . well, they're on other men's horses. Men who, uh, ain't here."

"From which we can draw two conclusions. The first being that whoever loaded them on these horses didn't know which mount went with which corpse."

McCoy nodded. "That's what I figure."

As if he hadn't heard, Trask went on, "The second being that in all probability there are other mismatched pairs somewhere in the vicinity." He drew in a deep breath. "More of my men who have been killed."

"Yes, sir, Doctor. I thought the same thing. That's why I sent some fellas to have a look around."

Trask was annoyed briefly by the way McCoy put his reasoning on the same level as his own, but he ignored it as he went down the steps to one of the men holding the reins. "They were shot, I take it?"

"That's right. Ventilated good and proper, in fact."

"Were these men all members of the same search party?"

"Yeah. They were checkin' out some of the high pastures north of here."

"Get them down."

Men sprang to carry out the doctor's order. Knives slid from sheaths and sawed through bindings. Hands grasped the corpses and lowered them to the ground. In a matter of moments, the four dead men were laid out on their backs.

Their faces were frozen in rictuses of death. Dark brown stains where blood had dried were visible on their clothes. Some had been shot only once, while the others were riddled with several wounds.

Trask studied them dispassionately. Loss of life bothered him only in its wasted potential. Someday when his research was complete, they could have been so much more.

A shout made him lift his head. Riders were coming in, leading two more horses carrying the same sort of grisly load. One of the animals had two bodies strapped to it.

Those dead men were cut loose and placed with the others.

The man who had come to get Trask studied them, matching up the corpses with the animals that had brought them back to the ranch headquarters. He turned to Trask. "They're all accounted for, Doctor, except one horse that could've wandered off after the fight. I don't reckon we'll find any more."

"Unless whoever did this strikes again."

McCoy went on excitedly. "We'd better send some more men up there right away."

Trask shook his head. "Whoever did this will be gone by now. I make no claim to being any sort of military tactician, but even I know that."

"You reckon it was that Jensen woman they were lookin' for? When she got away from here, a couple ranch hands were with her. They might've taken that missing horse for her to ride."

"Possibly," Trask said. Even as he spoke, he didn't believe it. He knew how unlikely it was that a woman and two cowboys had gunned down more than twice their number of hardened killers.

No, Trask thought as he felt anticipation begin to grow inside him, there was a much more plausible explanation for the deaths of his men.

Smoke Jensen had returned.

Chapter 43

Before the dead gunmen had been loaded on their horses, Smoke had checked the bodies and appropriated the boots that had belonged to the one with the smallest feet. They were still a bit too big for Sally, but they fit much better than the ones she'd been wearing.

"It'll always make me feel a little queasy, knowing that I'm wearing a dead man's boots," she said as they got ready to leave the line shack.

"Better that than tearing your feet up on rough ground," Smoke told her.

"I suppose you're right about that."

They took all the ammunition and several extra guns from the dead men. In a war like the one they might be facing, it was impossible to have too much firepower.

They searched saddlebags for supplies, but all they found were some jerky and pipe tobacco. Pearlie took the tobacco, although his pipe was back in the bunkhouse at Sugarloaf—if one of the varmints who had raided the ranch hadn't stolen it—and he strapped on a sheathed bowie knife one of the men had been wearing.

From the line shack, they took what was left of the

supply cache. It would keep them going for a few days. Up in the high country, the men could always rig snares to catch small animals, so they wouldn't starve. And water was plentiful in the small creeks that flowed from springs higher up.

Smoke, Sally, Pearlie, and Cal mounted up and headed higher in the rugged northern reaches of the Sugarloaf. Smoke knew that eventually they would reach the end of his range, but boundaries didn't mean much to him at the moment.

Keeping Sally safe did.

"What are you planning to do, Smoke?" she asked as she rode alongside him. "I know you're not going to keep running and hiding out from those men."

"I want to find someplace for you to stay where you won't be in danger."

"Danger doesn't bother me. I've faced it plenty of times before, remember?"

"I remember," Smoke said grimly. "I also remember seeing you lying there with an outlaw's bullet in you, looking like you were dead. I thought you were. I don't want you to ever go through something like that again."

"I know," she said, her voice soft. "And I love you for being so worried about me. But I also know the men at the ranch who were captured are in danger now, and so are the people in Big Rock. Those are your friends, Smoke. You have to do something about it. And you can't let your concern for me stop you."

"I don't intend to. There's a cave almost as high up on this mountain as you can go. Nobody can get near it without being seen. One man can hold off an army from up there, as long as his ammunition holds out. We're going to spend the night there, then tomorrow you and

Cal will stay there while Pearlie and I ride back down and deal with this."

"Hey!" Cal objected. "You're gonna leave me behind? I don't like the sound of that."

"I do," Pearlie said. "I'm just itchin' to take the fight to those polecats, Smoke."

"Your job is just as important, Cal," Smoke told the youngster. "I'm counting on you to keep Sally safe."

"Why not leave me up there alone, if you're bound and determined to keep me out of the fight?" Sally suggested. "You know I can handle a rifle, and if Cal goes with you and Pearlie, that's one more man on your side."

Cal grinned with pride at being described as a man. He looked like he was fit to bust about it, in fact.

"I'll think about it," Smoke said. "For right now, let's just keep climbing."

They did so, going higher and higher up the mountainside as the sun began to sweep down toward the western horizon.

Finally, not long before dusk, they reached the base of a long, rocky slope mostly bare of vegetation. It led up to a towering cliff.

Smoke pointed. "The cave is at the bottom of that cliff. Nobody can get at it from above, and with this open ground below it, a man with a rifle can pick off anybody who tries to attack this way."

"Is there any water up there?" Pearlie asked.

"No, but all our canteens are full. We'll leave them, and whoever stays will have enough to last for a few days if they're careful with it."

Sally said, "That's one more reason to take Cal with you and leave me alone up here. One person can make the water and supplies last twice as long as two."

"I suppose that's true," Smoke admitted.

"Of course, I'd rather you just take me with you . . ."

"That's not going to happen."

"That's what I figured," she said. "But I still think you should take Cal with you. You can leave Dog here with me. Nobody's going to be able to sneak up on me with him around."

"We'll talk about it in the morning," Smoke said, but he already knew that Sally was right. With the odds facing him, he would need all the help he could get. In a scrap, Cal, despite his youth, was a seasoned fighter and a good man to have on his side.

"The three of you stay here," Smoke went on. "I'll ride up and have a look at the place. I've never known any bears to den up in it for the winter, but you never can tell."

"It's too early for that," Pearlie said.

"Maybe. No point in taking a chance."

That was exactly what Smoke was doing—not taking a chance with his wife's life. He would be out in the open as he climbed that slope. If anybody happened to be watching through field glasses and decided to try a long-distance rifle shot, it would be aimed at him, not Sally.

In the fading light, his stallion picked its sure-footed way upward toward the cliff. Nothing happened, and a few minutes later he reached the top. The cave was more of an overhang than an actual chamber carved into the rock, but it had a small ledge in front of it where boulders had lodged in the past after toppling from the cliff. Those boulders provided plenty of cover. The open area under the overhang was about thirty feet wide, twenty deep, and the roof curved down from a ten-foot-high opening at the front.

It was a nice, cozy hideout. In the light that remained in the sky, Smoke could see that it was empty. Some old bits of brush showed that animals had denned up there at some time, but none recently.

That brush would serve as fuel for a cooking fire during the day, but it would have to be a cold camp at night. That high up, once darkness closed down, a fire could be seen for a long way, like a beacon.

Smoke scanned the slopes of the surrounding mountains and hills as far as he could see. Nothing out of the ordinary was moving. He lifted his arm and waved for the others to come on up. He was confident that Sally would be safe there for a while.

The thought that he and his allies might fail in their campaign against Jonas Trask and his men never entered Smoke's mind. He didn't have an arrogant bone in his body, but he possessed a quiet confidence that he and his friends would do their best . . . and in the past, their best had always been more than good enough to emerge victorious against all sorts of odds.

Although he would feel a little better about the situation if he knew how Preacher and Matt were faring in their mission to Big Rock.

Chapter 44

After the encounter with Cully, Preacher drove the wagon on down the street. He glanced at Louis Longmont's saloon and thought about how nice it would be to go in there and cut the trail dust from his throat with a beer.

He couldn't risk that, though. Longmont was too canny and observant. If the gambler/gunman who was one of Smoke's oldest friends was anywhere around, he would see through Preacher's meager disguise in an instant.

Preacher didn't want to venture into any of the usual haunts he visited whenever he was in those parts. He kept an eye out for someplace he'd never been and found it in a hash house with a painted sign that read Loo's.

He hauled back on the reins, brought the wagon to a stop, and climbed down, tying the team to a hitch rail. The mules stood there, heads drooping in weariness after a long day of pulling the wagon. He'd need to take them to a livery stable later, so they could be cared for properly, but they could wait while he tried to find out more about what was going on in Big Rock.

Considering how few people were on the street,

Preacher wasn't surprised when he went into the hash house and found that it didn't have any customers. The proprietor, a short, round-faced Chinese man, was the only person in sight. He stood behind the counter resting his elbows on it. His chin was propped in his hands. He showed a little interest when Preacher walked in but didn't straighten from his glum pose. "You want something?"

"Maybe a bowl o' chili and beans, if you got it," Preacher said. "Or some hash an' eggs 'd be good, too."

The little man perked up. He straightened and put his hands on the counter "You want to buy food? Really?"

"That's what this place is for, ain't it?"

"Yes, yes, of course, but no one comes in since those—" The man stopped short and frowned at Preacher. "Those men are friends of yours? The ones running the town now?"

"Nope. Never saw 'em before, and didn't know they was here until I drove in just now. Don't much like the looks of 'em, neither. I'm just a driftin' peddler and tinker, not an owlhoot like them." Preacher didn't bother keeping the genuine dislike out of his voice. He figured the fella would be more likely to talk if he thought his visitor was a kindred spirit.

The man put a finger to his lips. "Be careful. You must not anger them. They are very cruel when they are angry."

"Fine. How about that grub?"

"I have some stew I was heating for my own supper. I will be happy to share it with you. No charge. It will be good to have company. As I said, no one comes in anymore."

"That's mighty kind of you. I'll be much obliged to you, Mister . . . ?"

"Loo. Loo Chung How."

"They call me Art. It's a pleasure to meet you, Mr. Loo."

"Please, sit." Loo gestured at the several empty stools in front of the counter. "I will get the stew."

"How about coffee?" Preacher asked.

"Oh, yes. There is a pot on the stove."

"Gettin' to be more and more of a pleasure meetin' you, Mr. Loo," the old mountain man said with a grin.

A few minutes later, Loo put a big bowl of stew in front of Preacher. Hunks of roast beef floated in it, along with potatoes, carrots, and corn.

"No offense," Preacher said, "but this looks more like an Irish stew than a Chinese one."

"I cook what my customers like to eat, and I have grown accustomed to it myself."

Loo set a cup of coffee next to the bowl. Preacher sampled it and found it just the way he liked it—black as sin and strong enough to get up and walk off on its own hind legs.

Loo fetched stew and coffee for himself, and for a few minutes the two men ate in relative silence. Preacher commented on how good the food was, and Loo thanked him.

Then Preacher said, "What in blazes is goin' on in this town, anyway? Seems like there's gun-hung hardcases ever'where. What happened to all the reg'lar folks?"

"They are hiding," Loo said. "Well . . . staying in their homes, anyway. Only a few businesses are open, and not many customers visit them. I am here only because I live in the back. Where else would I go?"

"So they've got the whole town treed?"

Loo shrugged. "You could call it that."

"Well, what about the law? Don't you have a sheriff in these parts?"

"Sheriff Carson was taken unawares and captured when those men first arrived," Loo explained. "He is locked up in his own jail, along with his deputies and the mayor and the rest of Big Rock's leading citizens."

A relief to hear that Monte Carson was still alive, Preacher thought, even though he and Smoke and Matt couldn't count on any help from the lawman as long as Carson was behind bars. "Well, what in blazes is it all about? Most of the time when an outlaw gang comes in and takes over a town, they loot the bank and the other businesses and then take off for the tall and uncut. How long's this been goin' on?"

"They have been here for several days now. As for what they want"—Loo sighed and shook his head—"I cannot tell you, Art. They have not shared their goals with us. But I can say"—he lowered his voice to a con-spiratorial level—"it has something to do with Smoke Jensen."

Preacher arched his eyebrows. "The gunfighter?"

"Yes. He has a ranch near here. There is a rumor that the men responsible for this have captured Mrs. Jensen and are holding her prisoner."

"Smoke Jensen's wife?"

Loo nodded solemnly. "That is what I have heard. They want Jensen to surrender to them, but why he is so important to them, I have no idea."

Preacher couldn't help but look a little surprised, but he managed to keep his face from expressing the depth of shock he felt. He didn't like hearing that Sally was in the hands of the varmints. He had known her for so many years that she was like a daughter to him, just as

Smoke was like a son. She was part of the family and always would be.

He took a sip of the strong coffee and brought his anger under control. He wanted to march up to one of those owlhoots, shove a gun barrel in the owlhoot's mouth, and start demanding answers. As satisfying as that might be, it wouldn't accomplish much in the long run.

Trying to sound casual about it, he asked, "They got Miz Jensen locked up somewheres here in town?"

Loo shook his head. "I have heard she is still out at the ranch her husband owns. The men have taken it over, as well. The doctor is out there."

"Who's the doctor?"

"His name is Trask. That is all I know about him. He is in command at the ranch, while Major Pike is in charge here in town." Loo frowned. "I beg your pardon, Art, but you ask a great many questions."

"Yeah, well, I'm just sort of a nosy ol' cuss, I reckon," Preacher said. "Like to know what I've got myself in the middle of. I ain't lookin' for trouble, though. I can promise you that."

"You will not say anything to anyone about the things I have told you?" Loo was starting to look a mite worried. He didn't want it getting back to the outlaws that he had been flapping his jaws about them.

Preacher shook his head. "I don't plan on talkin' to those fellas. Don't have nothin' to say to them, and I'd just as soon steer clear of 'em."

Loo relaxed. "That is wise. You would like more coffee?"

Preacher pushed his mostly empty cup across the counter and nodded. "Much obliged." What he really wanted was to find Matt and share what he had learned, so the two of them could get out of there and find Smoke.

The sooner he knew that Sally had been captured, the better.

And the worse it would be for the men who had captured her, when they had to face the wrath of Smoke Jensen.

Chapter 45

Matt and Lorena Morton walked through the gathering dusk toward the cottage where she lived. It was only a few blocks away from the school, but she hurried them along anyway.

"Major Pike established a curfew the first day," she explained. "Anyone caught on the street after dark is supposed to be shot."

"Has that happened yet?" Matt asked.

"No. Everyone's had enough sense to obey the order. But I don't doubt that some of those men would be happy to carry out an execution if they caught anyone breaking the curfew."

Matt figured she was right about that. Innocent life probably meant less than nothing to a lot of those hired killers. But the curfew disposed of his worry that some of the townspeople might see them and Lorena's reputation might be compromised. No one from Big Rock was out and about that late.

The only ones who saw them were members of the gang that had taken over, and even though they watched the pair suspiciously, none of them seemed unduly alarmed by Matt's presence. The outlaws he'd had that fracas with earlier must have told the others that he was Lorena's brother.

They reached the cottage and went in. It was small but neatly kept. Lorena lit a lamp in the front room. Matt took off his hat and tossed it casually onto a chair, as he might do if he actually lived there, just in case any of the outlaws were watching through the window.

Lorena pulled the curtains tightly together, then turned to Matt. "You can at least have supper before you try to get out of town, can't you?"

"Sure. I don't know when Preacher will be showing up at the school, but he'll wait for me if I'm not there."

"I'm afraid all I have are some beans and cornbread . . ."

"That sounds fine," Matt said with a smile.

"And I can brew some tea."

"Even better," he said, although he would have preferred a hot cup of coffee. He wasn't going to risk hurting Lorena's feelings by saying that, however.

"Make yourself comfortable." She went into the kitchen.

Matt poked up the embers in the fireplace and got a little blaze going, then sat down on a divan.

Lorena came back a few minutes later, told him that the beans were warming on the stove, and took a seat on the divan, leaving a suitable distance between herself and Matt.

"I've heard a lot about your brother. He's very well-known here in Big Rock. He wasn't in the area when I arrived in town, though, so I've never met him. I'm afraid I haven't heard much about you."

"There's not that much to tell," Matt said with a smile. "I'm just sort of a drifter. Shiftless and no-account, if you want to know the truth."

"Somehow I doubt that," Lorena said.

"No, it's true," Matt insisted. "I've never held a job for very long. I've scouted some for the army, worked as a shotgun guard for a stage line, done some prospecting and trapping, even pinned on a deputy's badge now and then. But no matter what it is, after a while I get sort of fiddle-footed and have to move on."

"That's not the same as being shiftless. You just haven't decided what you want to do with your life yet. That's understandable. You're young."

"Not as young as you, and you're already a teacher. You know what you want to do. You've settled down."

"Goodness, you make that sound so . . . so stifling! I'm still capable of acting on impulse."

"Are you?"

Somehow she had gotten closer without him noticing. In fact, she was close enough that when she leaned toward him a little, her shoulder touched his. She lifted her head, and her breath was warm against his face as she said, "I think everyone should be spontaneous at times . . ."

"Do you now?" Matt murmured as he lowered his head to hers and kissed her.

She responded eagerly. There was definitely nothing sisterly about the kiss. Matt slid an arm around her, pulled her closer.

After a long moment she drew back. "I . . . I really should check on those beans. I don't want them to burn."

"All right." He didn't particularly want to let go of her, but he knew she was right about the food. Besides, he was in the middle of the enemy camp, and lives might well be at stake, including hers. He didn't need to let himself be distracted by a pretty girl and her hot, sweet kisses.

She stood up and went into the kitchen. A few minutes later, she called, "Supper's ready."

There was no dining room in the cottage, so they ate at the kitchen table. The beans and cornbread might have been left over, but they were good. So was the tea she brewed. Matt enjoyed the meal, and her company made it even better.

The atmosphere in the kitchen grew more solemn as she asked quietly, "Do you know why those men have taken over the town and your brother's ranch? Why would they kidnap your sister-in-law?"

"Only one reason I can think of," Matt replied. His voice was grim. "They want to force Smoke to surrender to them. They figure if they hold Sally's safety over him, along with that of all his friends here in Big Rock, he won't have any choice but to go along with whatever they want."

"That still doesn't explain why."

Matt's shoulders rose and fell in a shrug. "Maybe they just want to kill him. Smoke has made a lot of enemies over the years. Or maybe they want him to do something for them."

"Something illegal?"

"It'd have to be, if they believe they'd have to force him to do it." Matt pushed his empty plate away from him and took a sip of tea from the china cup. "Do you have any idea how many men they have here in town?"

"Oh, goodness. I've never tried to count them."

"Just a guess."

Lorena frowned in thought. "I've heard people say there were at least a hundred men in the raiding party that took over the town. I'd estimate that at least half of them are still here."

"Then fifty men, roughly," Matt mused. "Some of the bunch were probably killed during the fighting when they took over. That'd make it between forty and fifty men here, and an equal number out at the ranch."

Lorena nodded. "That sounds reasonable to me. Are you going to ask the army for help, once you and your friend get away?"

"By the time we reached the nearest army post and then got back here, it might be too late. That would probably take a week or more."

"How about sending a telegram asking for help?" Lorena suggested. "That would be quicker."

Matt shook his head. "They're guarding all the roads in and out of town, and they've got the railroad cut off. I'm sure they've pulled down the telegraph wires, too. No, I'm afraid Smoke and Preacher and I are pretty much on our own."

She stared across the table at him. "Three men against almost a hundred? That . . . that's insane!"

"Those are pretty hefty odds," Matt agreed with a faint smile. "But sometimes you just have to play the hand you're dealt. Anyway, Smoke's got a habit of coming out on top no matter what the odds. The first big fight he was in, he killed eighteen men."

"Merciful heavens!"

Matt shook his head. "Those men were responsible for the deaths of his first wife and his son. Heaven would have been the only thing merciful that day, since it sure as hell wasn't Smoke Jensen." Matt's jaw tightened. "If anything happens to Sally, there's gonna be hell to pay all over again."

Chapter 46

The little Chinese man explained that no one was supposed to be on the streets after dark. "Major Pike said that anyone caught like that would be shot on sight," Loo warned.

"Well, then, seems to me like the thing to do 'd be not to let nobody see me," the old mountain man said.

"How are you going to do that?"

"I'm pretty good at sneakin' around." Preacher didn't elaborate. He slid a coin across the counter and went on. "I know you said I didn't have to pay you for that meal, but I'd take it kindly if you'd let me do it anyway. Your business is bound to be pretty bad since those fellers took over."

"Business? What business?" Loo pushed the coin back to Preacher. "But you will insult me if you fail to accept the hospitality I offered."

"Well, I wouldn't want to give no offense . . ." Preacher scooped up the coin and put it back in his pocket. "Tell you what I'll do. When this is all over, I'll stop back by and let you pick out anything you want from that wagonload o' goods I got. There's all sorts of pots and pans and cookin' utensils and gimcracks like that. We'll call that me bein' hospitable to you."

Loo thought about it, shrugged, and nodded. "I think we can do that, but you must hurry now, Art. It will be dark soon."

"I know." Preacher put on the derby hat he'd gotten from Isaac Herschkowitz and left the little café.

The sun was down, but a reddish-gold arch remained in the western sky. He saw one of the gun-hung hard-cases leaning against a post not far away and approached the man, who straightened and moved his hand to the butt of his holstered revolver.

"Don't get all het up there, amigo," Preacher said to the man. "I know it's late and I'm s'posed to be gettin' off the street. But I got to put my team up. Can you point me to the livery stable?" He knew good and well where Big Rock's livery stable was, but he wanted to maintain the pose of being a stranger here.

"It's back up the street a couple blocks," the outlaw responded in surly tones. "Better get a move on, old-timer."

"Could you maybe go with me? That way if some o' your compadres see me, they'll know you got ever'thing under control and won't get no itchy trigger fingers."

The man scowled. "Ah, hell. The saloon's that way, and I was thinkin' about goin' and gettin' a drink anyway. Come on, you old coot."

"You boys sure like to point out that I'm a mite long in the tooth," Preacher said as he untied the team from the hitch rail and led the mules with the reins. The two of them started walking toward the stable.

"Long in the tooth?" the gunman repeated with a

laugh. "Hell, you're about as old as Methuselah, ain't you?"

"Reckon I could give him a run for his money," Preacher agreed. He didn't mention the fact that he didn't look any older than he had a decade and a half earlier when he had met Kirby Jensen for the first time, along with Kirby's pa Emmett. Preacher seemed to have reached a certain age and then just stopped getting older, something that he attributed to clean living. Of course, Smoke always laughed whenever Preacher made that assertion.

When they reached the livery stable and wagon yard, the gunman said, "Maybe you'd better ask the hostler if you can sleep in the hayloft tonight, old-timer. You don't need to be wandering around anymore. It's likely to be dangerous."

"I'm obliged to you for the advice. I'll do that."

The man nodded curtly and moved on toward the saloon.

Preacher sighed. He had hoped to lure the outlaw into the stable and then cut his throat, or at least knock him out, tie him up, and gag him—that would improve the odds by one, anyway—but it hadn't worked out.

That was all right, Preacher told himself. There would be plenty more chances for killing before it was all over.

He didn't recognize the young hostler who was working in the stable. That meant the youngster was less likely to know who Preacher was.

"You're out too late, mister," the hostler said as Preacher led the team and the wagon into the barn. "The sun's down, and it'll be dark in a few minutes."

"I know. I was hopin' maybe I could bed down in the

loft after we get this team unhitched. I'll give you a hand with that."

"Well, I don't know . . . I don't own the place, you understand. I just work here. But I reckon it's all right, since you'll be paying to have your animals stabled here." A bitter laugh came from the young man. "It's not like we can afford to turn away business. In fact, other than those fellas who've taken over the town, nobody's come in here for the past couple days."

"I don't reckon they're payin' for the feed their hosses eat, neither," Preacher commented.

The hostler snorted. "Not hardly." He looked at the wagon, noticing for the first time its distinctive appearance and went on in an excited voice. "Hey, you're the fella who brought those dead owlhoots in earlier today."

"Reckon I am," Preacher said. "But I didn't have nothin' to do with 'em dyin'."

"I'm surprised they didn't shoot you anyway, just for the fun of it." The young man glanced nervously at the open double doors and lowered his voice. "I'd better quit talking like that. Some of them might be out there. They could hear me, and then I'd be in trouble."

"Them owlhoot horses I led in," Preacher said, making it sound casual, "do they happen to be here?"

"Yeah. They're out in the corral, where we'll have to leave your team. All the stalls are full. We'd better get busy, too. There's not much light left."

Preacher and the young man, who introduced himself as Wendell, worked together for the next few minutes. They unhitched the mules and left the wagon where it was parked as they led the animals into the corral next to the barn. Preacher was glad to see that Horse was there. The stallion spotted him, too, and greeted him with a sharp whinny and a toss of the head.

"Huh," Wendell said. "Wonder what's got into that big fella?"

"Ain't no tellin'," Preacher said, but he knew the gray was glad to see him, and the feeling was mutual. Later, he would have to sneak Horse out of there, get to the school, and rendezvous with Matt. Then they would head for Knob Hill to meet Smoke.

The shadows were thick inside the barn. Wendell lit a couple lanterns and pointed to the ladder leading to the hayloft. "You can go up there any time you want. I'm surprised you don't just sleep in your wagon, though. I mean, what do you usually do when you're on the trail?"

Preacher hadn't even thought about that. He supposed ol' Ike could've had a bunk inside the wagon, or maybe a tent he pitched. Preacher wanted to be someplace where he could move around more easily, though. "Yeah, I do, but a nice pile o' hay is softer 'n a bedroll."

"Well, it doesn't make me any never mind," Wendell said with a shrug. "But say, if you're not ready to turn in yet, I've got a checkerboard in the office. What do you say to a game or two?"

"Now you're talkin'. Ain't much I like better 'n a friendly game o' checkers." And that would give him an excuse to find out even more about what was going on in Big Rock, he thought. Checkers and conversation just sort of went together.

Over the next couple hours they played several games, and Preacher heard again all about how the gang had raided the town several nights earlier, how Sheriff Monte Carson was a prisoner in his own jail, and how half of the outlaws had gone out to Sugarloaf, attacked the ranch, and taken Sally Jensen prisoner.

"They talk a lot about it," Wendell said as he studied the checkerboard, contemplating his next move. "I've overheard them saying things about Mrs. Jensen several times."

"Reckon they're proud of what they've done," Preacher said.

They wouldn't be proud when Smoke found out about it, though. If they hurt Sally—or even if they didn't—they'd be sorry.

Sorry they had ever crossed Smoke Jensen and the rest of his family.

Chapter 47

Matt stood at the window in the front room of Lorena's cottage and eased the curtain back. He had blown out the lamp a few minutes earlier, so the room was dark, allowing him to see what was going on outside, which appeared to be nothing.

"Do you see anything?" Lorena asked from behind him in a worried tone.

"Not a blessed thing. There's some light a few blocks away, probably from the saloons, but this end of town is plumb peaceful." At least that's what it looked like. He knew that appearances could be deceptive.

"There have been times at night, while I was trying to sleep, when I've heard men on horseback riding by in the street. I'm sure they were guard patrols."

"More than likely," Matt agreed. "I'll have to keep an eye out for them."

"If you're going back to the school, you'll be heading away from where the guards are most likely to be, won't you?"

"That's sure what I'm hoping."

"And you have to go now?"

Matt let the curtain fall closed and turned away from the window. He could make out the slender shape of Lorena standing a few feet away from him.

"Preacher and I didn't set a particular time," he explained. "We just said we'd meet at the school. If he gets there before me, he'll wait. Likewise if I get there first. I reckon if it got to be too late and one of us hadn't shown up, whoever was there might have to think about getting out of town before sunup. But that's not going to happen."

"What it amounts to . . . is that you could take an extra few minutes before you leave?"

"I don't see any reason why not." He smiled faintly in the darkness as he heard the rustle of cloth. Lorena came toward him. He reached out, and she moved into his embrace. He closed his arms around her as his mouth found hers.

The kiss was long, passionate, urgent. Her fingers clutched at the front of his shirt. When she finally pulled back, she whispered, "Take me with you."

Matt stiffened a little in surprise. "What?"

"Take me with you," she repeated. "I want to come with you when you leave Big Rock."

Matt moved his hands to her shoulders and rested them there. "I'm not leaving for good. I'll be coming back here. Me and Preacher and Smoke, and anybody else we can find to help us. Somebody's got to deal with those men who took over the town, and I reckon we're the only ones who can do it."

"I can be one of those who help you," Lorena insisted.

He shook his head, even though he wasn't sure if she could see him. "I was thinking more of the crew out at Sugarloaf. They're a pretty salty bunch."

"You think I can't be . . . salty? I have to deal with a whole schoolhouse full of unruly children every day!"

Matt almost laughed, but he sensed that she was serious. He didn't want to hurt her feelings. "It wouldn't be safe to take you along. You might get hurt."

"I'm willing to run that risk."

His tone hardened. "Well, I'm not. Besides, I'd be worried about looking after you, and that might make me let my guard down at just the wrong time."

"Oh. So I'd be a liability, is that it?"

Sounded like he'd succeeded in offending her after all, he thought. But it was better for her to be offended than to be shot on sight for violating the gang's curfew.

"I appreciate all the help you gave me earlier, Lorena, I really do. But from here on out, this isn't the sort of job a schoolteacher needs to be mixed up in. There's going to be gun work, and a lot of it."

"A job for a killer, in other words."

"To be blunt about it . . . yes."

She sighed. "I'm sorry, Matt. I don't know what came over me. I just thought . . . for a minute there, it seemed like such a grand adventure . . . and I've never really done anything exciting. . . ."

"Fighting outlaws isn't all that exciting. Mostly it's just scary. I don't reckon anybody ever gets used to the sound of a bullet whipping past their ears."

"No, I . . . I know I never would." She lifted her arms and cupped his face with her hands. "I shouldn't have put you in that awkward position. Will you accept a kiss as an apology?"

"You bet I will. And another one for good luck."

He left the cottage a few minutes later with the sweet taste of Lorena's lips still on his.

It took him only a fraction of a second to put those

kisses behind him, though. Instantly, all his senses were on hair-trigger alert, and his instincts were working at peak efficiency.

The cottage was completely dark, as were the houses close by. Matt threw a leg over the sill of a window in a small side room Lorena used as a sewing room, climbed out, and dropped the short distance to the ground, landing noiselessly. He figured that if any of the patrolling gunmen happened to glance at the cottage, they would be more likely to pay attention to the doors rather than the windows.

He looked back through the window, knowing that Lorena was in the darkened room even though he couldn't see her. He lifted a hand in a brief farewell and ghosted into the shadows under the trees.

Nobody was better than Preacher at moving like a phantom through the night, but he had taught Matt quite a bit about it. Matt stuck to the blackest areas and didn't take a step until his gut told him that nobody was watching him. His progress toward the school was slow but steady. Since the building wasn't far away, he figured it wouldn't take him long to get there, even being as careful as he was.

What he hadn't reckoned on was the low, frightened cry that drifted through the night.

Chapter 48

Matt's head snapped around. The sound had come from the direction of Lorena's cottage. He was pretty sure she was the one who had cried out.

Something had happened, he realized, and he could either go back and find out what it was, or he could continue to the school, rendezvous with Preacher, and get the hell out of Big Rock while he had the chance.

It took him less than half a second to make up his mind.

He broke into a run toward the cottage, less concerned with stealth than he was with speed.

The window he had climbed out of was still open. So was the front door. Lorena had lit a lamp once he was gone, and light spilled through the opening.

He reached the window, grasped the sill, and pulled himself up and through the opening with lithc athleticism. *Thump*. He landed on the floor of the sewing room, but he thought the sound of a man's harsh laughter from the front room probably covered it up.

"Where's that damn brother of yours?" the man demanded. "I was hopin' to teach him a little lesson before I give you what you got comin', schoolteacher."

Matt recognized the voice. It belonged to the man whose face he had gashed with that jagged piece of wood earlier in the day. Dixon, that was his name.

"Charles . . . Charles isn't here," Lorena said, "but he just stepped out. Please don't hurt him!"

"Where'd he go?"

"He . . ." Lorena hesitated, and Matt could practically see her mind working feverishly as he eased toward the door. "There's a girl . . . he's sweet on. He went to see her, to make sure she's all right." Her voice strengthened as she grew more sure of herself. "But he won't cause any trouble, I swear. He's a very . . . a very peaceable man."

Matt smiled grimly in the darkness at that.

"Well, I hope the gal was worth it," Dixon said. "I'm gonna wait here until he comes back, and when he does . . . well, Major Pike's orders were pretty clear, weren't they?"

Lorena sobbed in the front room. Matt wasn't sure if she was acting or not. She had no way of knowing that he had heard her cry and came back. As far as she knew, he had gone on to the school as planned. She had to answer Dixon's questions about her so-called brother, and she had to be convincingly scared for his life.

Acting frightened couldn't be too difficult under the circumstances. She had to be terrified of Dixon for her own sake, since she wasn't expecting any help from Matt.

Dixon made it worse. "Of course, if you was to make me happy enough before your stupid brother gets back, maybe I'd decide to show a little mercy and let him live, no matter what the major says."

Matt didn't believe that for a second. Dixon wouldn't want to risk his boss's wrath. He would force Lorena into cooperating with him, and then gun down "Charles Morton" anyway. It had to be what he was planning.

In a voice that shook a little with fear and revulsion, Lorena said, "I'll do whatever you want me to."

Dixon laughed. "I figured you would. C'mere . . ."

Matt had reached the little hallway between the front room and the kitchen. In the glow from the lamp, two shadows writhed, came together, then pulled apart as Lorena instinctively struggled against Dixon's brutish grasp.

That sight was all Matt could stand. Moving in an almost silent rush, he burst into the front room and crashed into Dixon in a diving tackle as he tried to pull Lorena closer to him.

Both went down, falling heavily against the divan. Matt's left hand clamped like iron around Dixon's right wrist, preventing the outlaw from drawing his gun. At the same time, Matt hammered a punch at the outlaw's face. The man twisted his head aside at the last second so the blow grazed his ear. He howled in pain anyway.

His left hand shot up and grabbed Matt by the throat. Matt aimed a knee at Dixon's groin, but again the outlaw writhed out of the way just in time, taking the knee on his thigh. He arched his back, bucked up from the floor, and rolled, taking Matt with him.

Matt wound up on the bottom with Dixon leering down at him. He was a good-sized man, and his weight and the brutal grip on Matt's throat allowed him to keep Matt pinned to the floor.

As the lack of air started to get to him, Matt levered his right leg up and scissored it in front of Dixon's head. He threw all of his strength into straightening the leg, and that tore Dixon's hand away from his throat. Dixon toppled to the side.

Matt couldn't hold on to the wrist of Dixon's gun hand, but he surged up and leaped at the outlaw again before Dixon had time to draw the revolver. Matt lowered his head and rammed it into Dixon's jaw. Dixon went over backwards. Matt slammed him to the floor as hard as he could.

The impact didn't knock Dixon out, but his gun was jolted out of its holster and went sliding away across the smooth hardwood floor.

Matt didn't have a chance to go after it. Dixon threw both arms around him in a bear hug and rolled over. Lorena cried out as they crashed into her legs and knocked her down.

Matt hoped she was all right, but he didn't have time to check on her. Dixon was putting so much pressure on his ribs it felt like they were starting to creak and bend. Matt head-butted him again. He felt Dixon's nose crunch and flatten. Dixon yelled and loosened his grip. Matt tore free.

Blood gouted from Dixon's broken nose, but the injury didn't slow him down. He brought up a leg and kicked Matt in the chest. Matt slid across the floor on his back. Dixon leaped after him, clubbed his fists together, and smashed them across Matt's face.

Matt's vision spun crazily from the powerful blow. A red haze seemed to drop across his eyes. He realized he was about to lose consciousness and fought it off. As Dixon lifted both fists to strike again, Matt hooked a punch to the man's belly. Dixon's breath gusted out, and he looked sick. Matt shoved him away to get some room between them and fought his way to his feet.

Dixon was still down. Matt was about to kick him in

the jaw when his other foot slipped on one of Lorena's throw rugs. He went down hard, giving Dixon the chance to recover his wits. He sprang at Matt and landed on the young man's belly with both knees.

A split second later, both of Dixon's hands closed around Matt's throat. Matt knew the outlaw wouldn't let go until he'd choked the life out of him.

A dull thud sounded. Dixon's eyes opened wide, bulged out, and then rolled up in their sockets. His hands came loose from Matt's neck as he rolled off limply to one side.

Lorena stood behind him, her chest heaving, both hands wrapped around the gun that had come out of Dixon's holster. Matt could tell from the way she held it that she had just used the gun barrel to hit Dixon in the back of the head and knock him out.

Matt was pretty breathless from the savage battle. He pushed himself up on one hand and summoned a grin for Lorena. "You cold-cocked him just in time—"

Outside the open front door, a man said, "Dixon, if you've come here to pester that schoolteacher again—"

The newcomer broke off his comment as he stepped into the doorway. Matt recognized him as Bracken, the man who had been with Dixon at the school earlier.

The outlaw took in the scene in a heartbeat—Matt on the floor, Dixon lying senseless nearby, Lorena standing with a gun in her hands. He couldn't know in that instant whether Dixon was alive or dead.

But he could see the gun, and Matt knew from what Lorena had told him that Major Pike's orders were clear.

Any citizen of Big Rock caught with a weapon was to be killed immediately.

Bracken was fast on the draw. He had to be in his line of work. His hand flashed to the Colt on his hip. The iron cleared leather and came up spouting flame just as Matt leaped to his feet and threw himself at Lorena, hoping to knock her out of the line of fire.

A sledgehammer blow crashed against his head. A black cavern opened up before him, and he toppled into it with no knowledge of what had happened to Lorena . . . or anything else except oblivion.

Chapter 49

Preacher and Wendell finished their checker games, and the young hostler turned in, stretching out on a cot in the tack room after turning the lantern down very low. It was unlikely that anyone would need anything else, unless one of the outlaws came in for his horse for some reason.

Preacher glanced to the tack room where Wendell had left the door open then climbed to the loft. In the faint glow coming from below, he could see the piles of hay. He knew how comfortable it would be to lie down on one of those soft mounds. It had been a long day and he was tired . . . but he had a lot to do and a ways to go before he could sleep—if he managed to get any sleep at all.

After a while, he heard snoring coming from inside the tack room. It mixed with the sounds of horses blowing, flicking their tails, and moving around a little in their stalls, but his footsteps made no sound on the hay scattered across the floor as he went to the small opening in the back of the hayloft. He unlatched the shutter-like door and swung it out, then leaned through the opening and looked and listened intently.

A few strains of music came faintly to his ears. In one of the saloons some outlaws must have forced the piano player to tickle the ivories.

Preacher didn't hear any hoofbeats or see anyone moving around. The alley behind the livery stable was shadowy and deserted as far as he could tell. The old mountain man knew if his keen senses didn't pick up on anything, it just flat wasn't there.

He turned around, wiggled his legs and body through the opening, hung by his hands for a second, and dropped to the ground.

The landing was a little more of a jolt than his old bones needed. He straightened from the crouch he had wound up in, but no harm was done. He could tell he was fine as he moved silently away from the big barn.

He paused as he reached the corral at the side of the building. A low whistle brought Horse to the fence. The big gray stallion stretched his head over the top rail and bumped Preacher's shoulder with his nose. Preacher scratched the silky hide and whispered, "I'm gonna get you out of there. Just hang on a minute."

Since the gate was on the front of the corral, he would have to leave the shadows and risk being seen, but it couldn't be helped. He wasn't leaving Big Rock without Horse. He would have to abandon his saddle and his other gear for the moment. With Wendell sleeping in the tack room, fetching the saddle without waking him would be a problem.

Preacher had a feeling that if he explained what was going on to the young hostler, Wendell wouldn't betray him to the outlaws, but it was just simpler without waking him. Besides, when Preacher was younger, he had ridden bareback many times.

Horse followed him on the other side of the fence as he cat footed around to the front, causing a slight disturbance among the other animals in the corral. Preacher hoped they wouldn't get too spooked, raise a big ruckus, and attract the attention of the gunmen on guard duty.

He reached the gate. Horse was ready on the other side. Preacher lifted the latch and swung the gate open just enough for the stallion to get through. Some of the other horses started toward the gate, following the big gray. Preacher closed it quickly to keep any of them from getting out.

"Good boy," he whispered. "Come on." He didn't have any reins to lead the stallion, but he didn't need any. Horse followed him without any more urging.

Preacher circled the corral again and felt a little relieved when he reached the gloom of the alley once more. He knew he wasn't out of danger yet, though. Horse couldn't move without making any sound like he could. The guards might hear the *clip-clop* of the stallion's hooves and come to investigate.

He had to take that chance and headed unerringly toward the edge of town where the school was located. He hadn't been lost in more than sixty years, no matter what the circumstances, and he wasn't about to start.

His route took him behind the sheriff's office and jail. Monte Carson was locked up in there, Preacher recalled from his conversations with Loo and Wendell. He paused to wonder if it might be possible to take the guards by surprise and rescue the sheriff and the other prisoners. Having more fighting men on their side would help with the overwhelming odds.

He shook his head, deciding it was too big a chance

to take. He needed to rendezvous with Matt, and then the two of them could find Smoke and have a powwow. They would decide together what to do.

He had just come to that conclusion when he heard something that made him stop in his tracks. A commotion broke out in front of the jail, and he heard the name *Jensen*.

Maybe they were just talking about Smoke, Preacher told himself. The hombres who had taken over Big Rock certainly knew that Smoke's ranch was nearby; that was the reason they had targeted the settlement, after all.

A man asked loudly, "Are you sure it's him?"

"Damn right I'm sure," another man replied. "I saw him shoot a fella up in Cheyenne last year. This is Matt Jensen, all right."

Preacher bit back a curse. From the sound of it, Matt had gotten himself captured.

Or worse.

Preacher knew he had to find out. He leaned close to Horse's ear and whispered, "Stay put," then moved carefully and silently along the side of the building.

"Somebody go fetch the major," a man ordered. "He'll need to decide what we do with Jensen."

That sounded like Matt was still alive. The old mountain man was grateful.

Matt was a prisoner, though, which wasn't good.

"No need to fetch the major," one of the outlaws said. "Here he comes now."

Preacher reached the end of the narrow passage between the jail and the neighboring building, staying back just far enough that the thick shadows concealed him. He could see a tall, spare man with a limp, striding along the street. Had to be the major the outlaws had been talking about—Major Pike, Preacher recalled.

"What's going on here?" Pike asked sharply as he came up to the knot of men in front of the jail.

Preacher counted seven or eight of them, all heavily armed. Although he couldn't make out what they were clustered around, other than a vague shape on the ground, he knew it had to be Matt. The thought made his heart slug heavily in his chest.

"I've got a prisoner here," one of them replied. "Helmond says it's Matt Jensen."

Enough light came through the front windows of the sheriff's office to reveal the frown that creased Pike's forehead. "Matt Jensen is Smoke Jensen's brother. Where did you find him, Bracken?"

"Down at the schoolteacher's house. Dixon and I saw him with her earlier. She claimed that he was her brother."

"Are you sure he's not, Helmond?" Pike asked. "Maybe you're mistaken."

"I'm as sure as I can be, Major," the outlaw called Helmond declared. "Why, I was as close to him in Cheyenne as I am to you now. Once I saw him draw his gun, I wasn't likely to forget him. He was fast as greased lightning."

Pike grunted. "His brother's faster."

"Maybe so, but I reckon this fella could shade just about anybody *except* Smoke Jensen."

Pike continued to frown in thought for a long moment before he said, "Either he's been hiding out somewhere all along—maybe with this schoolmarm you mentioned—or else he snuck into town recently. Either way, I don't like it. How bad is he hurt?"

"I think my bullet just creased him and knocked him out," Bracken said. "I came in down there at the schoolteacher's place—I was looking for Dixon—and found Jensen and Dixon on the floor and the teacher standing over Dixon with a gun in her hands."

"Is Dixon dead?"

"No, sir. He's got a goose egg on his head where she clouted him, but that's all. I didn't know that at the time, though. I remembered your orders about shooting anybody caught with a gun, so I threw down on the woman. Jensen jumped between me and her just as I fired. The bullet clipped him and put him down and out."

"What about the teacher?" Pike wanted to know.

Bracken hesitated, then said, "Well, she yelped and dropped the gun when I shot Jensen. I could have gone ahead and gunned her down, but once I had a second to think about it, the idea of shooting an unarmed woman . . . well, it didn't sit too good with me, Major."

"You had your orders," Pike snapped.

"Yes, sir, I know that. I'll go get her right now if you want me to—"

Pike silenced him with a wave of his hand. "No, never mind. Where did she get the gun?"

Again Bracken hesitated then said, "It was Dixon's. It fell out of his holster while he and Jensen were fighting."

"I see. And what was Dixon doing in the woman's house?"

When Bracken didn't say anything right away, Pike made a disgusted sound. "Never mind. I told the citizens they wouldn't be harmed if they cooperated. I can see that none of my orders are followed to the letter, are they?"

"Major, I'm sorry—"

Pike cut him off. "Tell Dixon I want to see him later. In the meantime, lock Matt Jensen up in there along with Sheriff Carson and the others. From everything I know about him, he's a dangerous man. At least he won't be running around loose anymore. That's something to be thankful for anyway."

"You bet, Major. We'll take care of it." Bracken

paused. "What about the teacher? Miss Morton, I think her name is."

"I'll want to ask her some questions. Bring her to the town hall tomorrow morning. In the meantime, put a guard on her house so she doesn't try anything else."

"Yes, sir."

Pike turned and limped away. Several of the outlaws bent down and took hold of Matt's arms and legs. They lifted his unconscious form and carried him out of Preacher's line of sight and into the jail.

Preacher drew back deeper into the shadows and cursed bitterly to himself. Maybe what had happened hadn't been Matt's fault, but the young man's misfortune had put Preacher in a hell of a spot.

Since Matt wasn't going to meet him, he could go ahead and slip out of Big Rock without waiting, head for Sugarloaf, and try to find Smoke.

On the other hand, he could try to rescue Matt and in the process release Monte Carson and the other prisoners, as he had considered a few moments earlier. He hadn't thrown down on the men in the street because there were too many others close by. He might have been able to down six or seven of the varmints, but not the twenty or thirty that would come arunnin' as soon as the shooting started.

There were probably only a few guards in the jail. He might be able to get the drop on them. The place would be locked up tight, so he had to figure out a way in. . . .

As those thoughts raced through his brain, he realized that he had already decided to try to rescue Matt and the others. In the long run, the potential benefit from it outweighed the risks.

Preacher slid along the side of the jail building, then moved along the back until he was underneath one of the barred windows. He listened intently, heard low-voiced talking from the men inside.

A moment later, light glowed through the window. He knew somebody had carried a lantern into the cell block. Heavy footsteps sounded.

Then a man ordered, "All of you men get back."

"How can we get back, the way you've got us crowded in here?" another man asked.

Preacher recognized Monte Carson's gruff tones.

"Do what I tell you, or we'll splatter buckshot all over that cell and make some room that way."

Men grumbled and cursed. Preacher supposed Carson and the other prisoners were moving back away from the cell door.

Carson exclaimed, "Good Lord! Is that Matt Jensen?"

"Yeah," one of the outlaws gloated.

"Is he dead?"

"No, but he will be if that damn brother of his don't cooperate with the doctor. Don't any of you move. If you so much as twitch toward this door, you'll get a load of buckshot in the face."

Preacher listened as the cell door clanged open, then a moment later slammed shut again. In between there was a dull sound like a sack of potatoes being dropped on the floor. That would be Matt being tossed into the cell, still unconscious.

The light disappeared and a door closed.

The door between the cell block and the sheriff's office, Preacher thought.

Quickly, he hunted along the alley until he found an old crate he could stand on. He placed it under the window, stepped up on it, and gripped the bars. "Monte!" he said in a low, urgent voice. "Monte Carson."

The men inside the cell had been talking together in

quiet, angry tones. They abruptly fell silent at Preacher's hail. He couldn't make out any details in the darkened cell. The prisoners were just vague shapes.

One of them moved closer to the window and the sheriff's familiar voice asked, "Who's that?"

"You mean you don't recognize these here dulcet tones o' mine?"

"Preacher!" Carson stepped up to the window and took hold of the bars, too. "Preacher, what are you doing here? I guess I shouldn't be surprised to see you, since Matt's here, too." Carson paused. "And Smoke? Is Smoke with you?"

"Last I seen of him, he was headed to Sugarloaf to see what's what out there. Me an' Matt slipped into town to do some scoutin'. You got a heap o' trouble here in Big Rock, Sheriff."

"I know," Carson said grimly. "Maybe even too much for you fellas to handle."

Preacher wasn't anywhere near ready to go along with that idea. "Can you tell how bad Matt's hurt?"

"From what I could see when they threw him in here, it looked like he has a bullet graze on his head. There was quite a bit of dried blood, but you know how head wounds are. They bleed like a stuck pig."

"If that slug just creased him, he'll be all right. Boy's got a hard head." Preacher tugged on the bars. "I don't reckon if I found a rope, ol' Horse could pull these here bars outta the window, could he?"

"I don't think even a whole team of wild stallions could do it," Carson said. "This is a stone wall, and they're set solid. It'd take dynamite to blow them out, and if you set off a blast big enough to do that, it would probably kill every man in here at the same time."

"Well, then, seems to me the only way to get you boys out is to unlock the door."

A humorless laugh came from Carson. "How are you going to do that?"

"How many guards out in the office?"

"From what I've been able to tell, there are always at least three. Sometimes four."

"That ain't too many. I got to get in there somehow . . . or get them out." Preacher thought about it for a moment, then asked, "Reckon they got a fire goin' in the stove? It's sort of a chilly night."

"I'm sure they do. They let us shiver back here, but I can't see them putting up with being uncomfortable."

"All right. That's what I needed to know. I got me an idea."

"Preacher . . . ?"

"Yeah?"

"Be careful," Carson said. "If you see that you can't get us out of here, then leave and find Smoke. You know what has to be done. It'd be a mighty tall order for two men . . ."

"You mean kill ever' damn one of them hardcases? Don't worry, Sheriff. We'll get around to it."

Chapter 50

Once again, Preacher patted Horse's shoulder and told the stallion to stay where he was. Horse gave an impatient toss of his head. He was ready to be out of there, running free across the range again.

"I know how you feel, old son," Preacher told him. "Just hold on a mite longer."

He went back up the side of the building to where he could see the area in front of the jail. Gun-hung men drifted away and ambled up the street toward the saloons. Preacher heard the door close, and a moment later a bar thumped down in its brackets.

Nobody was left inside except a few guards and the prisoners. It was time for Preacher to make his move.

As he'd moved to the back of the jail, he had noticed a drainpipe on the building next door. It was what had given him an idea in the first place. Climbing it wouldn't be easy, but it was his only chance. He gripped the pipe, muttered, "Up you go," planted a foot against the wall, and heaved and levered himself up.

I'm climbing this downspout like a dang go-rilla, he thought as he hauled himself upward. By the time he was able to reach up, grab the edge of the flat roof, and pull himself over it, he was winded and his heart was pounding. "Getting too old for this sort of thing," he muttered.

Of course, he had been saying that for nigh on to twenty years, and he was still at it, wasn't he?

Adventure kept a feller young. No two ways about it.

He lay there for a few minutes and caught his breath, then climbed to his feet and studied the gap between the building and the jail. Approximately eight feet separated them—quite a leap for an old-timer. Preacher knew that if he didn't make it, he was liable to break both legs when he fell—if not his damn fool neck.

But it was the only course open to him, so he took off the derby and with a flick of his wrist sailed it across the open space onto the jail roof. Then he backed off to get some distance, took a deep breath, and broke into a run toward the edge.

He'd been a pretty fast runner in his day. He'd had to be. More than once, his speed afoot was the only thing that had saved his life. He wasn't nearly as fleet-footed. His run was better than a shuffle, but not by much.

The muscles in his legs were still powerful, though. He reached the edge of the roof, pushed off it, and sailed far out over the shadow-cloaked passage below. He stretched his arms as far as they would reach . . . and landed with his head, arms, and shoulders on the jail roof. His hands dug in as they tried to find purchase on the slate shingles. He slid backwards, but only an inch or so before he got a firm enough grip to support himself.

From there it wasn't difficult to swing a leg up, hook a foot over the edge, and pull himself onto the roof. He rolled over, grateful for the support underneath him.

Yeah, way *too old for this*, he thought.

He'd made it, so there was no point in worrying about it. He climbed to his feet and looked around until he found the hat he had thrown over a few minutes earlier.

Walking as softly as possible, he carried the derby over to the round tin stovepipe sticking up from the roof. Sure enough, wood smoke drifted from it. The guards had a fire in the stove down below. It was exactly what Preacher needed.

He muttered, "Sorry about your hat, Ike," then tore the brim away from the derby, wadded up what was left, and forced it under the raised conical tin cover that shielded the top of the pipe from rain. He stuffed the mutilated hat into the pipe until it was completely blocked.

It wouldn't be long until the smoke from the stove began to back up into the sheriff's office. Preacher moved to the front of the building and stretched out on the roof to watch what happened below.

A minute or so went by before he began to hear angry voices through the roof and ceiling. He couldn't make out the words, but the tone of voice was obvious and so was the reason.

After a moment, a man said loud enough for Preacher to understand, "Don't do that, you idiot!" followed by coughing.

One of the guards had opened the door on the stove and let even more smoke billow out into the office.

The bar scraped in its brackets, and the door banged open. Men emerged onto the boardwalk, stomping heavily and coughing. A couple walked out into the street. Preacher slid back a little, knowing that instinct would make the men look up onto the roof. He didn't want them to spot him.

"I can't see anything." The guard's voice was hoarse from the smoke.

"Could be a damn bird got up under that stovepipe cover somehow," the other outlaw said. "One of us better climb up there and take a look. Something's got it clogged up, that's for sure."

"Climb up there how?"

"Well, go find a ladder, damn it."

The first man walked off grumbling while the one who had given the order went on. "Scanlon, you stay in there and keep an eye on the prisoners."

"Why me?" Scanlon asked between coughs. "That smoke bothers me just as much as it does you."

"Well, then, stand there in the doorway and watch the cell block door."

"That's crazy, Rawley. There's nobody in there."

"I'm just saying we don't want to disappoint the major . . . or the doctor."

"No," Scanlon agreed with a sudden note of worry in his voice. "We don't want to disappoint the doctor."

They were scared of the doctor hombre, whoever he was, thought Preacher. The gent had to be hell on wheels to make a whole crew of hardened gunmen leery of him.

Preacher waited patiently. Some of the smoke was probably drifting into the cell block, but the men being held prisoner there would just have to put up with it for a while. That was a small price to pay for their freedom.

The man Rawley had sent to look for a ladder came back after a few minutes, still muttering and cursing.

Rawley told him, "Prop it there at the side of the building." He pointed to the alley.

Preacher heard the ladder bump against the roof.

"Who's goin' up there, you or me?" asked the man with the ladder.

"You can, Nelson."

"Thanks." Nelson didn't sound grateful at all.

Preacher moved to the side of the building where the ladder was. The top of it projected about a foot above the edge of the roof. He reached behind him and drew the Colt from the waistband of his trousers at the small of his back. Reversing it, he gripped the barrel and cylinder and waited.

Nelson grunted with effort as he climbed the ladder. Clearly he wasn't in very good shape. Spending most of his time in saloons would do that. As long as he could get his gun out in a hurry and shoot accurately, that was all that mattered.

Nelson's hat appeared at the top of the ladder. His head was down as he watched what he was doing. In one quick movement, Preacher's left hand shot out, snatched the hat off Nelson's head, and threw it away. His right brought the gun butt down hard on the gunman's skull and he grabbed Nelson's collar to keep the outlaw from falling. Nelson slumped against the ladder.

Preacher put the gun down, got both arms under Nelson's arms, and hauled the man up and over the edge of the roof. He was senseless for the moment, but he might not stay that way, so Preacher picked up the Colt and walloped him again, harder. He knew he might wind up busting the fella's skull, but considering all the evil the gang had done in Big Rock, he wasn't going to worry too much about that.

He had made some racket knocking out the gunman and pulling him onto the roof, but no more than Nelson might have made clambering up. Rawley and Scanlon were still standing on the front porch, talking.

After a few moments, Rawley stepped out in front of the building again and called, "Hey, Nelson, what have you found up there? The smoke's still coming out of the stove down here."

Preacher didn't reply, and Nelson couldn't say anything since he was out cold.

"Nelson? Damn it, what are you—? Stay here, Scanlon."

"What are you gonna do?" Scanlon asked.

"Looks like I have to climb up there and find out what the hell happened to Nelson."

"Let me do it," Scanlon suggested. "I could use the fresh air."

Rawley didn't answer immediately. After a moment, he said, "All right. Hurry it up. I'm startin' not to like this."

Preacher heard the ladder rattle as Scanlon started up. He dragged Nelson over to the edge and lifted his head and shoulder between the ladder's side pieces. He grabbed Nelson's ankles.

Just as Scanlon glanced up, saw Nelson's head, and exclaimed, "Hey, what—" Preacher tipped the senseless outlaw over the edge.

Nelson plummeted, crashing into Scanlon and knocking him off the ladder.

Preacher went down right behind him, sliding down the ladder as much as climbing.

Scanlon was pinned to the ground with Nelson's dead weight on top of him. He was trying to yell but couldn't muster much volume from that position. Preacher silenced him with a swift kick to the head.

He'd caused enough commotion to alarm Rawley, who charged around the corner with a gun in his hand. "What the hell—"

Preacher tackled him, going low at Rawley's knees so that the outlaw tumbled over him and went down hard.

Rawley was tough and stubborn, and hung on to his gun as he rolled over and came back up. Preacher couldn't afford the sound of a shot, whether it hit him or not. He leaped at the man and closed his left hand over the cylinder of Rawley's gun, knowing the weapon couldn't fire if the cylinder couldn't turn.

Rawley hammered a punch into the old mountain man's body. Preacher grunted from the impact but didn't loosen his grip on the gun. He jabbed a right into the middle of Rawley's face. Blood spurted from the outlaw's nose as his head rocked back.

Preacher had learned how to wrestle from Indians who were expert at it. He got a foot between Rawley's ankles, grabbed the front of his shirt, and heaved. The throw sent the outlaw off his feet, and as the man went down, Preacher twisted his gun arm so that the fall put a lot of strain on his bones and muscles. Rawley cried out in pain and let go of the revolver.

A split second later, Preacher slammed the heavy gun against the side of Rawley's head. The outlaw went limp and sagged to the ground.

The plan had worked. With a little luck on his side, Preacher had managed to knock out all three guards.

All he had to do was go inside and free Matt, Monte Carson, and the other prisoners.

Preacher left the unconscious outlaws lying in the dark passage beside the jail and hurried to the door. Coils of smoke wafted from the opening. The air inside the sheriff's office was thick with it. He coughed but ignored the smoke as best he could. He knew from previous visits to Monte Carson's office that the keys to the cells were on a ring hanging on the wall behind the sheriff's desk.

He snatched the key ring from its nail and went to the cell block door. It was locked, so Preacher had to take precious seconds finding out which key opened it. His eyes stung and watered from the smoke as he tried one after the other.

The sixth or seventh key opened the door. He pulled it back and hurried into the cell block.

In the light that came from the office lamp, Preacher saw that Matt had regained consciousness. The young man stood at the barred door with Carson. He still looked a little groggy but was able to say, "Preacher, I sure am glad to see you."

"Likewise," Preacher grunted as he started trying keys in the cell door.

"Let me." Carson thrust his arm through the bars. "I know which one it is."

"Good idea." Preacher handed over the key ring.

Carson quickly sorted out the right one and thrust it into the lock. He was able to turn it from inside the cell, and the door came open.

Before the prisoners could charge out, figures appeared in the doorway between the office and the cell block.

A man's sharp voice ordered, "Mow them down!"

Carson grabbed Preacher's shirt and jerked him into the cell. The prisoners sprawled back away from the bars as gouts of flame blossomed from the twin barrels of a shotgun wielded by one of the men in the doorway.

Preacher felt the sting from a couple buckshot but knew he wasn't badly hurt. That condition might not last long, as more men with Greeners rushed into the cell block.

"Hold your fire!" the same man ordered.

The shotgunners moved aside to let him step forward, but they kept their weapons trained on the men in the cell.

Preacher saw that the man in charge had a limp and

knew he must be the major, the hombre he had seen earlier when Matt was captured.

The major had a pistol in his hand and pointed it at the prisoners. The cell door was still open, but if the men inside tried to make a break for it, they would be slaughtered. He slammed the door shut and pocketed the keys, ending any hope of escape.

Preacher knew he had failed, but he wasn't the sort to give in to despair. A setback just made him more angry and determined.

Unfortunately, there was nothing he could do at the moment to change things.

"Get up," the major said curtly. He frowned at Preacher. "I don't remember you."

"That's 'cause I wasn't in here before," the old mountain man replied. He stood up and brushed himself off, ignoring the pain in his leg and back where he had picked up a couple buckshot in the blast.

"Who are you?"

"A feller who ain't got no use for scum like you awaltzin' in and takin' over a whole town full o' good folks," Preacher replied defiantly.

A man said from the office, "Major, the three men who were on guard here are all in the alley, out cold. That old geezer must've knocked them out."

The major let out a scornful grunt. "That hardly seems possible."

"Possible or not, I done it," Preacher said. "Damn near got away with gettin' these boys outta here, too. Then you'da had a fight on your hands, believe you me."

"Then it's lucky I noticed the smoke coming from here and decided to investigate," the major said. "You were responsible for that, weren't you?"

Preacher just folded his arms over his chest, squinted one eye, and glared at the major.

The major holstered his gun and rubbed his chin "An old, old man who can still outthink and outfight men half his age . . . You're the one they call Preacher, aren't you? Smoke Jensen's friend?"

Preacher still didn't respond.

"It doesn't matter whether you deny it or not," the major went on. "I know who you are now." He laughed. "We've made quite a haul tonight without even meaning to. We have Jensen's brother and his mentor, as well as his wife and scores of his friends. He'll have no choice but to go along with the doctor's plans."

"Mister, I don't know nothin' about no doctor," Preacher said. "But I do know that when you went after Smoke Jensen, you done raised hell and shoved a chunk under the corner. It's sorta like layin' hands on a mountain lion . . . you might be able to, but then what're you gonna do with it?"

"Wait and see, old man. Just wait and see." The major jerked his head toward the door. He and the shotgunners began to back away. Over his shoulder, he ordered, "One of you men get up on the roof and clear that stovepipe. Open some windows and get this smoke out of here."

The cell block door slammed closed behind them, and the key turned in the lock with a sound of finality.

This is far from over, Preacher thought as he turned to look at Matt and Monte Carson. He saw the same thing in their eyes that he was feeling.

For the moment, it was all up to Smoke.

BOOK THREE

Chapter 51

The night got cold in the cave high on the mountain, but Smoke and Sally were warm enough snuggled together in Smoke's bedroll. Pearlie and Cal had to make do with wrapping up in blankets and having Dog sleep between them.

The big cur was an excellent sentry. No one came close enough during the night to alert his senses.

In the morning Sally built a small, almost smokeless fire, boiled coffee, and fried some bacon. It was a meager breakfast but better than nothing. After they'd eaten, she and Smoke stood in the opening and looked out over the rugged, beautiful landscape. Smoke didn't see anything moving. The morning sunlight didn't reflect off any metal.

"What are you going to do, Smoke?" she asked quietly as she slipped her hand into his.

"Now that I know you're safe, Pearlie, Cal, and I will circle around and head for Big Rock. Once we meet up with Matt and Preacher, we'll figure out a way to turn Monte Carson and the other prisoners loose. I figure we need to deal with the men Trask left in town before taking on the ones at the ranch."

"You'll be badly outnumbered wherever you go," Sally cautioned him.

Smoke smiled. "Being outnumbered sort of seems to be a way of life."

"Yes, I know, and you've never let it stop you from doing what you thought was right."

"If a man only fought the easy fights, the ones he knew he could win, it wouldn't take much courage, would it?"

She leaned against him, rested her head on his arm. "You've never lacked for courage," she said softly.

He put his arm around her and drew her closer. They stood like that for a few minutes, then Sally slipped out of his embrace and stepped back.

"I won't keep you from what you have to do. Go on and don't worry about me. Dog and I will be all right up here." She paused. "Just don't forget to come back and get us when it's all over."

Smoke grinned. "Not much chance of that."

The men got their horses ready to ride.

Smoke dropped to one knee next to Dog and rested his hand on the back of the big cur's neck, ruffling the thick fur. "You're staying here with Sally. You protect her, understand?"

Dog whined a little, deep in his thick throat.

"I know. But Preacher will be with us when we come back to get you. You've got my word on that."

Dog sat with his tongue lolling out. Smoke knew from the intelligence in the animal's eyes that Dog understood. The bond between Preacher and Dog was stronger, but Dog and Smoke got along well. Smoke knew Dog would follow his commands.

"Stay," he repeated as he stood up. "Stay."

Sally rested a hand on the big cur's head. "We'll be fine, Smoke." She had a rifle in her other hand, and a revolver was tucked into the waistband of the trousers she was wearing.

He put a hand on her shoulder, bent down, and kissed her. The kiss wasn't a long one, but it packed plenty of meaning into those few seconds.

He turned and went to where Pearlie and Cal were waiting. The three men started down the slope, leading their mounts. When the ground leveled out enough for them to ride, they swung up into the saddles and headed for Big Rock.

They rode like men on the dodge, staying in cover as much as they could to avoid being skylined. At different times in their lives, Smoke and Pearlie actually had ridden the owlhoot trail, so they knew what it was like to be hunted. Cal followed their lead.

Several times during the morning, they had to lie low in thick stands of trees while groups of armed men rode past in the distance. No doubt those were some of Trask's men, out looking for Smoke.

Passing a trail leading to Sugarloaf headquarters, it was difficult for Smoke not to follow it and head home. He knew that it made more sense to go to Big Rock first, find Matt and Preacher, and do what they could to whittle down the odds against them before setting out for a showdown with Trask.

At one point, Pearlie asked, "Smoke, you got any idea why this doctor fella wants you so bad?"

"None at all," Smoke replied honestly. "I never came across a doctor named Jonas Trask or anybody by that name in any other line of work, as far as I recall. Or a major named Pike, either. From what I've seen of the men working for them, they're the same sort of gun-wolves I've crossed trails with many times, but Trask and Pike have to be something different."

Cal said, "Well, when you come right down to it, no matter what brought them here, they'll still get what's comin' to them."

"You got that right, kid," Pearlie agreed.

Smoke didn't say anything. He wanted to settle the score for all the evil Trask and Pike had done, true enough, but a part of him also wanted to know *why* they had raided Big Rock and Sugarloaf.

A little later Pearlie asked, "Did you decide on a meetin' place with Matt and Preacher when you fellas split up?"

"Knob Hill," Smoke said. "I hope they've already found out what we need to know and will be there waiting for us."

Pearlie nodded. The hill had steep, rocky sides and was choked with brush, although there was a path to the top if you knew where to look for it. And once up on the summit, the elevation commanded a good view of the surrounding countryside.

They had to hide from one more patrol before they came in sight of the hill. Closer to Big Rock than to the ranch, they were cautious as they approached. Still in a thick clump of trees about two hundred yards from Knob Hill, Smoke reined to a halt. Pearlie and Cal did likewise.

"You fellas stay here," Smoke said. "I'll take a look around."

"I thought we was in this together," Pearlie protested.

Smoke smiled. "We are, but if I ride into trouble, I'll be counting on you two to gallop in and bail me out."

"It's usually the other way around," Pearlie said, "but I reckon that makes sense."

He and Cal sat on their horses in the trees while Smoke rode toward the looming, beetle-browed hill. His eyes moved constantly as his gaze roved over the countryside around him. He didn't see any movement, but that didn't really mean anything. He put more trust in the hair on the back of his neck. It told him that no one was watching.

He reached the hill and left his horse in the trees that grew around its base. There was no sign of other mounts, which was a little worrisome. He had been halfway convinced that Matt and Preacher were waiting for him.

He found the narrow game trail that led to the top and started the arduous climb, being careful not to disturb the brush too much. If anybody saw the branches waving around, it would be a dead giveaway that somebody was up there.

Once he got past the rocks and the thickets, the top of the hill was actually rather idyllic—level, grassy, and dotted with trees. It didn't take long to have a good look around and confirm that Matt and Preacher weren't there.

Not a good sign, but it didn't necessarily mean anything bad had happened to them. After all, they hadn't set a time for meeting. It was entirely possible that they were still poking around Big Rock.

Smoke went back down the hill and rejoined Pearlie and Cal. They could see on his face what he'd found.

"I wouldn't worry about it," Pearlie said. "If there's anybody who can take care of themselves, it's those two fellas."

"Yeah," Cal chimed in. "I'd hate to have to tangle with Matt and Preacher."

Smoke knew they were right. "Let's split up so we can

cover all the approaches to the hill. That way if either of them show up, we'll see them coming."

They climbed the hill and divided the surrounding landscape into rough thirds and found good places to stay out of sight while they kept an eye on Knob Hill. The afternoon passed in tedious fashion. Once Smoke spotted some riders about half a mile away and knew they were probably Trask's men. The patrol passed by at an angle, however, and didn't come close to the hill.

When the sun began to lower toward the western horizon, Smoke knew Pearlie and Cal would be rejoining him soon. He had told them that if no one showed up by the end of the day, they should come back to where they had left him.

Sure enough, less than five minutes apart, they came into the rocks and trees where he was hidden. Their glum silence was all the testimony Smoke needed. They hadn't seen hide nor hair of Matt and Preacher, either.

Pearlie scratched his angular, beard-stubbled jaw. "I would've thought they'd be here by now."

"Yeah, me, too," Smoke said.

"What are we gonna do?" Cal asked.

Smoke suspected that they knew the answer to that question as well as he did. There was really only one thing they *could* do. "We're going to Big Rock."

Chapter 52

The day had been one of the longest in Matt's memory. His head still ached from being knocked out the night before, but for the most part, he was able to ignore the dull throbbing.

It was harder to ignore the thought that he had failed and let Smoke down. Matt felt a lot of the same sort of admiration a younger brother felt for an older, even though they were adopted siblings and not blood relatives. The last thing in the world he wanted to do was disappoint Smoke.

Also, he was downright angry at the men who had raided the settlement and kidnapped Sally. They had a whole hell of a lot to answer for.

Preacher wasn't happy, either. He had lived wild and free his whole life, and being locked up behind bars didn't sit well with him. It put his nerves on edge. More than once during the day, he had muttered something about how being stuck in a cage gave him the fantods. He had those painful buckshot wounds to contend with, too. The little lead pellets should have been dug out already. The wounds were going to fester if they weren't tended to.

Monte Carson didn't have much sympathy for them. "We've been locked up in here for days. I've heard of men behind bars going crazy from it, and I'm starting to understand why."

His deputy Curley said, "Aw, you ain't gonna go loco, boss. You're too level-headed for that."

"I wouldn't be so sure of that," Carson growled. "I kind of understand why an animal caught in a trap will gnaw its own leg off, too."

Matt had to occupy his mind with something, so he did it by trying to come up with some way for them to escape.

Short of finding a few spare sticks of dynamite in his hip pocket, he couldn't think of a thing.

Late that afternoon, the jail had an unexpected visitor. Loo Chung How, the proprietor of the little café where Preacher had eaten the day before, showed up carrying a cast-iron pot with wisps of steam rising through gaps around the lid. The three guards on duty abandoned the desultory game of poker for matchsticks they were playing, stood up quickly, and rested their hands on their guns.

"What the hell do you want, Chinaman?" one of the gunmen demanded.

Loo held up the pot as a big smile wreathed his face. "Bringee supper for prisoners."

"They've been gettin' meals," another guard said. "Mostly cornbread and beans, but they ain't been starvin'."

"Special Chinese soup much better," Loo insisted. "Major Pike, he say all right to give to prisoners."

"You sure about that? If we go ask the major, he's

gonna back up your story?" The outlaw leered. "'Cause if you're lyin' to us, chink, we'll peel that yellow hide offa you a strip at a time."

"No lie," Loo insisted. "Major Pike, he say. You go ask."

"Ah, hell," the third guard said. "What's the harm in a pot of soup?" He went over to Loo. "Maybe we might want some of it, too. What's in there? Lemme have a look."

Grinning, Loo lifted the lid on the pot, letting more steam rise.

The guard leaned over it, then jerked back as his face contorted in a grimace. "Good Lord!" he exclaimed. "What the hell's in there? Smells worse 'n possum piss."

Another said, "Knowin' these Chinamen the way I do, I'll bet there's some dogs missin' lately."

"No dog," Loo said with an emphatic shake of his head. "Only good things. Squid, octopus, bird's nest . . . good soup! Special Chinese dish!"

"You know, makin' those fellas eat this mess might be the best way of gettin' them to cooperate," one of the outlaws mused. "Tell 'em that if they give us any trouble, we'll have the chink here boil 'em up another pot of it."

"Put that lid back on there," ordered the man who had smelled the pot's contents. "Come on."

Two guards accompanied Loo into the cell block after they unlocked the door with the keys the major had given them. Both carried shotguns.

Matt, Preacher, Monte Carson, and Curley stood up from where they were sitting on the floor in a corner. They looked surprised at the sight of the visitor.

"Got a treat for you boys," one of the outlaws jeered. "The Chinaman's brought you a special supper."

"Very special," Loo agreed. "Very good."

"Set it down on the floor," the gunman ordered. "Then

come over here and get the key. You're gonna unlock the door and push the pot inside." He gestured with the twin barrels of the Greener he held. "You inside, move back, way back. If any of you boys try anything funny, we'll not only kill you, we'll blow this little yellow man to pieces, too."

"We won't try nothin'," Preacher promised.

"You ain't smelled that soup yet." The gunman sneered.

Loo did as the guard told him, setting the pot on the stone floor, getting the key, and unlocking the door. All the while, he grinned and bobbed his head.

Preacher frowned slightly in thought.

"Toss that key ring back over here," the guard ordered.

Loo did so.

"Don't open the door any wider than you have to, to push that pot inside."

"No trouble, no trouble," Loo said. "Just good soup." As he bent to push the pot inside the cell, he glanced up, and caught Preacher's eye. "Very special soup, full of good things. Squid, octopus, and bird's nest. Reachee down to bottom of pot to find tastiest morsels."

Curley rubbed his jaw and said dubiously, "I dunno about eatin' squid and octopus and bird's nests."

"Very good, you see," Loo assured him.

"All right," one of the shotgunners snapped. "Now back off and slam that door, chink."

Loo did as ordered.

"How are we supposed to eat soup with our hands?" Curley asked.

Preacher said, "We can pick up the pot and pass it around. Drink the soup and then eat them tasty morsels."

"On bottom of pot," Loo said.

"Yeah, we got that," Preacher assured him.

Loo bowed, grinned, and backed away from the cell.

"All right, get the hell on outta here." The guard who issued the order aimed a mock kick at Loo's backside as the little man scurried out of the cell block. He didn't slow down until he was out of the office.

Chuckling among themselves, the outlaws followed him. The door between office and cell block slammed shut.

Curley looked askance at the pot sitting on the floor just inside the door. "Are we really gonna eat that stuff?"

"Sure we are," Preacher said, his voice loud enough to carry to the office just in case the guards were listening. "Let me at it. I et things a heap worse in my younger days, to keep from starvin'." He went to the pot, hunkered beside it, lifted the lid, and plunged his hand into it despite the heat of the contents.

"Hey," Curley objected with a frown. "I said I wasn't sure about eatin' the stuff, but that don't mean—"

Matt lifted a hand and motioned for the deputy to be quiet. A slow grin was starting to appear on his face as he realized what Preacher was up to.

The old mountain man drew his dripping hand out of the pot. He held something, but it wasn't a piece of squid, octopus, or bird's nest. The object was wrapped in oil-cloth tied tightly in place with twine.

Every man in the cell could tell by the shape of the thing that it was a gun.

Chapter 53

Night had fallen by the time Smoke, Pearlie, and Cal neared Big Rock. Smoke's keen senses and instincts had allowed them to dodge several more outlaw patrols as they rode toward the settlement. They reined in half a mile shy of the edge of town, stopping in the shadows under a grove of cottonwoods.

"According to what Trask told Sally, he's got Monte Carson and some other folks locked up in the jail," Smoke said quietly. "I'm going to see if I can get there without being seen so I can talk to Monte. I might even be able to get him and the others out."

"And let me guess," Pearlie said. "Cal and me are gonna get left behind again."

"Nope," Smoke replied with a grin. "Pearlie, you try to get to Longmont's Saloon. Louis will know what's going on in town, and he'll back any play we make."

"What about me?" Cal asked.

"Head for the livery stable," Smoke told him. "The outlaws probably have their horses there. Some of them, anyway. If a ruckus breaks out, you stampede those animals, Cal. That'll put Trask's men at a disadvantage if we have to make a run for it."

Cal nodded. "You can count on me, Smoke."

"I know that. Meet back here in a couple hours, if you can. And both of you, stay out of sight as much as possible. That bunch is liable to shoot anybody they find on the street."

Pearlie and Cal nodded in understanding. All three men knew what a big risk they would be running, but there was nothing else that could be done.

They left their horses tied loosely in the trees and split up to proceed on foot toward Big Rock. With luck they would be coming back for their mounts, but if they didn't, eventually the animals would get free and return to Sugarloaf.

Smoke employed all the stealthy tricks he had learned from Preacher as he made his way through the night. He used every bit of cover and shadow he could find. Covering the half-mile or so of ground took him more than an hour. Twice he had to lie absolutely still, not even breathing, while outlaw sentries walked past almost close enough for him to reach out and touch them.

He had just arrived at the back alley that led to the jail when nearby footsteps made him freeze again in a patch of shadow behind the hardware store. A man with a Winchester tucked under his arm stepped out of the narrow passage between the store and the neighboring building. He stopped and looked in both directions along the alley.

His attitude was casual. It was obvious he hadn't heard anything suspicious. He was just making a perfunctory check.

Smoke stood still, breathing shallowly. About fifteen feet away, the gunman was close enough that Smoke could be on him in two bounds.

It wouldn't hurt to start narrowing the odds. As soon as the man turned away, Smoke decided, he would go after the hombre and put a dent in his skull. He started to slide the Colt on his hip out of its holster. . . .

"Anything back there, Masters?" another man asked from closer to the street.

"Nope," replied the man Smoke was watching. "Not even a damn ol' alley cat movin' around back here tonight."

The other man chuckled as he strolled along the passage and stepped out to join Masters. "I reckon even the cats have heard they need to stay off the street or get shot."

Masters dug in his shirt pocket and brought out the makin's. The other man did likewise. Smoke's jaw tightened. From the looks of it, they were going to stand there and roll quirlies, stealing a few minutes from their scheduled rounds.

When they had rolled the cigarettes, the man from the street scratched a lucifer to life on the wall and set fire to both gaspers. The glare from the match didn't quite reach to where Smoke was standing with his back pressed to the wall, next to a stack of empty wooden crates.

"How much longer you reckon we're gonna be here in this burg?" Masters asked idly.

"Until the doc gets what he wants, I suppose."

"You mean Smoke Jensen."

"That's why we're here, ain't it?"

"Yeah, but I'm not sure exactly what Trask wants with him. From everything I've heard about Jensen, he's hell on wheels. I wouldn't want to be within a hundred miles of the man . . . unless I was gettin' well paid for it." Masters shrugged. "Which we are, I guess."

"Why Trask wants Jensen is his business, and I don't

want anything to do with that part of it. Our job is just to deliver him."

These two would be mighty surprised, Smoke thought, if they knew their quarry was standing less than twenty feet away from them.

"I don't mind tellin' you, that fella makes my blood run cold," Masters mused.

"Jensen, you mean?"

"No. Doc Trask." Masters lowered his voice. "You know he was responsible for what happened to Lonesome Dan."

"Dan volunteered," the other man snapped. "He didn't have to let Trask do whatever it was he did."

"You know, I've heard stories . . . Some fellas say there were more men that turned out like Dan."

"Shut up. Just keep your trap closed, Masters. You know we're not supposed to be talkin' about things like that. If the major was to get wind of it . . . well, you know how close him and Trask are."

"All I know is I'm ready for this job to be over and done with."

"No argument there. But Jensen's bound to surrender soon as he finds out the doc's got his wife." The other man dropped his cigarette butt and ground it out with the toe of his boot. "Come on. Let's get back to it."

They turned and walked back toward the street.

In the darkness, Smoke smiled grimly. Those killers were counting on something that wasn't true. Trask didn't have Sally. She was safe in that cave up in the high country, leaving Smoke free to deal with the outlaws without having to worry about her.

He drifted off into the shadows, setting out to do just that.

Chapter 54

Cal had been in the middle of plenty of ruckuses since he had met and gone to work for Smoke Jensen. Trouble just seemed to gravitate naturally to him and those around him. All of those perilous adventures had turned out all right in the end, and Cal had no doubt that this one would, too. He had that much confidence in Smoke.

At the same time, in the back of Cal's mind was the realization that everybody's luck ran out eventually. Maybe fate would finally catch up to Smoke and his friends.

With a little shake of his head, Cal put that thought out of his mind. Just considering the possibility was being disloyal to Smoke, he told himself sternly. Anyway, in a dangerous situation, it was best to concentrate on one thing at a time.

He didn't want to slip up and get caught and focused his attention on staying out of the outlaws' sights as he carefully made his way toward the livery stable.

He reached the big, cavernous barn and tugged on the back door. It was barred from the inside, which was no surprise at that time of night. The front door might be open, but Cal wasn't going to risk stepping out into the street where he would be in plain view if one of the invaders looked his way.

He moved silently along the side of the building until he reached a small window that opened into the tack room where the night hostler slept. Most of the time, his friend Wendell Barnes held down that chore.

Despite the chill, the window was open a couple inches to let in fresh air. Cal raised himself on his toes and hooked his fingers over the sill. He put his mouth close to the gap and called in a whisper, "Wendell! Wendell, are you in there?"

He had to repeat that several times before he heard somebody stirring inside. A voice thick with interrupted sleep muttered, "What the hell?"

"Wendell, don't strike a light!" Cal said. "It's Calvin Woods. I'm here at the window."

A dark shape moved on the other side of the glass. Whoever it was shoved the pane up, then a tousled, sandy-haired head thrust out and Wendell said in obvious surprise, "Cal? What in blazes are you doin' here? I thought you were out at the Sugarloaf." The young hostler's voice caught a little as he added, "I worried those damn gun-wolves might've killed you."

"It wasn't for lack of tryin' that they didn't," Cal said. "Move back. I'm gonna climb in there."

"Let me give you a hand."

With Wendell's help, Cal clambered through the window. Relief went through him when his boots hit the floor of the tack room. At least while he was inside, none of the outlaws would come along and shoot him on sight.

Wendell was fully dressed except for his boots, since the night hostler never knew when he might have to help somebody with a horse. He ran his fingers through his hair, a gesture barely visible to Cal in the gloom. "I really was afraid you were dead. Those fellas have been talking all over town about how they took over the ranch, wiped out most of the crew, and made Mrs. Jensen their prisoner."

"Well, part of that's a lie, plain and simple," Cal stated. "They don't have Miss Sally. Pearlie and I got her away from there when they raided the place."

"Then Pearlie's alive, too?"

"Yep."

"Then why do they keep sayin' that about Mrs. Jensen bein' their prisoner?"

"I don't know," Cal admitted. "Maybe that's what they want you folks in town to think so you'll be more likely to cooperate with 'em. Or maybe they really believe it because that's what their boss told them for some reason. I reckon all that can be hashed out later"—his voice took on a grim edge—"after Smoke gives 'em what they've got coming."

"Where *is* Mr. Jensen?"

Cal opened his mouth to answer the question but then hesitated. What if Wendell sold them out to the gunmen who had taken over Big Rock?

He realized how ridiculous that idea was. He and Wendell had been friends for several years. They had played checkers and pitched horseshoes together. Wendell wasn't going to betray him or Smoke.

"He's somewhere around town," Cal replied. "He and Pearlie and I snuck in tonight to do a little scouting."

"What about Mrs. Jensen?"

"She's someplace safe." He was vague about that answer not because he distrusted Wendell but rather because the fewer people who knew where Sally was, the safer for her.

A fella couldn't be tortured into telling something he didn't know, Cal thought bleakly.

"Now I've got a question for you. Have you seen hide or hair of Matt Jensen or Preacher today?"

A frown creased Wendell's forehead as he repeated, "Matt Jensen? That's Smoke's brother, right?"

"Yeah."

Wendell shook his head. "I haven't seen Matt Jensen in quite a while. Nor Preacher. He's the old mountain man, Mr. Jensen's friend?"

Preacher was more like Smoke's adopted father, thought Cal, but it wasn't the time to go into that. He just nodded.

"Noooo . . ." Wendell said, shaking his head slowly. "There was an old man who came into town yesterday, but he was a peddler, not a mountain man. He had the bodies of three of those outlaws with him, though, slung over horses tied to the back of his wagon. He had the whole bunch in a ruction for a while, until they decided he was harmless."

That sparked Cal's interest. Smoke had told them about the battle he and Matt and Preacher had had with three men guarding the road outside of Big Rock. He wondered if there could be any connection between that fight and the peddler Wendell had mentioned. . . .

A thought suddenly occurred to Cal. "What did that peddler look like? Did you see him?"

"Oh, yeah. I saw him, all right. I even played checkers with him. His wagon's parked in the barn, and his mules are out in the corral. He's kind of a scrawny old-timer, looks like he's been through a lot in his life. He said his name's Art."

Cal stiffened and caught his breath. He had heard the story of how a young fur trapper named Art had been captured by the Blackfeet many, many years ago. They held a grudge against him for killing so many of their warriors, and they had planned to burn him at the stake.

Instead Art had saved his own life by starting to preach to the Indians. He had kept it up for hours on end, all night and into the next day, and his captors had come to believe that he was touched in the head. Since it was bad medicine to harm a crazy man, they'd let him go instead of killing him . . . and once that story got around, Art's fellow trappers had dubbed him Preacher.

The name had stuck.

With his heart pounding a little, Cal realized the ped-dler who had driven his wagon into Big Rock had to be Preacher. He didn't have any idea how the old mountain man had gotten involved in that masquerade, but it was the only answer that made any sense. "That peddler—where is he now?"

Wendell shook his head. "I don't know. After he brought his wagon in yesterday evening, he asked if he could sleep up in the hayloft. I thought it would be all right, so I told him sure, to go ahead. That's the last I saw of him. When I got up this morning"—Wendell's shoul-ders rose and fell in a shrug—"he was gone. I don't have any idea where he went. Is that important, Cal?"

That explained why Preacher hadn't kept the rendez-vous with Smoke out at Knob Hill, Cal thought. Some-thing had happened to the old mountain man, or else he wouldn't have vanished from the stable's hayloft.

The question was whether Preacher was hiding out somewhere else, had been captured by the outlaws . . . or was dead.

Chapter 55

Several blocks away and on the other side of Big Rock's main street from where Cal was talking to Wendell Barnes, Pearlie stopped. The Sugarloaf foreman hated sneaking around. He wasn't good at it, and it went against his personality, which tended more toward barging into trouble head-on and bulling his way straight through it.

However, he couldn't afford to do that. With the odds facing him and Cal and Smoke, they had to be careful. If they got themselves captured, there was no telling what would happen to them. Or to Miss Sally, and that was even more important in Pearlie's mind. Every man on the Sugarloaf crew would give his life for her, or for Smoke, and Pearlie was no different. That was the sort of loyalty those two inspired.

Whether he liked it or not, he stuck to the shadows, listened carefully, and made sure it was safe before he took a step as he approached the back of Longmont's Saloon.

Louis Longmont and Smoke had been friends for years and had fought side by side in many battles. The gambler was also a fast gun, fast enough to shade just about anybody on the frontier except the very top level pistoleers. Pearlie couldn't even begin to imagine him giving up meekly to Trask's hired killers.

For that reason, he worried that Longmont was already dead. It would be a blow to Smoke if it turned out to be true.

The saloon's rear door was locked, Pearlie discovered when he carefully tried the knob. He bit back a curse as he listened to the noises that came faintly from inside the building. He heard men talking, the clatter of the roulette wheel, the tinkling strains of music from the piano. It sounded like a normal evening in the saloon, but he suspected the only ones enjoying it were the outlaws who had taken over.

He moved along to a window. The room on the other side of it was dark. Probably a storage room, he thought, drawing the bowie knife from the sheath at his waist. He worked at the wood with the razor-sharp point until he was able to wedge the blade between the window and the sill. He put pressure on it until, with a rending sound, the catch on the window gave and it slid upward a couple inches.

Pearlie grimaced at the sound, but a little noise couldn't be helped. He didn't think it had been loud enough to have been heard in the saloon proper. He hoped it hadn't been, anyway.

He sheathed the blade and raised the window far enough for him to climb through it. He had just gotten inside when he heard a heavy footstep on the other side of the door leading to the rest of the saloon.

Moving quickly, he put his back to the wall and stood where the door would conceal him if it opened. He drew his gun and held it up beside his head with his thumb looped over the hammer, ready to draw it back.

Sure enough, the knob rattled and the door opened. Light spilled into the room from the other side, throwing a man's shadow on the floor. He stepped into the room, advancing far enough that Pearlie could see his face in profile.

Instantly, Pearlie recognized the lumpy, craggy features. They belonged to a man named Glenn, who was one of Louis Longmont's bartenders. He wore a white shirt with sleeve garters, a string tie, and a vest. He didn't glance in Pearlie's direction as he muttered to himself, "Where the hell's that crate o' rye?"

Pearlie relaxed. He had worried that one of the outlaws might have heard him breaking in at the window and come to investigate, but clearly it was just a coincidence that Glenn had come into the storeroom at that moment. In the light that slanted through the open door, Pearlie saw crates of bottled liquor stacked around the room.

He knew he had to take a chance. Staying where he was, behind the door, he whispered, "Glenn! Glenn, don't holler or jump. It's me, Pearlie!"

Despite the warning, the startled bartender jumped a little. He quickly got the reaction under control, and didn't yell in alarm. With wide eyes, he turned his head to look over his shoulders and opened his mouth to say something, only to stop when Pearlie held the index finger of his free hand to his lips.

Glenn's surprised look disappeared and he nodded his head just slightly to let Pearlie know that he understood. "Dadgummit, how come I can never find anything when

I'm lookin' for it?" He rummaged through the storeroom
and moved crates around.

"That's good," Pearlie whispered. "If any of those hardcases are watchin' you, they'll think you're still lookin' for
whatever it is you came after."

"Got a crate of Maryland rye back here somewhere,"
Glenn said, keeping his voice low and barely moving his
lips. "Thought you was dead, Pearlie."

"Not hardly. And neither's Smoke."

Glenn's breath hissed between his teeth. "He's back?"

"Damn right he is," Pearlie said.

"Those gunnies out at the ranch . . . they got Sally."

"No, they don't. She's safe, Glenn."

The bartender sighed. "Well, thank the Lord for that.
A lot of folks here in town have been worried about her,
the way those varmints keep boastin' about her bein' their
prisoner."

"That's what they were after, but it didn't happen.
Reckon they're tryin' to make folks think it did, anyway,
so Smoke'll get wind of it and surrender to save her life."
Pearlie grunted. "They don't know Smoke Jensen."

"What can we do to help?" Glenn asked. He continued
pretending to search for the whiskey.

"Let Louis Longmont know that Smoke's back. I'd
like to talk to him if I could."

"That's just it," Glenn said regretfully. "Mr. Longmont
ain't here. He's gone to Denver. Won't be back for another
four or five days."

Pearlie breathed a curse. A formidable ally was gone.
In the inevitable showdown that was coming, they could
have used Longmont's help.

Nothing could be done about that bit of bad luck, so

they would have to prevail over the invaders without the gambler.

Pearlie moved on to the other thing that had brought him there. "Have you seen Matt Jensen or Preacher around here in the last day or so?"

"Matt and Preacher?" Glenn sounded surprised. "I sure haven't, and I haven't heard any talk about them. Are they supposed to be here in Big Rock?"

"They were headed in this direction yesterday," Pearlie explained. "They were supposed to get the lay of the land and then meet up with Smoke again. But they never came back."

"Damn," Glenn breathed. "You think that bunch killed them?"

Honestly, Pearlie couldn't imagine any owlhoots getting the best of Matt or Preacher, but there had to be a reason the two men had vanished. "I don't know."

"Well, if they were captured, chances are they're locked up in the jail. That's where Trask's gunman put Monte Carson and the mayor and the other members of the town council."

"The jail . . ." Pearlie said. Smoke had been headed there to talk to Sheriff Carson. If Matt and Preacher were there, maybe Smoke already knew about it. Shoot, he might've even busted them out already, thought Pearlie, although he hadn't heard any commotion.

"Pearlie, are you gonna fight back against the outlaws?" Glenn asked.

"Yeah, that's the idea, as soon as Smoke figures out how to go about it."

"Well, when the time comes, plenty of men in town will pitch in to help you," Glenn declared in a grim, angry voice. "We've got scores to settle with that bunch.

We managed to hide a few guns when they went through town gatherin' 'em up, and we can fight with shovels and pitchforks and anything else we can get our hands on."

"Can you pass the word to be ready when hell breaks loose?"

Glenn made a face. "That ain't gonna be easy. They've got the whole town locked down at night. Nobody's supposed to be out. I can let the swamper and the girls who are still here know, though."

A bartender, a swamper, and a few saloon girls, thought Pearlie. It wasn't much of an army, but sometimes a fella had to make do with what he could get. "You do that. Meantime, I'm goin' back out that window and see if I can get to the jail. Smoke may be there—"

Another footstep sounded outside the storeroom, and a harsh voice asked, "What the hell are you doing in there, bartender? You've been gone a long time."

Pearlie pressed his back against the wall again. He nodded to Glenn. They had said everything that needed to be said.

"I can't find that damn rye," Glenn told the man who had questioned him. "I know it's supposed to be here— Ah, there it is!" He chuckled as he bent over to pick up a small crate. "If it'd been a snake, it would've bit me."

"I've got a forty-five bullet that's gonna bite you if you don't get a move on," the outlaw said.

Glenn went out and drew the door closed behind him. Pearlie let out the breath he had been holding.

He holstered his gun and went swiftly to the window.

He had just thrown a leg over the sill when somewhere in Big Rock, guns started to roar.

Chapter 56

Preacher had felt more than one item in the bottom of the iron pot, under the noxious Chinese soup Loo had brought to the jail. He tossed the gun to Matt, who caught it deftly, and plunged his hand back into the pot. He brought up a second gun, handed it to Monte Carson, and went fishing a third time, coming up with what appeared to be a dagger. Once it was unwrapped from its oilcloth covering they could see it sported a short but very sharp blade.

"That's it," Preacher said. "But we're a lot better off than we were a few minutes ago."

The guns were .32 caliber Smith & Wesson revolvers, not as powerful as the .44s and .45s Preacher and Matt were used to, but deadly enough in the right hands.

When it came to gunplay, there weren't many hands better than those of Matt Jensen and Preacher.

"Good Lord," Curley said as he looked at the weapons. "That little Chinese feller risked his life smugglin' those in here. What if those outlaws had taken that soup away from him and tried to eat it themselves?"

"I reckon that's why it looks and smells like it does," Matt said with a grin.

"Yeah, Loo was makin' sure they wasn't tempted," Preacher added. "He's pretty smart, seems like."

In fact, it has been Loo's subservient attitude and the singsong voice he had adopted that had tipped Preacher off. He hadn't spent a lot of time with Loo Chung How, but enough to realize that the man was putting on an act. The look Loo had given him when he was talking about the tastiest morsels being in the bottom of the pot had confirmed it.

Preacher took the .32 back from Monte Carson, checked the cylinder, and tucked the gun into his waistband at the small of his back. The Smith & Wesson was fully loaded, which meant only five rounds.

Preacher usually kept the hammers of his Colts resting on empty chambers, so he was accustomed to having only five bullets in each gun. Between them, he and Matt had only ten shots. They would just have to make each and every one of those bullets count.

Monte Carson frowned. "Damn it. I wish he'd been able to fit another gun into that pot. I don't feel right being unarmed."

"You'll get a chance to grab another gun, Sheriff," Matt said. "And probably pretty soon, too."

"We're makin' a break for it?" Curley asked.

Preacher nodded. "That's right. I've been sittin' here all day, abuildin' up a heap of mad. I expect you fellers feel the same way. It's time we done somethin' about it."

"We've only got two guns, Preacher," Matt said, echoing the thoughts that had gone through the old mountain man's mind a few moments earlier. "Ten shots. That's not much to take on almost half a hundred hardcase killers."

"And a little pigsticker. You forgot about the knife."

Preacher rubbed his chin, which was bristly with silvery beard stubble. "But I reckon you're right. Startin' out, we won't try to do nothin' 'cept get out of here. Then maybe we can get our hands on some more guns, arm the rest of these boys, and, well, we'll see how it goes from there."

It seemed like a reasonable plan. Over the next few minutes they figured out exactly what they were going to do.

Once everyone understood, they got in position. Preacher and Matt were close to the bars. The other men were scattered around the cell, although with so many of them there wasn't room to spread out too much.

They doubled over and started moaning and groaning, first one man, then another and another until the whole cell block sounded like it was full of men who were dying, and painfully, at that.

After a few moments, the cell block door was unlocked and thrown open, and one of the guards loomed there with his hand on the butt of his holstered revolver. "What's that unholy racket?" he demanded angrily. "What's wrong with all you in there?"

"We're . . . we're sick!" Matt gasped as he hung on to the bars in the cell door. "We ate that soup . . . and now our guts are being ripped out!"

The outlaw threw back his head and guffawed.

"Serves you right for eatin' that vile swill the Chinaman brought!" He gloated. "No wonder you're sick. There were probably things in there no white man should ever eat!"

"Please," Matt begged. "You've got to do something. . . ."

"Listen to me." The guard strode closer to the cell, angry again rather than amused. "I don't have to do a damn thing." He lifted the hand from his gun and used it to point an accusing finger at the prisoners. "This is your own damn fault, so you're just gonna have to—"

Matt lunged, reaching through the bars to seize the outlaw's wrist. He jerked the man toward the bars and used his other hand to bring up the Smith & Wesson. He jammed the .32's short barrel between the man's teeth just as the outlaw opened his mouth to yell. Some of those teeth broke under the impact.

With their faces only inches apart and the barred door between them, Matt said, "I'll bet if I pulled the trigger right now, your head would muffle the shot so much those other fellas out in the office wouldn't even hear it."

The outlaw's eyes bulged from a combination of surprise, pain, and fear. His life hung in a delicate balance, and he knew it.

"Now here's what you're going to do." Matt's voice was low enough that the other outlaws couldn't hear it. "You're going to call your friends in here. Tell them to bring the keys because that soup poisoned us and we're dying. We're important hostages, and the doctor wouldn't like it if we all died."

"You got that?" Preacher added.

The guard managed to nod, although it wasn't easy with the gun shoved in his mouth.

"If you yell and try to warn them, you'll die," Matt went on. "You may ruin our plans and keep us from escaping, but you won't know one way or the other because you'll be dead. Do what you're told and there's a chance that you might live through this." He paused to let that sink in on the outlaw's brain, then went on. "I'm taking the gun out now. You know what to do. Live or die, it's your choice."

He pulled the gun back. A mixture of blood and spit

dribbled from the guard's mouth. He stood with his jaw hanging open for a few seconds, breathing hard. Then he swallowed and called thickly through the open door into the office, "Bass! Crandall! Get in here, and bring the keys! These . . . these prisoners are all dyin'. We gotta do something!"

Curses and rapid footsteps sounded. The other two outlaws rushed into the cell block, one of them carrying the key ring, and as Preacher and Matt had hoped, they hadn't taken the time to grab the shotguns. Their revolvers were holstered, too. They skidded to a stop as they found themselves looking down the barrels of the .32s.

A third gun was aimed at them, as well. Monte Carson had reached through the bars and plucked the first guard's Colt from its holster. His finger was taut on the trigger as he pointed the weapon at the other two outlaws.

"Don't yell, and don't reach for your guns," Matt warned them. "You'll be dead before you hit the floor if you do."

Since the first man was disarmed, Matt let go of him. He stepped back, groaned, and held a hand to his ruined mouth.

"Carter, you idiot," one of the other men said. "What the hell have you done?"

"I . . . I didn't have any choice," Carter said. "They were gonna kill me."

"What do you think the doctor's gonna do when he finds out about this?"

Carter's eyes had been wide and scared. At that thought, they fairly bulged out of their sockets. Whatever fate might await him at the hands of Dr. Jonas Trask obviously terrified him more than anything else in the world.

Matt and Preacher could never have predicted what happened next.

Carter lurched in front of the other two guards, shielding them with his own body, and croaked, "Kill them!"

Chapter 57

The other two guards clawed at their guns.

Matt didn't like the idea of killing an unarmed man, but he knew that with Carter in the way, the outlaws would use him for cover and might have time to wipe out the men in the cell. He targeted the shouting Carter first and sent a .32 slug into the man's left eye. The bullet popped the orb and bored on into Carter's brain, instantly ending his life. He dropped like a puppet with its strings cut.

"Everybody get down!" Preacher yelled.

The gun thunder was deafening in the cell block as everybody opened up at once.

Bullets whined off the bars and ricocheted around the room. Matt felt the wind-rip of a slug passing within inches of his ear. The Smith & Wesson in his hand cracked spitefully as he triggered it, as did the gun Preacher held. The louder roar of .45s added to the terrible racket.

The two outlaws staggered back against the stone wall behind them as bullets pounded into their bodies. Bloodstains bloomed like crimson flowers on their clothes. As death claimed them, the guns slipped from their fingers and thudded to the floor. One man slid down the wall, leaving a gory stain on the stone. The other pitched forward loosely and let go of the key ring as he toppled. The keys clattered toward the cell, stopping just short of it.

Gunsmoke was thick in the air, stinging eyes and noses. The guns fell silent, but clamorous echoes still rebounded from the thick walls.

Matt had emptied the .32. He jammed it behind his belt and dropped to one knee as he reached through the bars. He stretched his hand toward the keys but couldn't quite reach them.

"We got to get out of here," Preacher said. "Them shots'll make the rest of those varmints come arunnin'."

"I know," Matt grunted as he strained against the bars and tried to get just a little more extension on his arm. His fingers still couldn't quite reach the key ring.

"I've got one round left in this gun," Monte Carson announced.

"I'm empty. Still got that little knife, though." Preacher took the dagger out and handed it to Matt. "Try that."

The knife proved to be just what Matt needed. He held the end of the handle and hooked the tip of the blade into the key ring to pull it closer.

A second later, he was on his feet with the ring in his hand. Carson took it from him and thrust the right key in the lock. A twist of the key and they were free.

The question was how long they would stay that way.

The first thing to do was get out of the jail. They couldn't afford to get trapped in there again. A siege would end only one way. They needed to be out where they could move around if they were going to have any chance.

As Carson unlocked the other cells to release the rest of the townspeople, Matt and Preacher hurried into the sheriff's office. They grabbed Winchesters from the rack of rifles and shotguns on the wall and stuffed their pockets full of cartridges from a box Matt found in the desk. He dumped a box of shotgun shells on the desk and told the men to help themselves to the scatterguns in the rack.

Only a couple minutes had passed since the shots died out in the cell block, but he was worried that was already too long. He blew out the lamp, plunging the office into darkness, and went to the window to look out.

The street appeared to be deserted. How was that possible, he wondered? Could it be that the rest of the outlaws hadn't heard the shooting from the jail? He couldn't bring himself to believe that.

They had the opportunity to get away. They had to seize it. Besides, they couldn't stay there. . . .

"Is everybody armed?" he asked the men crowding into the office.

He got a round of agreements in return.

"All right, we're getting out of here. I'll lead the way. If any shooting starts, hunt some cover and fight back the best you can."

Curley said, "I'll be glad to get some of those varmints in my sights. They got a lot to answer for."

A couple townsmen lifted the bar from the door. Matt levered a round into the Winchester's firing chamber, twisted the knob, threw the door open, and charged out onto the boardwalk, crouching low to make himself a smaller target.

Nothing happened.

He stopped a few yards into the street and turned from side to side, ready to open fire if he needed to. Big Rock remained quiet and peaceful.

The newly released prisoners couldn't take it anymore. They poured out of the office onto the boardwalk and into the street, despite Preacher's warning. "Hold on a minute, dang it—"

Matt knew why the old mountain man was upset. It had to be a trap. That was the only explanation that made sense. Major Pike or someone else among the outlaws had reacted quickly to the shooting in the jail and had set up an ambush.

That thought raced through Matt's brain at the same instant as Preacher shouted, and all of it was too late. With a crash like the world ending, dozens of guns went off. A deadly hailstorm of lead ripped through the former prisoners. Men cried out in pain and went down.

Albert Pike was in the room he had taken at the hotel, reading one of Jonas's books. He knew that his mind was nowhere near the same level as Trask's, but he tried to educate himself so he could at least vaguely grasp what Trask was talking about most of the time.

That particular volume was about how you could tell what a man's personality and capabilities were by studying the shape of his skull and the bumps on it. That seemed a little crazy, but Trask had been saying for a long time that the key to everything about a man could be found in the brain. He believed that if you could study the brains of men with shared characteristics, you would be able to see the similarities in them. Since the brain rested inside the skull, Pike thought maybe there was something to the theory in the book he was reading. . . .

Gunshots made him lift his head and slam the book closed. Nothing theoretical about guns going off. That was real, and Pike knew exactly what it meant. Somebody in Big Rock was fighting back.

He had been expecting it. In fact, he *welcomed* it. There was no better way to kill the spirit of a conquered people once and for all than to let them have a moment of hope . . . and then crush it utterly and completely.

He might have to kill half the town tonight, Pike thought as he stood up. If he did, the half that was left would never give him any trouble again.

He was buckling on his gun belt when somebody pounded on the door. Pike called for the man to come in.

"Major, there's been a jailbreak," Cully reported breathlessly as he stood in the doorway.

"I'm not surprised." Pike clapped his flat-crowned hat on his head. "What's being done about it?"

"We held our fire until they all came out into the street, then opened up on 'em."

Pike nodded in curt approval. It was a good tactic, the sort of thing he might have ordered himself if he had been on hand.

"Did it work?"

"We got some of 'em. The others took cover. It's settled down into quite a fight."

"One that we'll win," Pike declared. He shrugged into his coat. "Come on."

Matt threw the Winchester to his shoulder and fired the rifle as fast as he could work its lever, swinging the barrel from left to right and spraying bullets at the muzzle flashes from the darkened buildings across the street.

Something hot kissed his cheek, leaving behind a streak of fiery pain.

Bullets would be getting even closer if he didn't move.

He lunged to the side and broke into a zigzagging run, continuing to fire the rifle as he dashed for cover. Spotting a water trough, he threw himself full-length behind it. He squirmed forward until he could thrust the Winchester's barrel around the end of the trough and return the outlaws' fire from there.

Preacher ran along the boardwalk until he reached a rain barrel not far from Matt's position, kneeling behind it and firing over the top. Matt looked back along the street toward the jail and saw several dark forms sprawled in the dirt in front of the building. Those men had been chopped down in the first volley and hadn't been able to make it to cover.

The others had scattered and were putting up a fight from various places along the street where they had taken shelter. Shots were coming from the jail, so Matt knew some of the men had made it back inside. He didn't see Monte Carson and Curley, but there was no time to check on them. He had bigger problems to worry about.

"Preacher, they're going to try to get behind us!" Matt called to the old mountain man as both of them paused to reload their rifles. "There are too many of them!"

"Damned if I don't know it!" Preacher replied. He jacked the rifle's lever, then thumbed one more cartridge through the loading gate. "I'm gonna fade back and see if I can fight a delayin' action in the alleys."

"Be careful."

"We done gone way past the time for that!" Preacher turned and ran for the nearest alley. Bullets from across the street chewed splinters from the boardwalk and the posts that held up the awning over it.

He never broke stride, though, as Matt watched the old-timer disappear into the black maw at the mouth of the alley, so he probably wasn't hit. He seemed to have a guardian angel watching over him, although he would have scoffed at that idea.

If it was true, that guardian angel had his work cut out for him. Only a few seconds after Preacher disappeared into the alley, a thunderous fusillade of gunshots erupted back there.

Chapter 58

Smoke was on his way to the jail when he heard a brief flurry of gunshots from that direction. He didn't know what was behind the sudden violence, but it wouldn't surprise him if Matt and Preacher were mixed up in it somehow. They seemed to find trouble wherever they went.

I'm a fine one to talk, he thought with a faint smile as he hurried toward the jail. He still stayed behind cover as much as he could, not wanting the outlaws to realize he was in town until he found out what was going on.

More guns began to boom—a lot more. It was a full-fledged battle. He was more convinced that he was going to locate Matt and Preacher very soon.

He was behind the building next to the jail when half a dozen men suddenly rounded the corner of a building up ahead and charged into the alley. At the same instant, a running figure burst into view from the narrow opening beside the jail. In the moonlight, Smoke got a good look at the newcomer. The man was clean-shaven and wasn't wearing the usual buckskins, but Smoke knew him right away as Preacher.

Unfortunately, the old mountain man was between Smoke and the outlaws who were bristling with guns.

Smoke called, "Hit the dirt!" as he drew his Colt with smooth, eye-blurring speed.

Preacher threw himself to the ground. The rifle in his hands was spitting fire and lead even before he landed. Smoke's gun roared at the same time. The outlaws were trying to bring their guns into action, but only a couple got shots off before bullets scythed into them.

The light wasn't very good for shooting, but there had never been men any more deadly accurate than Smoke Jensen and the old-timer called Preacher. Slugs thudded into flesh, smashed bone, ripped through veins and arteries and vital organs. In the time it took for a heart to beat twice, all six outlaws went down.

Preacher scrambled to his feet and exclaimed, "Smoke! Is that you, boy?"

"It's me, Preacher," Smoke said as he began to reload with swift efficiency. He didn't have to think about what he was doing. The movements came to him automatically.

Preacher was doing the same with the Winchester. He told Smoke, "It's good to see you. We got a mite of a problem on our hands."

"Three or four dozen killers out to shoot you to pieces?"

"Yeah, that's about the size of it. We was tryin' to break outta jail without raisin' a ruckus, but I reckon you can hear how that done turned out."

"Where's Matt? Is he all right?"

Preacher jerked his head toward the main street. "He was fine last I seen of him."

"How about Monte Carson?"

"Yeah, he— Behind you, Smoke!"

Smoke whirled and dropped to one knee as Preacher

stepped up beside him and lifted the rifle. Smoke hadn't holstered his Colt, so he just shot at the four hardcases who were about to open fire on them. At the same time, Preacher cranked off three rounds from the Winchester.

The four would-be killers died without firing a shot.

A shotgun boomed behind them. Smoke and Preacher spun toward the sound. Smoke's finger was taut on the trigger, but he held off as he saw a small, chubby figure holding a Greener. A few feet away, one of the original six outlaws Smoke and Preacher had shot it out with was sliding down the wall, his chest a bloody ruin from the load of buckshot it had received.

"I thought all them was dead!" Preacher exclaimed.

"Looks like we didn't finish them all off," Smoke drawled, "but that hombre sure did."

The man with the shotgun stepped closer, grinning.

Preacher said, "Loo, is that you?"

"When I heard all the shooting, I knew you were enjoying that Chinese soup I brought you," Loo Chung How said. "I thought you might need a hand, so I got my old varmint gun and came to help."

"As if you hadn't risked enough already," Preacher muttered. "You sure got here at the right time." He turned to Smoke. "I'll explain all this here later, Smoke, but right now this is a new pard o' mine named Loo Chung How."

"Pleased to meet you, Mr. Loo," Smoke said with a nod. "Things back here seem to have quieted down. Let's go see if we can find Matt."

Cully followed Pike downstairs and out through the lobby. The major could tell that Cully was holding himself back a little to keep from getting ahead of him.

The limp didn't slow him down much, but it was always there.

It would have been much worse if not for what Jonas had done for him, however. Pike knew that and would always be loyal to Trask and would fight to help him achieve his goals. He would die for the man if it came down to that.

But it wasn't going to tonight, Pike told himself. Whatever was happening on the streets of Big Rock, he was confident that he and his men could handle it.

Muzzle flashes spurted on both sides of the street. Pike drew his gun as he strode forward.

Beside him, Cully said, "Be careful, Major. We don't want to find ourselves in that crossfire."

Pike stopped and frowned in thought. After a moment he said, "Matt Jensen was with the schoolteacher when he was captured last night, wasn't he?"

"That's what I heard."

"Find her," Pike ordered. "The wives and children of the men who were locked up in the jail, too. Gather them and bring them here."

"Women and children, Major?"

Pike's head snapped around. "Sometimes in war you're forced to use weapons you'd prefer not to, but you do whatever is necessary to win."

Chapter 59

With his gun still drawn, Smoke hurried along the dark passage. Preacher and Loo had decided to stay on guard in the alley in case any more outlaws tried to get behind them.

As Smoke reached the street, he saw his adopted brother still stretched out behind the water trough. One bound landed Smoke behind the rain barrel Preacher had been using for cover.

"Matt!" Smoke called.

Matt twisted his head to look around. In the moonlight, Smoke saw the grin on the younger man's face.

"Smoke!" Matt exclaimed. "I'm mighty glad to see you! Not really surprised, though." An angry edge came into his voice. "Those outlaws keep talking about how Sally's their prisoner."

"They're lying or else they just don't know any better." Smoke had explained the same thing to Preacher. "She's safe. She's hidden out where they'll never find her."

"That's mighty good to hear," Matt said in obvious relief. "Now we can concentrate on handling things here without worrying about her."

"That's the idea." Smoke aimed over the top of the barrel and fired at a spot just above one of the muzzle flashes from across the street.

During the next half-hour, the battle settled into something of a standoff, with the outlaws on one side of the street and the former prisoners on the other. Smoke and his allies were still greatly outnumbered, but they had decent cover and were making a good fight of it. The ones who had retreated back into the jail had plenty of ammunition, but the same wasn't true for those who had taken cover elsewhere along the street. They would run out of bullets after a while.

Suddenly, something happened to tip the balance further than it already was. Shouted commands to hold fire went along the far side of the street. Gradually the outlaw guns fell silent. Smoke didn't know what was going on, but he was pretty sure it couldn't be anything good.

He was right. Men carrying torches came into view around a corner up the street. They formed two lines, and between them, clearly visible in the garish light as they were pushed along at gunpoint by men behind them, were a number of women and children. The hostages huddled together in fear as they stumbled along.

One of the townsmen hidden behind a parked wagon let out a strident cry. "Margaret!"

A woman in the group sobbed, "Ben!"

The man straightened from his crouch and started to leap out from behind the wagon, but another man with him grabbed his collar and hauled him back.

"Stay down, you fool!"

Watching the drama from up the street, Smoke recognized Monte Carson's voice and was relieved that his old friend was still alive.

Carson continued. "They'll gun you down if you go out in the open."

From behind the terrified hostages, a man shouted in a loud, commanding tone, "Everyone cease fire!"

All the guns were silent. The only sounds in the street were sobs from the hostages and angry, frightened curses from the defenders.

"Matt Jensen!" the powerful voice went on. "Matt Jensen, do you hear me? This is Major Albert Pike!"

Matt looked over at Smoke and said quietly, "Trask's second in command."

Smoke nodded to show that he understood.

Matt raised his voice. "I hear you, Major. You should let those people go! Threatening them isn't going to get you anything but more trouble!"

"You're wrong, Jensen," Pike replied confidently. Limping around the group of hostages, he held a gun in his right hand and his left was clamped around the arm of a nice-looking young woman with long brown hair. He stopped and put the gun to the woman's head. "You and your friends have ten seconds to throw your guns into the street and step out with your hands up, or I'm going to kill Miss Morton! That will be the signal for my men to open fire. We'll slaughter every one of these prisoners of war!"

"You're damn crazy!" Matt cried. "Those aren't prisoners of war! Those are women and children!"

"There are no innocents in war," Pike intoned.

"This isn't a war!"

"That's where you're wrong, Jensen." Pike pushed the gun harder against the young woman's head, hard enough to make her cry out in pain. "All of life is war, and those who don't realize that have already lost."

Smoke didn't know who the woman was, but Matt

obviously did, which came as no surprise. If there was a good-looking female within a hundred miles, she and Matt usually wound up bumping into each other.

Smoke's brain continued to race as a couple tense seconds ticked by. He realized that they had a trump card to play. He raised his voice and called, "Pike! You've been looking for me!"

"Who—"

Smoke stood up from behind the rain barrel and stepped out into plain sight. "My name is Smoke Jensen!" He knew he was taking a chance. Probably several dozen guns were aimed right at him.

But he knew that Dr. Jonas Trask wanted him alive, for whatever reason the doctor had in mind. It was why Trask had gone to so much trouble, had wreaked so much havoc, caused so much death and destruction. A dead Smoke Jensen wouldn't do Trask or his men any good.

Pike looked surprised. "Smoke Jensen. At last."

"That's right. I'll surrender to you and let you take me to your boss . . . but first you've got to let those women and children go."

"Smoke, no!" Matt exclaimed. "They're all loco—"

"Maybe, but they know what they want," Smoke cut in. "And I'm it."

Out in the street, Pike said, "You ask me to give up an advantage, Jensen, with no guarantee that I'll get anything in return."

As he noticed something, Smoke stepped out farther. "You want a guarantee, Major? I'll give you a guarantee. You don't agree to this bargain and I'm going to kill you five seconds from now. No matter what happens to anybody else in this street, *you'll* be dead."

Pike laughed. "You think you can do that?"

"I know I can."

For the first time, Pike looked a little less sure of himself in the firelight. "Throw your gun down."

"Let the hostages go first."

Pike hesitated. Smoke didn't know if he was going to accept the deal or not. A lot of lives hung in the balance.

Abruptly, Pike shoved the young woman away from him and let her go. She fell to her knees for a second but scrambled up and ran toward the buildings. He nodded to his men, and the other women and children broke loose, streaming for safety. The husbands and fathers who had been fighting for Big Rock hurried to meet them, drawing them in and leading them to cover.

"All right, Jensen. I did as you asked. No one else has to die. Throw your gun down."

"Smoke, no!" Matt shouted.

"I gave you my word," Smoke said to the major. He tossed the Colt to the dirt at his feet.

From behind the outlaws assembled in the street came a shrill, unholy yell, like the war cry of a Blackfoot going into battle, followed by a familiar voice shouting, "Powder River and let 'er buck!"

A wave of gunfire slammed into the outlaws, and in the blink of an eye, bloody chaos erupted in the street.

Chapter 60

Smoke had been waiting for that to happen. When he had first started negotiating with Pike, he had been prepared to surrender to the major in order to save the lives of the hostages.

Then he had seen movement in the shadows farther along the street, back where no one except him was watching. He had seen moonlight wink on gun barrels and knew somebody was sneaking up on Pike and the other killers.

Preacher. Had to be. And the old mountain man wasn't alone. Somehow he had rallied a force to join the fight.

Smoke had concentrated on doing whatever it took to get the women and children clear, knowing that as soon as they were, all hell would break loose.

And it was exactly what was happening.

Pike howled a curse and jerked his gun up. In the torchlight, Smoke saw the major's face contort with insane hatred. He knew that being tricked had infuriated Pike so much the major wasn't going to hold back, no matter how much Trask wanted his quarry alive.

Smoke dived to the street as Pike fired. The bullet whipped through the air just above him. His hand closed around the butt of the Colt he had dropped a few moments earlier. He rolled and came up on one knee as Pike triggered a second shot. The slug burned through the air next to Smoke's left ear.

Smoke fired once, putting the bullet right in the middle of Pike's chest. The major rocked back under the impact. His gun sagged. He struggled to lift it again, but it slipped out of his fingers and thudded to the ground. Pike fell to his knees and toppled slowly to the side like a tree falling.

In the time it took for Pike to die, Smoke had shifted his aim and killed two more outlaws.

Men had scattered so much that he could see the attackers who had come up behind Pike's men. It was an oddly mixed group with Preacher leading them. Smoke saw Pearlie and Cal on either side of the old mountain man. Loo Chung How was with them, too, along with Glenn the bartender and Chet the swamper from Longmont's Saloon, Wendell Barnes from the livery stable, and several other townies. Wendell didn't have a gun, but he wielded a pitchfork with deadly effect, plunging the sharp tines into a gunman's body, ripping them loose, and striking again before the men he attacked knew what was happening.

That element of surprise turned the tide. Big Rock's defenders were still outnumbered, but they tore into the enemy with such speed and fury that the balance began to tip back almost right away. Smoke and Matt, fighting side by side, led the attack from the other direction, swarming against the outlaws holed up on the other side of the street. It was a bloody, vicious battle, filling the air with gun smoke and the cries of wounded and dying men, and seemed to last for a long time even though it was over in a matter of minutes.

When the shooting finally died away, the street was littered with corpses. Some good men had died, but the outlaws' grip on Big Rock was broken. The settlement was free again. Pike and most of his men had met the same fate that sooner or later claims all tyrants.

Preacher strode up to Smoke and gripped his arm. "You all right, boy?"

"I am now," Smoke replied.

Preacher slapped Matt on the back. "Looks like you come through fine, too."

"Yeah, thanks to you, old-timer," Matt said with a grin.

"Smoke! Smoke!" Cal said as he came running up.

"Good to see you, Cal." Smoke nodded to his foreman and added, "You, too, Pearlie."

"We were on our way to find you," Pearlie drawled, "when we ran into Preacher. He sorta whipped the whole thing into shape."

"You saw us sneakin' up back yonder, didn't you, Smoke?" Preacher asked. "That's why you was astringin' that feller along."

Smoke nodded. "That was the idea. We were lucky that it worked out." His voice took on a grim edge as he added, "But we'll need some more luck, because this isn't over yet."

They held a council of war in the sheriff's office— Smoke, Matt, Preacher, Monte Carson, Pearlie, and Cal. Everyone had been brought up to date on what had happened over the past day and a half, and they were discussing what to do next.

"We can't be sure none of Trask's men got away," Smoke cautioned.

Carson said, "Considering the number who were killed in the fight and the ones we've got locked up, not many of them could have made it out of town."

"How many doesn't really matter," Smoke stated. "If even one man escaped, there's a good chance he lit a shuck for Sugarloaf to warn Trask about what happened here."

"If Trask finds out that Pike is dead and the town isn't under his control anymore, he's liable to get all the men he has left and head this way," Matt commented.

Smoke nodded. "That's right, so until we know for sure, the town's got to be ready for trouble. That'll be your job, Monte."

"They won't take us by surprise again, Smoke," Carson vowed. "You can bet a hat on that."

"I know. In the meantime, the rest of us are going to find out just where things stand."

Pearlie asked, "We're headed for Sugarloaf?"

"That's right."

"Good," the foreman said. "We got some scores to settle with that varmint Trask."

Carson shook his head. "Even with Trask's force cut in half, the five of you can't take on the ones who are left. You'd be outnumbered almost ten to one."

"We're not going to just charge in there blindly," Smoke assured the lawman. "If we see that Trask is on his way to Big Rock with his gun-wolves, we'll turn around and rattle our hocks back here to help you defend the town. But if he doesn't know what happened here and is still dug in at the ranch, we'll send word to you. Bring everybody you can round up who's willing to come along and help clean up that bunch."

"I like the sound of that," Carson growled. "My head still hurts a little from that wallop Trask gave it."

Smoke looked around at the others. "Everybody understand what we're doing?"

They all nodded.

Pearlie said, "Cal and me will fetch the horses we left outside of town."

"No telling where my horse is by now," Matt said. "But I reckon I can find a good one among all those outlaw mounts."

"And that stallion o' mine is waitin' down at the stable," Preacher put in. "He'll be glad to get out and stretch his legs."

Smoke smiled at the old mountain man. "When this is all over, you'll have to tell us how you wound up pretending to be a peddler."

"And a tinker. Don't forget that. I never did get to fix nothin', though."

"That's all right, Preacher," Matt told him. "You're handier with a six-gun than with any other tool."

Preacher nodded. "Damn right."

Chapter 61

The hour was getting close to midnight by the time the five men approached Sugarloaf headquarters on horseback. They hadn't run into any patrols, and they certainly hadn't seen or heard any sign of a large force heading for Big Rock. It appeared that none of Trask's men had escaped during or after the battle for the settlement.

Smoke wanted to be sure of that before he made up his mind on a course of action and led the way to the top of a ridge from which they could see the valley where the ranch house and the other headquarters buildings were located. A few lights were visible in the main house, but the rest of the place was dark.

Preacher said, "Looks like most ever'body done turned in."

Matt said, "It doesn't look like they're getting ready to ride to war, that's for sure."

Before leaving Big Rock, he had stolen a few minutes to check on Lorena Morton and apologize for the danger in which she had found herself a short time earlier. She had told him not to be ridiculous, that none of what had happened was his fault—which was true enough.

The blame for everything could be laid at the feet of Dr. Jonas Trask.

With luck, he would be answering for it soon.

Smoke leaned forward in his saddle, resting his hands on the horn as he studied the ranch headquarters and frowned in thought. An idea had come to him, prompted by what he had done back in Big Rock. It would be a huge gamble, but if it was successful, it could give them an advantage in the fight to come.

He straightened, took off his hat, and ran his fingers through his thick ash blond hair. As he tugged the hat on again, he said, "I'm going to give myself up to Trask."

Startled exclamations came from the other four men. Smoke lifted a hand to silence them.

"What the hell are you talkin' about?" Preacher asked. "After all we've gone through to keep that there loco weed from gettin' his hands on you, you aim to just ride in and say 'Here I am, boss'?"

"Something like that," Smoke replied with a smile at the old-timer's outrage. "But there's a little more to it."

Preacher snorted. "There dang well better be."

Matt said, "No matter what you've got in mind, Smoke, giving yourself up doesn't sound like a good idea to me."

"Look," Smoke said, attempting to explain his reasoning, "Trask has got to have a mighty important reason for wanting to get his hands on me, otherwise he wouldn't have gone to so much trouble. Hiring all those gunhands had to cost him a fortune. I want to find out what he's got on his mind, and the easiest way to do that is to let him tell me."

Pearlie rubbed his chin and said slowly, "I dunno, Smoke. Sounds awful risky to me."

"Yeah," Cal said. "What if he shoots you as soon as you ride in?"

"If all Trask wanted was to see me dead, he could have sent those hundred men after me to kill me, instead of taking over Big Rock and Sugarloaf."

"Unless he wants to be the one to kill you himself," Matt pointed out.

Smoke couldn't argue with the younger man's logic. He shrugged. "I suppose that's possible. But my gut tells me there's something else at the bottom of this. Something more than a thirst for vengeance on me is driving Trask."

"Mebbe you're right," Preacher said, "but what good does it do for you to surrender?"

"It'll make Trask think that he's won. He'll let his guard down, and maybe his men will, too. Then, when Cal gets back from Big Rock with Monte Carson and the rest of the men who'll be siding him, I'll be right there to strike a blow at the heart of the enemy while the rest of you attack."

"I'm riding to Big Rock?" Cal asked.

"That's right," Smoke said. "Actually, now that I think about it, you and Pearlie are both going."

"Dadgum it," Pearlie said. "I wanted to shoot some of those fellers."

"You'll get your chance," Smoke assured him. "Getting word to Monte is an important job. I'm sending two riders because at least one of you has got to get through and bring those reinforcements back."

"All right," Pearlie said with grudging acceptance. "We'll make it. You can count on that."

"I am," Smoke told him.

"And there's a chance the ball won't start until we get back here, right?"

"A good chance. That's the way it'll be if everything goes according to plan." Smoke looked up at the stars and gauged the time. "It'll be a little while before dawn by the time you get back. That'll be a good time to hit them."

Matt suggested, "Why don't you wait until then to ride down and surrender?"

"I'll wait awhile," Smoke said, "but I want to have a chance to talk to Trask and find out what's behind all this before hell starts to pop."

"Still sounds plumb loco to me," Preacher said, "but I know once you've got your mind made up, there ain't no changin' it. Pearlie, you and the boy rattle your hocks on back to Big Rock and fetch Monte. Don't lollygag none."

"No chance of that." Pearlie turned his horse toward town. "Come on, kid."

He and Cal rode away, vanishing in the night.

Once they were gone, Matt said, "So Smoke, what do Preacher and I do while you're down there having your little parley with Trask?"

"You'll wait here. The two of you will lead the attack when the others get back. Even with reinforcements, you'll be outnumbered, so you'll have to hit them hard and fast if you're going to have any chance of winning."

"We can do that," Preacher said. "Ain't gonna be easy waitin' up here until dawn, though."

"Smoke's got the harder job," Matt said. "Staying alive until then."

Smoke chuckled at that.

The stars wheeled through the ebony sky overhead as the three men waited, talking quietly among themselves. The conversation was of little consequence. Preacher explained how he had run into Isaac Herschkowitz and decided to take on the role of a traveling peddler and tinker. Mostly, though, it was the sort of talk a family would share while sitting around enjoying each other's company.

Finally, Smoke lifted a hand in farewell and nudged his horse into motion.

As he started down the slope, Preacher called after him, "Wonder what you're gonna find down there."

So did Smoke, but he still didn't have any answers. Major Pike might have known what Trask's goal was, but Pike was dead.

Actually, the only thing Smoke was sure of was that whatever awaited him at Sugarloaf, it wouldn't be anything good.

Chapter 62

Jonas Trask was asleep, his slumber haunted by nightmares of the war as usual, when someone pounded on the door of the room he had claimed as his own. He cried out, lost for a second on seas of blood, then struggled to wakefulness and sat up in bed. He ran his fingers through his tangled hair.

The darkened window told him it was still night. Whoever was out there in the hall had better have a good reason for disturbing him, he thought. "What is it?"

"Hate to bother you, Doctor," came the voice of one of his men, "but, uh, something's happened. You need to come see."

Trask got out of bed and stomped to the door. He was dressed in shirt, vest, and trousers, although he had taken off his boots before stretching out. He jerked the door open and snapped at the unshaven, clearly nervous outlaw who stood there. "Don't be mysterious. Tell me what this is about."

"Smoke Jensen just rode in and surrendered."

The words struck Trask like a physical blow. The news was what he had wanted all along, of course. Getting his hands on the legendary Smoke Jensen had been his goal for a long time, ever since he had first postulated his theory. But a part of him had been doubtful that it would ever happen.

"You're sure it's Jensen?" he asked when he'd recovered enough from his shock to speak again.

"Yeah, I've seen pictures of him in the illustrated magazines. It's Jensen, all right."

"Where is he now?"

"Sitting on his horse in front of the house with a dozen men around him, holding guns on him."

"Get more men," Trask ordered curtly. "A dozen might not be enough where Smoke Jensen is concerned. I'll be down in a moment."

The gunman nodded and turned away.

Trask put his boots on, then went to the dresser and lit the lamp. He buttoned his shirt collar, picked up a string tie, and fastened it around his neck. He ran his fingers through his hair again to get it in some semblance of order.

It was a momentous occasion. He wanted to dignify it by looking presentable.

He didn't put on his gun belt before he left the room. He wasn't going to need a weapon, he thought. He was fairly proficient with a revolver, but more than anything else he was a man of science and reason. *Those* were his true weapons.

He smiled as he went down the stairs, knowing that he was going to meet his destiny.

The biggest danger in riding in like Smoke had done was trigger-happy guards. It was why he had identified himself as quickly and as loudly as possible. He wanted all the outlaws around to know that he was the man Trask was after, and that they needed to keep him alive.

It had worked. He was sitting his saddle in front of the house—*his* house, he thought as he tamped down the fires of anger burning inside him—and waited for the man who had brought hell to Sugarloaf.

A tall, lean figure with a shock of dark hair stepped out onto the porch. He was well-dressed, although his clothes were a little rumpled as if he had slept in them. His eyes blazed with the fires of madness as he gazed intently at Smoke. "It really is you," the man said by way of greeting. "You're Smoke Jensen."

"That's right. And I reckon you're Jonas Trask."

"*Doctor* Jonas Trask," the man corrected.

Smoke shrugged slightly as if the title didn't mean anything to him. In truth, it didn't. No man responsible for so much death and destruction deserved to be called *Doctor* as far as he was concerned.

"You have my wife," Smoke said harshly. He knew that wasn't true but wanted Trask to think he believed Sally's life was in danger. It would make Trask more likely to believe Smoke's surrender was real.

"She has not been harmed," Trask said. "You have my word on that. I wish her no ill will, and I regret any inconvenience we've caused the lady. I had to ensure, though, that you would accept my invitation."

"Invitation?" Smoke repeated. "Is that what you call it? Seems to me more like you declared war on this whole part of the country."

"Not at all. You have to understand. The mission in which I'm engaged will change the course of medical history. It will change the world. Some small . . .

sacrifices . . . are necessary for progress to take place. They always have been."

Smoke still wore his gun. Even though he was surrounded by gun-swift killers, he knew he could have his Colt out and put a bullet in Trask's brain before any of them could stop him. For a second, he considered doing just that, to make certain whatever evil scheme Trask had in mind would never come about.

He discarded the idea. He wasn't ready to die yet, not when he still had plans of his own to put into action. "What is it you want?" he asked in a hard, flat voice.

"Why don't you come in?" Trask suggested. "I'd like to explain everything to you." He smiled. "I realize I'm inviting you into your own house. I don't mean to insult you by doing that. It's just the situation."

"All right." Smoke started to swing down from the saddle.

Trask held up a hand to stop him. "I'm sorry, but I have to insist that you hand over your gun first. You see, I've studied your life as a pistoleer with great interest, Mr. Jensen. I know you're quite possibly the fastest man with a gun who has ever lived."

Smoke didn't like being unarmed, but he had known all along that was a possibility. He held up both hands, then reached across with his left to take the Colt from its holster. One of Trask's men stepped forward and snatched the gun out of his fingers.

"Thank you," Trask said. "Now, please come in."

Smoke dismounted. With more than a dozen guns still trained on him, he climbed the steps to the porch. Several of Trask's hired killers were up there, too, flanking the so-called doctor. They kept Smoke covered as he followed Trask inside.

They went to the parlor, where Trask lit a lamp. As the

yellow glow filled the room, Smoke caught his breath at the sight of a man who had been standing in the darkness. The man was tall, with arms and shoulders that appeared massively powerful. His eyes were open, but like the rest of his features, they were utterly devoid of expression.

Trask noticed Smoke's reaction. "Don't mind Dan. He's my servant."

"He was just standing here in the dark."

"Yes, Dan doesn't require sleep anymore. One of the unexpected effects of his involvement in my project."

That made no sense to Smoke, but he supposed if he waited, Trask might explain it. In the meantime, he didn't look at the big man called Dan. As Preacher would have put it, the sight of those empty eyes gave him the fantods.

Several of the outlaws followed them into the parlor. Trask said, "I'd send these men away so that we could discuss this matter in private, Mr. Jensen, but I'm afraid I can't run the risk of you doing something foolish. I don't expect you to understand—yet—the great honor I'm about to bestow on you."

"I want to see my wife," Smoke said. That seemed like something a prisoner in his situation would demand.

Trask shook his head. "I'm afraid that's not possible, but I give you my word, on my sacred oath as a physician, that she is unharmed. Perhaps you'll see her later."

Trask was lying and Smoke knew it. Trask didn't have Sally, and even if he did, he had no intention of letting Smoke see her. All he cared about was his damned *project*, whatever it was.

"Could I offer you something to drink?" Trask went on.

"I don't want anything to drink," Smoke snapped. "I just want to know what the hell this is all about. What's so important about me that you'd go to all this trouble just to get your hands on me?"

Trask smiled. "Well . . . to tell the truth, it's not actually *you* that I want to get my hands on, Mr. Jensen. It's your *brain.*"

Chapter 63

Smoke's blood seemed to turn to ice in his veins. He could tell that Trask meant that bizarre statement literally. "What in blazes are you talking about?"

"I need your brain, Mr. Jensen," Trask said. "To study. To serve as the basis for a surgical procedure that will change the world." He extended both index fingers and gestured with them as he went on in an eager voice, like a professor warming to his subject. "You see, you have a unique ability. You can draw and fire a gun with greater speed and accuracy than anyone else in the world. The secret to that ability lies in your brain. I'm convinced that the same secret can be found in the brains of a great many men. All I need is the key to unlock it. When I have that key, which I'll learn from studying you, I'll be able to perform delicate surgeries on the brains of other men and give them that same ability."

Smoke's thoughts whirled crazily inside his head. He said slowly, "Hold on a minute. You're saying you want to see how my brain is built, so you can whittle on the brains of other men and make them the same as mine?"

A pleased grin spread across Trask's face. "Exactly!

I'm so glad you're able to grasp my theory. I was afraid it might be beyond your capabilities."

"Even if you were able to do that . . . what good does it do you?"

"Why, it should be obvious," Trask replied with a little shake of his head. "Slowly but surely, I'll create an army of men who are as good with a gun as you are. Men who will have no thoughts of their own but will obey my every command." He turned his head to look at the massive, stolid Dan. "I've mastered that part of the procedure already. It took a while, but Dan here is the culmination of that area of study. Now you'll provide what I need to complete the project."

Smoke saw that Trask's men were glancing at each other nervously. He had a hunch they had never heard the scope of the doctor's mad scheme explained in such detail before. It appeared they didn't like what they were hearing.

"Just what is it you plan to do with that army of yours, Doctor?" Smoke asked.

"Why do I have to *do* anything with them, Mr. Jensen? Isn't it enough to create one of the greatest scientific and medical achievements of all time? Why, this process could unlock all sorts of capabilities in the human brain! It could transform the world!" Trask shrugged. "Of course, to properly fund such continuing research will require a great deal of money, so I was thinking perhaps I could take over an area here in the Southwest—Colorado, Utah, and New Mexico and Arizona Territories, say—and use their natural resources to further my work."

"In other words, you'll have the biggest, deadliest outlaw gang of all time."

Trask spread his hands. "If you want to put it in such crass terms . . ."

One of the gunmen said, "Hold on a minute, Doc. You're gonna do this brain stuff to us? Make us where we can't think no more, like Lonesome Dan?"

"Anyone who undergoes my procedure will be a volunteer and will have his family suitably compensated," Trask replied curtly. "Unless, of course, there aren't enough volunteers. Then I'll take whatever steps are necessary."

Smoke smiled grimly. "That means he's going to start carving on your brains, boys, whether you like it or not."

"Nobody's cuttin' on my brain," a second man said. He started backing toward the door.

Trask held up his hands and tried to sound mollifying. "Don't jump to conclusions. No one will die from my procedure. I give you my word about that. The only one who'll die is . . ." His head swung around so he could look at Smoke. "I'm afraid that in order to properly study your brain, Mr. Jensen, I'll have to remove it from your skull and perform an extensive dissection of it. There's no way for you to survive that. I'm sorry."

"So am I," Smoke said. "I'm sorry somebody as pure-dee loco as you ever got loose to cause so much trouble."

Trask's face hardened. Clearly he didn't like being accused of being insane. He looked at the three outlaws. "Five hundred dollars to each of you if you'll take Mr. Jensen to the operating room." To clarify, he added, "What used to be the dining room."

The gunmen forgot their misgivings for the moment. The promise of five hundred dollars was enough to accomplish that. Instead of backing away, they moved toward Smoke.

Smoke glanced at the window. The curtains had enough of a gap between them for him to see that the sky outside had started to turn gray. It wouldn't be long until dawn. Pearlie and Cal ought to be back from Big Rock with Monte Carson and the other men, and Preacher and Matt ought to be leading the attack on the ranch any time.

If they didn't, Smoke was just going to have to out-fight the outlaws, whether he was unarmed and outnumbered or not. There was no way he was going to let them put him on some operating table so Trask could take a scalpel and start cutting his head open. . . .

Outside, the pre-dawn gloom suddenly erupted in gunfire.

The racket made the three outlaws whirl toward the window. Smoke reacted instantly, too, and dove at the gunmen. He crashed into the closest one and closed his right hand around the cylinder of the man's Colt. His left fist slammed against the outlaw's jaw. As the man sagged, Smoke wrenched the gun out of his grip.

The other two men were swinging around toward him again. Their guns came up.

Trask shrieked, "Don't shoot him in the head!"

Smoke flipped the gun up and caught the butt in mid-air. It roared and bucked against his palm as he triggered it. Flame gouted from the muzzle and almost touched the shirtfront of an outlaw as the slug punched into his chest. He toppled backward over a chair.

The third man got a shot off. Smoke felt the bullet pluck at his shirt as he fired again. His slug left a red-rimmed black hole in the center of the outlaw's forehead as it bored on into the man's brain. His knees folded up and dropped him to the floor.

The man whose gun Smoke had taken tried to struggle to his feet. A swipe of the Colt's barrel put him down, out cold, leaving Smoke alone with Trask and Dan.

Although the shots might bring other men on the run. From the sounds of the ruckus outside, the rest of Trask's hired killers had their hands full.

Trask appeared to be unarmed. He extended his hands toward Smoke "Why are you doing this? Don't you understand I'm offering you the chance to be part of something wonderful? You'll be more famous for helping me change the course of history, Mr. Jensen, than you ever will be as a gunman!"

"I don't want to be famous," Smoke said. "I just want to be left alone to live my life. And if that means putting a crazy man where he belongs—"

"Don't call me crazy!" Trask screamed. "I'm not crazy! I'm the most brilliant medical mind that's ever lived!"

Smoke kept one eye on the door and the other on Trask. "Sorry, Doctor, it's over—"

"No, it's not!" Trask pointed at Smoke. "Kill him, Dan! But don't hurt his brain!"

Chapter 64

During the fight between Smoke and the outlaws, Lonesome Dan had stood motionless and expressionless, seemingly paying no attention to what was going on around him, but at Trask's command, he lurched into motion. With surprising speed, he launched himself at Smoke.

Smoke didn't want to shoot, but he had no choice. The Colt roared again. A slug ripped through the meaty part of Dan's right thigh. Smoke waited for the leg to go out from under Dan and spill him to the floor.

But other than a twitch of the leg, Dan didn't show any reaction. He didn't fall, and he didn't slow down. He kept barreling at Smoke like a runaway train.

It felt about like a runaway train when Dan crashed into him and drove him over backwards.

They landed on a divan, which toppled over from the impact. Dan's long, sausage-like fingers groped at Smoke's throat. Smoke twisted away from them. The collision had made him drop the gun, so he had to fight barehanded. He smashed a right and a left into the man's broad face.

Dan didn't seem to feel the punches any more than he had the bullet in his leg. Smoke tried to writhe away from him, but he was pinned against the wall. Dan's right hand closed around Smoke's throat.

The man's strength was incredible. Dan would crush his windpipe in a matter of seconds. Smoke's hand fell on the barrel of the fallen gun. He swept it up, smashed the butt across Dan's face. Bone shattered under the blow, but Dan didn't let go. Smoke hit him again and again, pounding until Dan's face barely resembled anything human.

Finally, the terrible punishment began to take a toll. Dan's grip loosened enough for Smoke to pull free. He lifted his leg, planted his boot against Dan's chest, and shoved hard, sending Dan flying through the air for a short distance before the big man crashed to the floor. Breathing hard, swallowing to work some of the soreness out of his neck, Smoke started to get to his feet.

In shock and disbelief, he saw that Dan was clambering up, as well. The man's broken, bloody face still showed no real emotion.

Smoke was so horrified he almost didn't notice Jonas Trask lunging at him.

Lamplight flashed on the scalpel he held as he slashed at Smoke's throat with the razor-sharp instrument. Smoke threw up the Colt in time to block the attack, but just barely. The scalpel glanced off the gun and raked a fiery line down Smoke's forearm.

Smoke ignored the pain and shot a left into Trask's jaw. The crazed doctor wasn't as big as Smoke, but he was fighting with the strength of madness. He shook off the punch and swiped at Smoke with the scalpel again. Smoke jerked back just as the blade swept in front of his face. Trask bored in on him, hacking wildly.

At the same time, Dan reached for Smoke again, still following the last order Trask had given him. The big man got in the way of one of the doctor's wild swings. The scalpel bit into his throat and ripped across it. Blood geysered from severed arteries. As Dan staggered, for the first time he showed a reaction to something. His eyes widened as if he realized something terrible had just happened. One hand went to the blood welling from his ruined throat, and he made a grotesque gurgling sound.

"No!" Trask yelled as he stepped back. "Dan, I didn't mean—"

Dan's tree trunk of an arm swept out with blinding speed and smashed into Trask's head. Smoke heard a sharp crack. Trask flew backwards, slammed into the parlor wall, and dropped in a crumpled heap.

Dan swayed back and forth for a second, then fell. The floor shook a little as he landed.

In the eerie silence that followed, a tiny whimpering sound caught Smoke's attention. He reversed the Colt so that he was holding it normally and turned toward Trask. The man lay motionless, but his eyes were open and he was conscious. His head was twisted at such a gruesome angle on his shoulders that Smoke didn't see how he was still alive.

He stared up at Smoke and whispered, "Jensen . . . Jensen, you have to . . . help me. . . . You have . . . deft hands. . . . You can . . . perform surgery. . . . I'll tell you what to do. . . ."

Smoke checked the gun's cylinder—two rounds left. The shooting had stopped outside. He swept the curtains back. The sun had started to peek over the horizon. In the wash of reddish-gold light, he saw Preacher, Matt, Pearlie, Cal, and Monte Carson walking toward the house. They had a few new bullet grazes, but Smoke could tell they were all right.

The battle for Sugarloaf was over.

"Jensen . . ." Trask rasped behind him. "You can . . . save me. . . ."

Smoke turned his head. "You want me to perform surgery?" He swung around. "I reckon I can do that. I can remove the thing that caused all the pain."

The Colt roared once in the parlor.

Smoke walked out into the morning sun to meet his family and friends. They would have a lot of work to do, cleaning the place when he brought Sally home.